The Accordo

Roberta L. Smith

This novel is a work of fiction. Names, characters, incidents and some places are a product of the author's imagination. All elements are used fictitiously.

The Accordo

Copyright © 2012 by Roberta L. Smith

Cover Artwork by Ronnell D. Porter

Cover artwork copyright © 2012 by Ronnell D. Porter

All rights reserved.

No part of this book may be reproduced or transmitted in any form or by any means, electronic or mechanical without permission of the author.

ACKNOWLEDGEMENTS

Many thanks to the wonderful people who helped make this story come together. To Richard Barbour who is always willing to read my books in draft form and give his honest opinion. To my critique group friends: Jim Elstad, Holly LaPat, Dwight Norris, and Hazel Stearns. Their valuable feedback is a big reason this novel got written in the first place. Thank you, Antonio Di Matteo, for saying yes to this project and making sure the Italian in the story rings true. And to my husband, Chuck, thank you for always thinking I can write great novels and encouraging me.

Other books by Roberta L. Smith

The Secret of Lucianne Dove

Chapel Playhouse

The Accordo

Prologue

1637 – Country Villa Outside Florence Italy

When they had finished making love, Lavinia Rossi Zanetti held the coverlet to her breast, rose on one arm, and stared at her beloved. He lay on his back, gulping the air, sweat upon his brow. She watched and waited for his breathing to grow calm. Then she leaned down and kissed him softly on the mouth.

Keeping his eyes closed, he grinned.

"You have a pleased-with-yourself smile," Lavinia said, her voice low, almost a whisper. She still wasn't smiling, but she added, "You should see mine."

Agostino reached for her with one hand and stroked her long unruly hair. "I am pleased. Always pleased when I am with you."

She took his hand, held it to her cheek, and gazed upon his face. *Such a beautiful man. I love your fine features. Your strong chiseled bones. Thick eyebrows. Short black beard. You are perfection.*

Perspiration caused his dark hair to cling to his forehead in ringlets. She drew a finger through the sweat then lightly traced his nose from bridge to tip. She drew her finger along the crevice where his lips met and he kissed it. Her finger went under his chin, traced his throat and stopped in the middle of his naked chest. She extended her fingers and pressed her hand to his body as her mind indulged itself.

Here. Your beating heart. Caged thirty-five years in this chest. Muscle, bone, blood, skin. All temporary. That is for certain.

She sighed so softly she felt, but hardly heard, the vibration of her vocal chords.

And what about our devotion to each other—you and I, Agostino? Has that already been lost? It pains me to think so. But if we live until whatever ripe age we live to be, when we die, does the devotion die then anyway? The church would have our souls exist, but would throw them in hell for our wanton actions, our sins of the flesh. Oh, perhaps not you, my love. For have you ever done anything wrong? Have you ever sinned? Aside from loving me, that is. Perhaps that is sin enough to send you to hell.

I don't believe the church is right. I don't. And I have to say, I hate God. But if the church is right, then there is no doubt that we will be separated in the afterlife. And I cannot bear that. I cannot allow that. I will not lose you.

She removed her hand.

The sun had long set and the lone candle in the room cast a shadow with dramatic effect. The contrast of dark and light, the stillness with which Agostino lay, and the rich blue and gold of the divan made the scene worthy of a Caravaggio painting—worthier still, of a Zanetti painting. After all, this man belonged to her.

She reached for a vessel of hearty red wine that sat on a nearby table and poured several ounces into a waiting goblet. She moved the goblet back and forth under Agostino's nose.

"It is your favorite."

He opened his eyes, sat up, and reached for the wine. He saw that there was only one cup. "What about you?"

"We shall drink from the same, but I've had my fill for now. Sip it. Savor it—as if it were your last."

She could say those words. He wasn't a suspicious man. If he were, he might have wondered about her meaning as well as the gentle tone in her voice. Lavinia was a strong woman, an outspoken woman. Gentle was not her approach to life. She guided the cup to his lips.

He swallowed—once, twice. She took the goblet from him and placed it back on the table before he could drink more.

"Please join me," he told her.

She didn't answer, but took hold of each of his wrists and pressed them to the divan. She leaned in, forcing him to lie back. Her face and his face were nose to nose. She looked into his eyes and could see that he had no idea what she had done. Light from the candle danced in his dilated pupils.

"You have not expressed your opinion of the painting," Lavinia said. "It is finished. Did you not notice?"

"*Amore mio*. You did not tell me, but swept me away with your charms. When I am here, I only notice you."

She stood, clutching the coverlet about her, and took the candle. She moved to a portrait of Agostino that was propped upon an easel. He adjusted his gaze to have a look.

"*Bellisimo. Bellisimo!* You have outdone yourself. She will love it." There was pride in his voice that Lavinia did not like. It was pride in the wonderful gift he would be giving the latest object of his affection, Catherine, not pride in Lavinia's prowess as an artist.

But his pride did not matter, she reminded herself. It was true that Catherine would love the painting. Lavinia had taken the money and done the work, but the painting would be delivered to the unsuspecting Catherine on Lavinia's terms. She had gone to great lengths to learn the last name of this Catherine.

"And the portrait of myself?" Lavinia said as she moved to a second easel that supported another painting. In it she looked a good ten years younger than she was now. She had given her eyes a haughty, piercing stare. The clothing was shear and seductive. One tender hand, the left, lightly touched her chest in contrast to the stark nature of the eyes.

"You are a wonder," Agostino said. "A woman, but still a painter of merit."

Lavinia's eyes narrowed. Even with all his years of knowing her, he still believed being a woman made her work inferior to that of a man.

"And you are a great healer—for the male of the species," she replied, coming back to the divan.

"What do you mean?"

She gave him a calculated smile, placed the candle on the table, and sat.

"Oh, of course," he said, tugging a lock of her hair. "How you do tease and yet it is true. I am one of life's mysteries. Why should I be blessed with the gift to heal? Why any man?"

Lavinia shrugged. She didn't bother herself with such questions. Why should a person be able to sing or play the piano or write music or books? Why was one man good at amassing money and another good only at having none? In her own case, why had she been born with the ability to paint if a woman was not to do so? From an early age her work had shown brilliance.

Her father had been a painter. Although not of great talent, he had been able to make a living, and he recognized in his daughter the greatness that was not in him. He might have reacted with jealousy and taken steps to thwart her talent except for the fact that he saw her as an extension of himself and wanted her to become known at the right time. He taught her what he could but knew she needed a teacher who was the best if she was to become one of the greats.

He devised a plan. When Lavinia was eleven he had her disguise herself as a male in order to gain access to the art world's premier instructor, Guiseppe D'Addario. The teacher had a reputation as a brute, one without fondness for females who thought they could do more than raise children and keep a house. But a task master was what Lavinia's father wanted. Soft words would not help Lavinia become a great artist. Little did he, or she, know that D'Addario's reputation had been understated.

Their scheme went undetected for just over three years before

Lavinia's feminine charms became too difficult to hide, and once D'Addario realized Lavinia's true sex, it sent him into a rage. Lie to him? Belittle his stature as a master artist and teacher? A female in his class? He resolved to teach her a lesson she would not forget and it had nothing to do with art.

She fought him off, only to lose, and afterwards her father sued D'Addario in court for having deflowered his daughter. After a lengthy four month trial, Lavinia's father lost his case. A thumbscrew had been placed on Lavinia's right thumb and tightened to excruciating effect. It was the court's way of making sure a person told the truth. Did it never occur to them that a person would lie to stop the pain? Did it never occur to them to apply the screw to Guiseppe D'Addario as well?

She was publicly humiliated and the humiliation did not end with the trial. She was branded a lascivious woman even though she was merely fourteen and had been a virgin at the time of the rape.

In hindsight, even at that young age, she saw that the offensive label had its upside. She was notorious and notoriety helped to sell paintings. The experience may have been painful. It may have left her changed. But she was now a skilled artist and one of renown. She wondered if everything of value came with a price. She wondered if prices were always as steep as the one she had paid. She wondered if somewhere, unbeknownst in her sleep perhaps, she had made a deal with the devil to be a success.

She glanced at her thumb, long healed—not because of time, but because of Agostino—and rubbed it. Advantages aside, the rape and her attacker's acquittal had left her bitter and ruthless. She did things that no one knew about. Hatred and rage burned within her belly and only three things soothed her: the presence of her beloved Agostino; being lost in the process of creating her art; and inflicting the pain she felt upon men. Yes, sometimes, when she was unable to contain herself, when Agostino missed a visit and when the creative process had been spent, she went into the city in search of appropriate victims.

And now Agostino had told her that she must share him with another. She wasn't naïve. She had probably shared him with many. But this was the first time he had told her about it. This was the first time he had shared a name. This new woman, this Catherine, meant something to him and that was a reality Lavinia would not live with.

Agostino's arm fell limp from the divan. Lavinia stroked his cheek. An "ahh" escaped his lips.

She stood up and dropped the cloth that had been covering her body. She was a portrait painter and the eyes of all the paintings in the room were upon her. *We are here for you*, they seemed to say. *We shall be your witnesses.*

Lavinia giggled like a girl, clasped her hands to her chin and did a little spin. This was to be her wedding night. Not in the traditional sense, but in a more lasting sense.

Agostino had asked her to marry him many times, but she had liked their arrangement as it was. He was hers and she was his. Of that, she'd had no doubt. Now the situation had changed because of Catherine. Now it was a marriage for all eternity that she desired.

Men were so clueless, she thought. Why did she love such a clueless man? For all the times he had been in the workroom of her villa, whether to pose for her, to look at the work she had done, have a cup or two of wine or to make love, he hadn't noticed that she'd arranged the paintings in a special way—with the portraits of the two of them at the core.

And if he had noticed, what would she have said?

Nothing. She would have shrugged and smiled cryptically.

Lavinia walked over to a full-length mirror and gazed into the glass. She appraised her body and face. She was forty-two, had years ahead of her to paint, but without the exclusive devotion of Agostino she felt she had nothing to live for. Her beauty had faded. Her hips looked too wide now and there was superfluous flesh upon her thighs. They dimpled in the flickering candlelight. Her breasts looked fine, but for how long? Time had etched shallow lines around her mouth and downward from the corners of her eyes. The blush in her cheeks had vanished and the once-rich, deep brown color of her eyes had dulled. Was all this the reason Agostino felt drawn to Catherine?

No one ever sees the physical changes as they happen, she told herself. No one feels eyelashes replace or fingernails grow. No one feels it when the brows begin to gray, or the jaw line wants to sag. It's the internal things you feel. It's the events that rip you apart that you notice. And any event that thwarts your plans for happiness helps mold you into something you never expected to be.

A thin moan escaped from Agostino's mouth and Lavinia's eyes shifted in the mirror so that she could see him lying on the divan. She watched and waited. He did not moan again. He did not move. The drug she had given him must have worked. He was breathing. He was unconscious, but alive. It was very important that he be alive.

She heard footsteps approach in the hall and her eyes went to the door. It was time. She felt her chest heave with excitement. The moon had waxed and the practitioner was here. She had one last plan to carry out—one last arrangement to follow through.

She lifted the goblet from the table and took a swallow. Pulling the coverlet around her, she sat on the divan. She engaged Agostino's right hand and entwined their fingers. She waited.

The footsteps stopped and there came a rap on the door. The rhythm: Tap. Tap. Tap. A short pause. Two quick taps.

Lavinia took a breath. "We are ready," she said. "You may come in."

Chapter 1

Mickey McCoy climbed out of bed two hours earlier than normal. It was five o'clock on a Tuesday morning of what would be a bright summer day in Lake Tahoe. Marjorie would rise in an hour and begin her day with a brisk, hour-long walk. Afterward, they would have a leisurely breakfast together on the patio where they would enjoy each other's company along with a sweeping vista of the lake.

Mickey stretched his stiff, sixty-eight-year-old joints this way then that before he tossed a robe over his pajamas and ambled into the study. He sat at his desk and fired up the computer.

He didn't understand it, not yet. He didn't know Italian, not even a little bit, but for the past month, every dream he dreamed was in that romantic language. He knew it had to mean something. His life had been filled with mysterious, inexplicable experiences; this had to be one more. There was no such thing as a coincidence in Mickey's book. And what might seem humdrum in the normal course of living—a wacky dream for instance—probably wasn't mundane at all if given the proper scrutiny. Mickey was intrigued. He believed in the strange, the weird, and the meaningful. Things occurred for a reason, and it just so happened he'd been blessed with abilities that allowed him to learn what those reasons were. Maybe not always, but from time to time.

He pulled up the Internet and found a site that translated Italian into English and vice-versa. Now what? The Italian words in his dreams all ran together in his head. What was it he thought he could learn?

He folded his arms across his chest and reclined. The cursor blinked at him. In jest, he blinked back.

"Eye-ewe-toe," he said, phonetically sounding out the only word that had stuck in his head from last night's dream. "I-ew-toe. Iewto."

With no expectation of getting a comparable word in English, he typed and clicked the button for a translation.

No exact match found, came the reply.

He typed the word into a search engine and snared a website about martial arts. That didn't help. His dreams had nothing to do with martial arts. He leaned back. What had he dreamed about exactly? Nothing in particular; disjointed pictures that vaporized with the waking of consciousness.

He typed "Italy" in the search engine and poked about. Enticing photos of everything Italian appeared on screen: beautiful villas, gorgeous vistas, historic landmarks, Renaissance art.

Maybe, just maybe, my mind is telling me Marjorie and I need a little trip.

It could be as simple as that.

The phone rang unexpectedly and he snatched the receiver before a second ring could disturb his wife.

"Is this Mickey McCoy?" a male voice asked.

Mickey checked caller ID. The identity of the caller was blocked.

"Who's this? Do you know what time it is?" Mickey asked.

"I'm sorry to disturb you, but this is urgent . . ." The caller hesitated. "Ah, official police business."

"Police business?" Mickey felt skeptical. "*Official* police business."

"Yes. My name is John Carroll. Officer John Carroll."

An image of Alice from *Alice in Wonderland* drew through Mickey's mind. She jumped down a hole to chase a white rabbit. Lewis Carroll had written the story. The man's name was probably genuine. But what about the rest of the image? Was Mickey about to be drawn down a rabbit hole?

"Are you Mickey McCoy or not?" John Carroll sounded irritated.

"I am. Do I know you?"

"No. No, you don't. But, um, someone told me about you."

Mickey leaned back in the chair. He tried to discern what was really going on. He didn't believe the man was a police officer, but someone probably had told him about Mickey or he wouldn't have called. He wouldn't have had his phone number otherwise. And a crank caller wouldn't have known his name.

Marjorie wandered into the study, yawning. "Who is it?"

Mickey motioned at the phone and shrugged. "Not sure," he mouthed. "Who told you about me?" he asked the caller.

"I got your name from my cousin. Dean Stern. He's a detective in Brookdale."

Mickey knew Detective Stern, although they hadn't spoken in more than a year.

"Do you remember him?"

"Of course I remember him. I'm old, not dead."

"I wasn't implying . . . He said you could be cranky."

"I don't mean to be," Mickey said. "But you call at the crack of dawn, tell me it's urgent, and you still haven't told me what you want."

"I was told this sort of stuff is right up your alley."

So that was it. Officer Carroll was embarrassed to say what he wanted because it had something to do with the paranormal.

"I can't confirm that until you tell me what it is. *Specifically*," Mickey said.

"Is there any chance I could get you to come to Los Angeles?"

"Without an explanation?"

"There's going to be a murder."

"Going to be?"

"Yes. It's just a matter of time."

"Doesn't that happen every day in L.A.?"

"This murder will be different."

For a moment Mickey wondered if this wasn't one of those cat-and-mouse games where the killer lets you know what he's about to do so you can frantically try to stop him, only you're always too late and you drive yourself nuts in the meantime. That would be a rabbit hole.

"How do you know this?" Mickey asked.

"That's hard to explain—"

Mickey heard the caller sigh.

"Look. I'm not really a police officer. I'm a security guard and I was fired for trying to protect the people I work with. They didn't understand. My boss didn't understand. And I'm afraid, Mr. McCoy. I'm afraid for them all."

Mickey could feel genuine fear coming through the phone. The caller was sincere. Not a killer. He softened his tone. "Where will this murder take place?"

"Where I used to work. In the city art museum. The Brahms Museum of Art. It's a little museum. You can see all of it in six or eight hours."

"And just what is it you think I can do?"

There was a pause. When John Carroll spoke again, his attitude had shifted. "I guess ... I guess nothing. I think my cousin was wrong about you. He said you could read minds. You don't seem to pick up on anything I'm thinking. And if you can't do that much, then the rest of what he said must be a load of crap."

Mickey didn't answer. His eyes were closed and he was trying to see if he could sense anything about John Carroll. All he could feel was the man's fear and now his anger at thinking he'd been lied to.

"Mr. McCoy? Mr. McCoy, are you there?"

"I could read your cousin's mind because it was an open book. What else did he tell you about me?"

"He said you see ghosts."

"And you need me to see a ghost. You think that will save someone's life?"

John Carroll hung up. Mickey held the receiver for a thoughtful moment before he placed it back in the cradle. He had mixed feelings about the conversation. If he could help the man, he certainly wanted to do that. But he wasn't feeling any urgency. He wasn't sensing anything that told him someone's life was in danger.

"What was that about?" asked Marjorie. She moved around the desk and gave Mickey a good morning kiss on the cheek.

"A man asking for my help. He wants me to save someone's life."

"Really? Whose?"

"I don't know."

"And how would you save this person you don't know?"

"I don't know that either. He hung up on me before he explained."

"Hmm. Maybe you should call him back."

"Can't. His phone number was blocked."

"Then I guess you can't." Marjorie's expression changed to hopeful. "Can you?"

Mickey chuckled. Sometimes he knew things he had no way of knowing. Marjorie was aware of this but her question struck him as funny.

"Not this time," he answered.

"That's too bad."

Marjorie caught sight of the computer monitor. "Italy!" she said, moving behind Mickey for a better view. "Oh, I love Italy. I love everything about it. The country, the cities, the art, the food . . ."

Mickey rolled the chair to one side so she could have a better look and he could admire her as she prattled on. They had been married for more than a year and were, he supposed, an elderly couple. He didn't like the term because it conjured an image of being decrepit and frail, which neither of them was. Both of their minds remained sharp and they were both well. Marjorie was in her sixties and was more vibrant and spry than he was, but not by much. She looked lovely in her silk nightgown—her figure perfect, her honey-blonde hair natural-looking, her skin spotless though gently lined.

She was kindhearted and loving and whenever Mickey looked at her, he felt blessed.

Marjorie placed her hands on Mickey's cheeks. "You haven't heard a word I said."

"I have. You love Italy. You've been there fifty times."

"I've been there once."

The phone rang.

"Is it him? Did he call back?" Marjorie asked as Mickey saw that the caller ID was once again blocked.

He answered with "John Carroll?"

"*Si*. John Carroll. *Ho chiamato mio cugino*."

"Are you speaking Italian?" Mickey's voice was full of surprise.

"No! I don't speak Italian."

"You don't?"

"My cousin said not to judge a book by its cover. I need your help. *Aiuto*."

"Iewto?" Mickey asked, recognizing the phonetic sound of the word that had also been in his dream.

"*Si. Voglio il suo aiuto. Aiutami. Per favore*."

"This is very frustrating. Why can't you speak in English?"

"I am speaking English! I'm asking for your help. Please, Mr. McCoy. Help me. This is very important. Come to L.A."

Chapter 2

On Tuesday nights Lollietta's Mexican Restaurant in Santa Monica remained closed. It was the slowest day of the week, slower than Monday for some reason, and not worth the expense of staying open. The owner, Harvey Lack, liked money and hated to miss a day of revenue, but that was the way it was.

One Tuesday night, while he was at home not working, he happened to catch a local cable show on television. It was one of those amateur ghost hunting reality shows, if ghost hunting could ever be termed "reality," where a group of youngsters (people in their twenties were youngsters as far as Harvey was concerned; he was forty-eight) took cameras and recorders into places that were supposed to be haunted. They walked around in the dark reacting to sounds and, in Harvey's opinion, their own imaginations, trying to capture evidence that ghosts really did exist.

Harvey would have found the show boring and changed the channel except for the fact that he got a brilliant idea. He would get his restaurant on the show! Ghosts were good for business. It seemed every hotel and restaurant had one nowadays. Why should Lollietta's be left out? The Paranormal Seekers Society—the name the kids called themselves—could do their little ghost hunt on a Tuesday when the restaurant wasn't open. The restaurant would get some free publicity, maybe gain the business of all those hungry people who operated in "la la land," and the Paranormal Seekers Society would have another episode to air.

"Everybody wins," he said as he watched the program come to an end.

He found the number for the ghost hunters on the Internet and grabbed the phone. He had to leave a message, but someone soon called him back.

"Yes, it's quite haunted," Harvey told the girl on the phone whose name was Kelly. "Well, let's see." Harvey racked his brain for bits of fiction that would interest the girl. He berated himself for not having gotten his act together before he set the ball in motion.

"Footsteps. Always the footsteps. Had a waitress quit because of that. She was there alone, closing up. Saw a ghost too. Yes, an apparition." He remembered a story he'd heard somewhere and used it. "At one of our tables, the shoelaces of patrons in athletic shoes get tied together as they eat. Yes, there are workers there you can speak to."

Harvey made a mental note to prep Jose. He knew Jose needed his busboy job. His wife had just had a second baby. Jose would go along with Harvey's plan. He wouldn't rat him out.

As it turned out, Jose didn't need prepping.

"But Señor Lack, your restaurant *is* haunted. For real," Jose said. "I smell perfume in the men's lavatory. And sometimes the door shakes for no reason. And once, once there was a big X on the floor."

"In blood, I suppose," Harvey said.

"I don't know. It was *rojo*. I cleaned it up right away."

Why Jose had never told Harvey Lack this, he didn't say. Harvey didn't believe him.

****

Kelly—twenty-five, cute, and spunky—watched her husband Dennis with admiration as he interviewed Jose with the camera rolling. Dennis was in his late twenties and had the eye-appeal of a well-muscled former college football star. He kept his blond hair short and stayed in shape. He was the group's founder and leader.

Jose seemed nervous which was normal. He fidgeted as he spoke. Nearby, Harvey watched with a smile and nodded his head. Something about his demeanor didn't seem right to Kelly and she decided he was anything but normal.

Once Dennis had finished with Jose, he began an interview with Harvey. "How did the restaurant get the name Lollietta's?"

Harvey looked briefly surprised by the question. "Well, it's my wife's name. Ex-wife. This was her restaurant."

"Ex-wife?"

"She left me some years ago." Harvey displayed a sad face. "For another man. I got the restaurant."

Yeah, poor you, thought Kelly.

After their interviews were finished, Harvey and Jose left the restaurant and the paranormal seekers set up their equipment. Jugs and Carl were the technical team, but Kelly helped them place cameras in the spots Harvey had said had the most activity: the kitchen; the hallway leading to the two restrooms; inside the men's restroom where Jose had had his experiences; and table number seven where the shoelaces of patrons would mysteriously get tied together. When the set up was complete, Jugs filmed Dennis for the show's intro.

"We are at Lollietta's restaurant in Santa Monica where we have been called in to verify or debunk claims that a mysterious spirit haunts the place. At least one waitress was so frightened that she quit, and Jose, who has worked at the restaurant for three years, says he often smells the perfume of the spirit in the men's room."

At this point the interview with Jose would be edited in for the broadcast. Then a clip of Harvey's interview telling about the restaurant and his table seven shoelace story.

A short pickup with Elyse came next. At age fifty-five, she was the "elder" of the group. She was a large woman who favored loose-fitting, floor-length dresses, big hoop earrings and lots of bracelets.

Her hair was shoulder-length, straight, and powder white.

Elyse looked straight into the camera with heavily outlined turquoise eyes. "Ghost hunting can be fun when something you can't explain happens. It can also be dangerous. That's why I always do some visualization before we begin. I do it at home where I'm comfortable, in my meditation area. I visualize white light around each of us and do a prayer for protection."

The investigation began at eight and by eleven the entire team was bored.

Kelly mugged for the stationary camera in the kitchen. "I'm not feelin' it," she said. "Of course, unlike my husband and Elyse, I don't have a psychic bone in my body. Yes, you could say I am psychically challenged. But I haven't heard anything or seen anything and I've done EVP work until I'm blue in the face. Does my face really look blue? Hmm. Anyway, we've told you what EVP stands for before, but I will tell you again in case you forgot. EVP stands for Electronic Voice Phenomena which is a fancy way of saying you can hear a disembodied voice speak on the recorder. Sometimes we hear the voice live and sometimes we only hear the voice on the recorder. Hopefully, when we review the evidence, we'll hear something." She gave the camera a wink before walking over to Elyse who was sitting on a kitchen stool.

Carl walked in with a hand-held camera. "This place is the pits," he said. "What do you say? Wanna do a little bit? We need something to spice up the episode."

"Sure," said Elyse, turning her eyes on Kelly. "Did you know, that right where you're standing . . ."

Kelly looked down.

"That's where McGregor strangled his young bride of barely three weeks?"

"Who is McGregor?"

"He owned a farm on this property around a hundred years ago. His kitchen was right where this modern kitchen is today."

"Really?"

"And after he strangled her, he cut her up right in the sink."

"And served her to the customers?"

"No, silly. This was a farm, not a restaurant. He fed her to the hogs out back. Of course, those hogs wouldn't have consumed all the bones. They're still lying around somewhere."

Kelly's eyes got big.

"But McGregor's bride went into the light. She doesn't like Mr. Lack so she isn't here."

"Is this true?" Kelly asked. Elyse could make you believe anything.

Elyse shrugged her meaty shoulders. "It's what came to me. And I'm psychic, you know."

Kelly furrowed her brow and stared at Elyse. "So there are no ghosts here?"

Elyse took a moment to answer. "I'm not sure. I haven't seen any, but I'm sensing the high-pitched sort of vibration you get when a spirit is around."

"I wouldn't know," Kelly said.

"Okay, that's good," Carl broke in. "At least it's something."

Kelly looked at Elyse. "Did you just make that up?"

"About McGregor? I told you, it came to me. We can do some fact checking later."

"No, I mean the sensing of a spirit. Do you sense one?"

"It's not real clear yet, but, yeah, I think there is one among us."

"Then let's go tell Dennis and see what he says."

Chapter 3

Mickey landed at Bob Hope Airport in Burbank and rented a car. He and John Carroll were to meet at Denny's on Hollywood Way. The entire flight, Mickey had played the conversation with John in his mind. The man never fully explained what it was that had him in such a panic. But because he sounded so sincere on the phone, Mickey made the decision to come to Los Angeles. He hoped there was something he could do to help. Depending upon how the meeting went, he would know soon.

At a little before eleven, Mickey pulled into the restaurant parking lot and found a space near the entrance. "I'm meeting someone," he told the girl at the register.

"You must be the first to arrive. All my singles are at the counter."

"I'm a little early."

Hugging her menus, she led Mickey to a table set for two toward the rear of the busy restaurant.

"How's this?" she asked.

Mickey was about to tell her it was fine when he spotted a large man sitting alone one table over and another table back. He faced away from the dining area with shoulders hunched, weight upon forearms that rested on the table. The index finger of his left hand nervously tapped his right hand, which was balled in a fist. Something told Mickey this was who he was supposed to meet. Maybe the young girl had simply forgotten about him because she'd been jammed with other customers.

"I think I'll move over there," Mickey said, gesturing at the other table. The girl glanced over her shoulder, gave him a funny look, and shrugged.

"Sure. If you want. Your server's name is Bonnie and she'll be right with you."

She handed Mickey a menu and headed back to her station. Mickey moved to the other table, but didn't sit down.

"John?" Mickey said.

The man looked up with baggy, forlorn eyes and didn't reply. For a second Mickey entertained the idea that he was wrong. The energy of this person was low and quiet, the opposite of John on the phone, and he looked so old—older than Mickey'd pictured him. His hair was thin and gray. He had a large nose and saggy jowls. The clothes he wore were simple: a green plaid, short-sleeve shirt extended over khaki-colored pants. He wore no jewelry—no ring and no watch.

"I'm Mickey McCoy."

The man motioned toward the chair opposite him.

As Mickey sat he noticed that John had already eaten. The plate had been shoved aside, a crumpled napkin tossed in with leftover pancake syrup. A three dollar tip lay in the center of the table.

"I was about to leave," John said.

Mickey frowned. "But I'm not late. In fact, I'm early and I came a long way to see you, at your request."

"I'm aware of that."

Bonnie appeared with a carafe of hot coffee. She grabbed the tip money and stuffed it in her skirt pocket. Then she lifted the carafe a few inches and said, "Coffee this morning?"

"Please," Mickey said.

Bonnie had to swipe a clean cup from another table. She filled it, ignoring John's cold, half-empty one.

"Do you know what you want or do you need another minute?"

"Just a couple of scrambled eggs and sourdough toast," Mickey said.

She wrote it down. "All right. Be up in a jiff." She stashed her order pad and reached across the table for the dirty plate. A knife fell, clattering on the table before it hit the floor.

"Whoops." Bonnie grinned. "Someone'll have to get that later." She walked away, plate in one hand, carafe of coffee in the other.

John leaned over to pick up the knife, giving Mickey a view of the dining room. He caught sight of a thin, good-looking woman in her forties seated alone at a booth. Everything about her screamed money. She had salon-styled, auburn hair and her clothes looked like something out of Vogue. She was smoking, which was what made Mickey notice her. Smoking in restaurants was prohibited in California and he found it strange that none of the employees, nor anyone sitting nearby, told her to put the cigarette out. She exhaled, her green eyes coolly cast upon Mickey.

John placed the knife on the table and his imposing torso blocked Mickey's view once again.

"I'd apologize for thinking I should go if this weren't so serious."

"I don't want an apology. But an explanation of why you asked me here would be greatly appreciated."

"You aren't what I expected."

"And what was that?"

John answered with an analytical stare. Finally he sighed. "I don't know. I'm at my wit's end. Time is running out, and I remembered my cousin talking about you." He shook his head. "I'm grasping at straws."

Mickey was growing more frustrated by the minute. Beating around the bush was not his style. He wished John would come to the point.

"What is it you need my help with?"

John took a deep breath. "I lost my job a couple months back and . . ."

"And?"

"I was a security guard at the museum." He paused again.

"The art museum you mentioned on the phone."

John nodded. "I was in charge of the schedule and I scheduled people the way I had to. I didn't let people switch. I reprimanded them if they did it anyway."

"That sounds reasonable."

"Well, it made them mad. I couldn't tell them why I scheduled them the way I did. No one would believe me. You won't believe me."

"Try me."

"They thought I was a control freak. Called me sexist. Said I was discriminatory. I know it looked that way, but I was trying to save lives."

"The way you scheduled people saved lives?"

John shifted in the chair; the movement of his body reminded Mickey of a big bear. "You really don't seem like the kind of guy my cousin said you were. If what he said was true, you'd know what I was talking about without me having to tell you."

"It doesn't work that way."

"Then, tell me, how does it work?"

There was silence. It was a valid question; one Mickey had asked himself many times. But he had no black and white answer. Certainly not one that would satisfy John.

"Maybe I should go to the museum and take a look around," Mickey said. "See what I can see. That's where you think these future deaths are going to take place."

"They will." John stood.

Or maybe I should fly home and forget all this nonsense, Mickey thought. But that would mean he'd come a long way for nothing, and he was intrigued.

"You could at least give me your phone number," Mickey said. "Just in case."

John shook his head. "I'll contact you if I change my mind. I'm sorry I can't compensate you for your time."

Mickey said, "I don't do what I do for money."

John gave Mickey one last look before he lumbered away. He

passed the table with the auburn-haired woman and she watched him go. Then she looked at Mickey. She wasn't smoking any longer. Maybe someone had told her to stop.

Bonnie arrived with Mickey's eggs.

"Here you go; anything else?"

"That was quick," said Mickey, checking his plate of food. "I'm fine. Ah, you can leave the check." She did.

Mickey took his fork and, looking up, saw that the woman with the auburn hair was gone. Two men were being seated where she'd been. He placed a bite of the eggs into his mouth and tried to catch sight of her. He couldn't, and he found it odd that she could disappear so quickly.

When he was close to finished eating, his cell phone rang. He grabbed it and checked the ID. Detective Stern was returning his call.

"Finally," Mickey said.

"Mickey McCoy. As I live and breathe. It's been a while."

"A year. I'm in Los Angeles."

"So my cousin convinced you to pay him a visit."

"He did. But then he held out on me. He's afraid I won't believe him. Afraid I'll think he's crazy."

"You? Think someone else is crazy? Now that's crazy."

Mickey smiled. "I won you over, didn't I?"

"Oh, yes. You certainly did."

"So what do you know about this?"

"Probably not any more than you do."

Mickey heard someone say something to Stern and Stern reply with "I'll be there in a minute." The detective came back on the line. "Where were we?"

"You were explaining everything in great detail."

Stern laughed. "I would if I could. The truth is, I hardly know my cousin and I don't know what he wants."

"Why'd you tell him to call me?"

"I was in L.A. a few months ago with my girlfriend. She likes art. We went to the Brahms and I ran into him. It was a fluke really, because he's a lot older than me and I didn't recognize him or anything like that. I happened to notice the name badge and said something. I didn't expect it to be my cousin because I thought he worked for this rich, high society matron. He'd worked for her for as long as I knew. Turns out she died and I thought, so that's why you're working here. But no. Lo and behold, she left the estate—her home—to him. He invited us to dinner so we could see it. Heart House. It's a pretty impressive place. Ever hear of it?"

"Maybe. A long time ago."

"Okay. So we went. He showed us around and while we're there my girlfriend heard a baby crying."

"A baby."

"She heard it, I didn't. Okay. Maybe I did. Faintly. You know how I feel about this kind of stuff."

"I know." Mickey smiled.

"So she asked about it and his words to her were, 'It's an echo from the past.' Wouldn't go into any more detail than that. But it was enough to get my girlfriend started. She told him about you and how you helped me solve this case because you have ... super powers." Stern said the last two words with a teasing tone and laughed.

Mickey smiled, eyes skyward.

"And before you correct me, yes, I know it's the other way around. I really helped you."

"Doesn't matter," Mickey said.

"Anyway. He got an earful about you while we ate. It was a nice time. My girlfriend and I went back to Brookdale and I forgot about it. Now, four months later, he calls and says he needs to talk to you. He'd been fired from his job and he was worried that people were going to get killed there. At first I thought he was telling me he was going to go back and shoot his coworkers. You know? But that wasn't it. He wants to save them and it has something to do with the paranormal. What was I supposed to do? Tell him not to call?"

"No, of course not. I just wish he'd be more forthcoming."

"Super powers gone dormant?"

"Apparently so."

Stern laughed and Mickey heard someone speak to him again. This time Stern told Mickey he had to go.

****

Mickey drove to the Hollywood Roosevelt Hotel on Hollywood Boulevard and checked in. Staying there was Marjorie's idea. She was stuck in Tahoe because of the yacht club's annual charity fundraiser, but planned to join Mickey as soon as she could. That would only happen, of course, if he remained in Los Angeles.

He looked at his stuffed suitcase. He had come prepared for a lengthy stay.

He hung up his shirts and his slacks. He put toiletries in the bathroom. Maybe he was on a fool's errand. In his experience, if the cosmic powers that be wanted him to help someone, they usually let him know in some unusual, but specific way. A vision. A dream. An encounter with someone on the "other side." But Mickey was getting nothing. Not even a hint of what was going on.

Mickey called his wife.

"I miss you, honey," Marjorie said. "How did the meeting go?"

"It came and it went, that's about all I can say. Didn't learn a whole lot except he's afraid. He's afraid of what he knows and he's afraid to tell anyone what he knows because it's something weird."

"And he doesn't understand that's your specialty?"

"Apparently not. So unless something happens to change my mind, I don't think I'll be here long. I'm going to pay a visit to the museum where he worked, but then I may catch the first flight home."

Mickey checked his watch. It was a little after one. He had time to visit the museum now. "Might even be home tonight," he said.

The clock radio switched on unexpectedly.

Tomorrow. Tomorrow . . .

It was the famous song from *Annie*.

Tomorrow. Tomorrow . . .Tomorrow. Tomorrow . . .

The song was stuck in a loop. Mickey stared.

"Mickey? Are you still there?"

"Marjorie," he said. "Don't expect me tonight. Something's changed."

"What?"

Tomorrow. Tomorrow . . .

"Okay. I get the message," Mickey called to the radio and it switched off.

"I'm going to visit the museum tomorrow," he said, and he explained about the radio.

"So something's happened. That's a good sign."

"Yes. That's good."

"I love you."

"I love you, too." They hung up.

Mickey stretched out on the bed, hands behind his head. What now? Did he while away the hours with a little sightseeing perhaps, or take a nap?

This time the television mysteriously clicked on. Mickey rose to his elbows. He saw a man with a smiling face on screen.

"I'm Harvey Lack and this is Lollietta's Mexican Restaurant in Santa Monica. Here you can enjoy authentic Mexican cuisine at family friendly prices."

The shot changed to a family of four enjoying dinner. One child held a taco; the other had a fork full of refried beans. The mother lifted a Margarita, the father a bottle of beer. "We love it," they shouted at the camera.

The low budget commercial ended. A still photo of the Santa Monica pier came on screen. An announcer said, "And don't miss tomorrow night's episode of *The Paranormal Seekers Society*, featuring a visit to Lollietta's. Right here on KVXT."

The television switched off.

Mickey smiled. He knew where he would be eating dinner tonight.

Chapter 4

Mickey sat at a table for two in the center of Lollietta's dining room. The restaurant buzzed with festivity, the chatter of cheerful customers blending with the music of a strolling guitar player. Huge murals of Mexican village life dressed up mustard-yellow walls. Mosaic table tops of blue and green Talavera tile added to the decor. He'd had better Mexican food though. The guy on the commercial might call it authentic, but that wasn't the word Mickey would use. It was just okay and much too oily. It reminded him of what people said about poorly-running cars that were for sale: "If it don't go, chrome it."

He took a sip of water. He wanted a clear head in case something unusual were to happen. But he'd been sitting for almost two hours and if something didn't occur soon, he would switch to Dos Equis amber and call it a night. He snatched a tortilla chip. The salsa was all gone and he found the chip completely stale. That was it. Enough was enough. He searched for his server to flag her down so he could order a beer. He would stay long enough to enjoy it, and then if nothing happened, he was out of there.

His server brought the beer. Mickey took a sip and berated himself for his impatience. Paranormal events happened in their own time; he knew that. Besides, he had nothing better to do. Well, except maybe catch up on his sleep. He was tired and disheartened. He'd gotten up early for the flight only to have a disappointing meeting with John. And then when the television seemed to direct him to come here, he'd been too stimulated to take a nap. Now nothing was happening and he hated it when his expectations weren't fulfilled.

He took another sip and then another. When the bottle was half empty he suddenly detected the pungent odor of lilacs. Had someone new sat nearby or were his olfactory nerves playing games? He looked around and saw no one he hadn't seen before.

He sat back, put the bottle of beer to his lips, and discovered a Mexican woman with a round figure and a lovely face three feet away, staring at him. She wore a colorful skirt and a beautifully embroidered white blouse, a name badge pinned on the bodice. She looked to be about forty-five. Her expression was sad and yet commanding. It said, *Do you see me? Really, really see me? I see you and I want your help.*

Mickey stared back. There was no doubt she was the source of the perfume. But what did she want?

After a second or two he saw that she had no legs. Her head and torso were midair with no support. She was a ghost. *Lollietta,* he heard in his head.

"Lollietta," he said softly.

A server walked toward her and strolled right through without hesitation. There was no impact, although it appeared the server sensed something because he took a quick glance behind him as he continued on his way.

What is it? Mickey asked silently.

Lollietta nodded, turned, and Mickey scrambled from the table to follow. She led him to the short hallway outside the restrooms and paused at the entrance to the men's room. Glancing at Mickey one last time, she disappeared by passing through the closed door. A moment later a man exited, waving his hand in front of his nose, making a horrible face.

"I wouldn't if I was you," he said. "It was fine a second ago, then all of the sudden this stench came out of nowhere. The plumbing must have backed up or something. Oh, jeez."

Mickey waited for the man to go before he went inside where he was greeted with the stink of decaying flesh.

"Oh, God." Mickey put his hand over his nose and mouth and nearly gagged. Lollietta was nowhere to be seen, but a big red X practically glowed on the floor.

****

"You know I can't call the police," Mickey told Detective Stern, once again seated at the table, cell phone to his ear. "What am I going to say, that I smelled a foul odor in the men's room? They'll tell me to call a plumber. Besides, it's gone now."

"I—"

"Don't you have connections? Tell them to bring a cadaver dog. That'll get them a warrant."

Stern sighed. "I'll see what I can do and call you back."

Mickey closed his phone and asked his server to bring him coffee and more chips. Fresh ones this time.

It took over an hour, but just as Stern called back and was saying, "I called a friend, who called a friend. I talked to the guy, but I don't know him and I don't know if I convinced him enough to follow through . . ." a disgruntled-looking guy in a blue dress shirt and gray tie entered the restaurant. He walked past the greeter without batting an eye and entered the dining area. He had cop written all over him.

"He's here," Mickey told Stern before hanging up. He stood and waved the man over.

"So what's this about?" the cop asked Mickey, showing little patience as he reached for a chip.

"Stern explained, didn't he?"

"Yeah."

"It's just like he said."

The cop stared at him. "You're psychic and you smell a rat."

"A dead body, actually. She's buried in the men's restroom, under the tile floor. Did you bring Duchess?"

The cop did a double-take. "How do you know the name of the

dog?"

"Maybe Stern told me."

"He wouldn't know. Department just got her and I didn't tell him."

"Then, Detective Clark Hanigan, the answer should be obvious."

Bull's-eye. Go ahead and ask me, how did I know your first name? Stern only knows your last.

The cop didn't ask. Instead he gave Mickey an icy stare which melted into one of puzzlement. "Okay, I'm bringing Duchess in, which probably isn't even legal. But we'll let a judge decide if it comes to that."

He walked out and returned with a brown and white Springer Spaniel on a leash.

"Sir. Sir. Dogs are not allowed," Mickey heard the greeter tell the cop.

"She's a seeing eye dog, of sorts," Hanigan answered as he briskly walked past, straight to Mickey. "Where?" he asked.

Mickey led him to the restroom and opened the door. The odor was gone.

"I don't smell anything," Hanigan said.

"Neither do I, now," Mickey responded. "But Duchess will."

As if on cue, the dog flopped on her belly and signaled with three barks—exactly where Mickey had seen the red X.

****

By three a.m. the restaurant was swarming with cops. A warrant had been obtained, the floor dug up, and Lollietta's body—wrapped in a clear plastic wardrobe bag—had been found. She was completely decomposed. Forensics would have to confirm the identity, but it was clear from the clothing on the skeleton, the name badge on the blouse, and the purse found with her, ID inside, that she was the long-lost wife of restaurant owner, Harvey Lack.

Despite the late hour, members of the media and a great many spectators stood outside the restaurant watching the police come and go. Reporters asked for answers from anyone they could.

"We found a body," Detective Hanigan announced when he was ready. "Indications are it's the missing wife of the restaurant owner. He's been brought in for questioning. Beyond that, I can't say."

"How'd you know there was a body there?"

Hanigan frowned. He'd told Judge Oliphant he'd stopped to use the restroom and didn't want to leave Duchess in the car. The dog signaled and he followed through. He couldn't very well say a psychic had called a detective-pal in Brookdale who called a cop friend he knew who called him and begged for a favor. His lie would probably hold up to scrutiny, but he wasn't about to share it with the media.

He scanned for Mickey and found him among the crowd. Once Mickey saw Hanigan looking his way, he gave him a small salute. For a moment Hanigan wondered if Mickey would want credit for having known there was a body buried in the men's room. But when Mickey turned away, that concern vanished.

Funny old buzzard, Hanigan thought. *How did you really know there was a body under that floor?* He'd be checking the time line of the victim's disappearance, when renovations had been done to the restaurant, and also among the things to investigate, he'd find out if there was any connection between the restaurant and Señor Mickey McCoy. Yep. He would check that too.

And you won't find any, Mickey thought as he got in his car.

Chapter 5

JoAnn Hernandez worked graveyard shift at the Brahms Museum of Art and hated it. The tasks of a security guard lacked the more glamorous—at least she thought of them as glamorous—duties of a police officer. She'd tried to get into the academy three times, but always failed the agility test. JoAnn couldn't run to save her life, let alone the life of anyone else.

She'd felt lucky to get the museum job. At the time, it seemed the only game in town. When John Carroll hired her, he had explained he only had an opening for the graveyard shift and she had claimed not to mind. Her thinking was she could make it work until a slot for days opened up. But man, was she ever bored. Time dragged with no one to talk to and it was torture just coming to work. There were only so many times you could make your rounds and feel like you were accomplishing anything before you knew your job was crap.

John Carroll had since been canned and JoAnn felt guilty about that. She'd joined forces with the other female guards to complain about how he assigned the shifts. Women always got graveyard. Period. No discussion. JoAnn was low on the totem pole, but there were others with seniority, even more than John Carroll, who still had to work it when they didn't want to. Seniority didn't matter to John, and the men who requested night watch because it paid a little better were ignored as well. Security personnel weren't union employees and John could do what he wanted. Now that he was gone, JoAnn found herself no better off because she was still at the bottom of the pecking order. She'd helped get the guy fired for nothing.

Sitting at the console with its bank of eight alternating security screens, she glanced at the clock. Ten to eight. Ten more minutes until she could go home. It had been a slow night, with the usual strange sounds coming from gallery seventeen. That had stopped intriguing her long ago. Everybody who worked graveyard heard them and no one could explain what they were.

She'd been forewarned on night one by none other than John Carroll himself, "You may hear what sounds like a woman talking. Crying, too. Go ahead and check it out, but don't let it scare you. There is nothing for *you* to be afraid of."

Very little scared JoAnn. And the weird sounds were a welcome relief from the boredom—until they'd become boring too. She did as John said, however. She always checked out gallery seventeen when she heard them, and, like everyone else, never found the source.

"Hey, JoAnn." Stan had arrived for work.

"Hey, Stan," JoAnn answered.

"Catch any art thieves last night?"

"Two."

"Any bums trying to keep warm?"

"A couple."

"Any ghosts in gallery seventeen?"

It was a running joke. No one believed in ghosts except for JoAnn, and she'd only *suggested* that maybe—maybe—a ghost was responsible for the noise. She'd never said it was a fact.

"You should catch the morning news when you get home," Stan said.

"Why?"

"They found a body in the men's room of Lollietta's restaurant. Under the floor."

"Oh, yeah? Why should I care about that? You think I did it?"

Stan chuckled. "No. They interviewed those guys from that cable show you like. Those ghost hunters."

"*The Paranormal Seekers Society?*"

"That's it. I guess they just did an investigation of the place and it's gonna air tonight."

"They found the body?"

"No, but they're taking credit for it. Just thought you'd like to know."

"Thanks."

****

When JoAnn walked into her apartment she switched on the television and tuned to the local news. It took a few minutes for the stories to cycle to the one she wanted, but finally she caught the coverage of what had taken place in the wee hours of the morning at Lollietta's Mexican Restaurant.

The screen displayed a photo of the building, its neon sign glowing, police lights flashing red and blue. Next, footage played of workers from the medical examiner's office carrying someone's bagged remains from the restaurant. Clutching a microphone, a news reporter braved the cold night air to explain that a fluke had led police to find what was believed to be the body of Lollietta Lack, missing for more than five years.

Little more was known at this point and the story changed to a short, in-studio interview with Dennis Curry, founder of *The Paranormal Seekers Society*.

"It seems there's been a proliferation of interest in ghost hunting. How did your interest come about?" asked the reporter.

"To tell you the truth, I'm not a big believer in ghosts. I know that sounds odd coming from me, but I do think claims concerning the paranormal are exaggerated. I started *The Paranormal Seekers Society* to debunk those claims."

"So you've never seen a ghost?"

"I've seen what appeared to be a ghost. More than a few times actually. But I think there are always explanations for such things."

"Which are?"

"That's the thing. I don't know. Nobody knows. But it's like anything. Cell phones. The Internet. Flying. All of this would blow a person's mind if that person was transported from the time of, say, Henry the Eighth."

"Interesting analogy. Time travel."

Both the reporter and Dennis laughed.

"But you know what I'm saying," Dennis continued. "It's a matter of technology, knowledge catching up with the phenomena."

"Tell us about your experience at Lollietta's."

"We did sense a presence in the men's room which is where the body was found. You'll see if you watch the show, that's where we got the strongest indications of a spirit being present. And that's where police found someone's remains. It's pretty interesting."

"But you didn't notify police?"

"No." Dennis smiled. "We sensed a spirit, not a body."

The reporter shook Dennis' hand. "Thank you, Dennis, for joining us on such short notice. We appreciate it. Now if someone has a place they'd like for your group to investigate, what should they do?"

Dennis explained how to contact the PSS. A phone number and e-mail address were shown on screen and the segment ended.

JoAnn turned off the television. Mulling over what she'd seen, she went into the bedroom and changed clothes. Then, sitting at the breakfast table eating a bowl of cereal, a brilliant idea flashed in her brain. Wouldn't it be cool if the PSS investigated gallery seventeen? She might even get to be on TV. After all, she was the one who heard the noises night after night and no one could explain them. The PSS was a small outfit. They needed places to go. Gallery seventeen was perfect. Perfect! She would give them a call.

Chapter 6

Kelly Curry did not know how to cook. She was easily distracted and things usually got burned. The broken smoke alarm in the kitchen was proof of that. Ten months ago she had whacked it with a broom when its siren scream couldn't be shut off quick enough for her. Now there it hung, by a wire, for anyone who came inside her kitchen to see. There was no point in fixing it; she would just break it again. She'd done so three times before she finally told Dennis to just let it be.

Bacon sizzled in the pan. Four strips, all for Dennis. Leaning against the stove on one hip, spatula in hand, Kelly was still dressed in the flannel pajamas she preferred when temperatures in the house dipped into the sixties at night. She and Dennis loathed consuming energy. Blankets, thermals, and flannels did a perfectly adequate job of keeping their bodies warm.

Grease spattered and she crinkled her nose at the aroma of the food.

"Piggy strips," she muttered, combing fingers through her short, dark hair.

"You don't have to cook bacon for me," Dennis said as he entered the kitchen, dressed for work in a suit and tie. He wrapped his arms around her, chest against her back, and planted a kiss on her cheek.

"You like piggy strips. You like cholesterol."

"Cereal is fine. I like a happy bride. You've got the fire too high." He reached for the dial and turned the flame down.

Kelly tapped his hand with the spatula and he stepped back. She returned the flame to where she had it. "You're running late. Gotta get this done."

Dennis laughed. "Had to watch myself on TV."

"That little interview you did at five-thirty this morning?" Her voice said she thought they could have conducted it just as easily at a more appropriate hour.

"Yep. That's the one." He sat down at the table where a glass of orange juice was waiting for him. Kelly left the stove to get him some coffee from the brew station. When she placed a mug before him, he grabbed her again, pulled her toward him and kissed her stomach.

She giggled as she looked up at the clock. "It's after eight."

"I know. I'll get there soon enough."

"Oh, yeah?"

"I've got most of that report done and I don't meet with Slocum until . . ." He made the noise he always made when he thought about his day job. Kelly called it his sigh-groan hybrid.

"Accountant by day, ghost hunter by night." She grinned, arms resting on his shoulders.

"I'm so glad I married you," Dennis said.

"Me too. Now if we could just nail down more places to investigate. Places with real ghosts in them. Our marriage would be perfect."

"Our marriage is fine. And I've been thinking. Maybe we should give up the ghost business."

Kelly took a step back. "No way. You love it. You know you do."

"I don't love it. You do. It's tedious and not much happens."

"The restaurant turned out okay."

"Too bad there isn't footage of me saying, 'She's under the floor tiles. Dig her up!'" He rolled his eyes and took a sip of coffee.

"You did say you saw a woman's face in the mirror and you felt she wanted something."

"I thought I saw a woman's face. My brain said she wanted

something. I imagined it."

"Whenever anything happens, you say you imagined it. I disagree."

"It hardly matters. The camera didn't capture her in the mirror and that's what viewers want. Evidence. Also, Elyse's little McGregor story should be cut. It makes us look like a bunch of amateurs."

"We are amateurs."

"You know what I mean."

"Jugs doesn't have much else."

"Did Elyse fact check to see if any of the stuff that, quote, came to her, unquote, might be based in fact?"

"I haven't heard."

"She won't. You'll have to."

"I don't mind."

Dennis put the orange juice to his lips and his eyes got big. He gulped, pointing with his free hand. The sound of sizzling bacon got louder.

Kelly looked behind her. The bacon was burning, dark smoke rising in the air. "Damn!" she yelled, running to the stove, grabbing the heated handle of the cast iron skillet. With a yelp, she immediately let go. The skillet struck the corner of the stove and searing-hot grease flew in all directions. It scorched the wrist and palm of her right hand. She jumped back to avoid further injury as the pan hit the floor. Her eyes filled with tears from the pain.

Dennis rushed to her and took her hand by the fingers.

"I'm such a klutz!"

"It's not your fault. I distracted you." He stared at the injury. It was red and ugly with blisters beginning to show. He pulled her to the sink and ran cold water over her burns.

"Bandages and Neosporin in the bathroom?" he asked as he turned off the burner.

Kelly nodded and Dennis left the room. The cool water helped soothe the burn. She ignored her cell phone when it rang.

Dennis returned with first aid. He dressed the wound, put ice in a tea towel and pressed it against the bandage. "I think I should take you to urgent care."

"I'm fine now. Besides, I'm too busy. There's a load of books coming into the store today. You better get to work. Sorry about breakfast."

"Breakfast is not what I'm worried about. And for your information, as of this moment, I hate bacon. Awful stuff, those piggy strips."

Kelly laughed. "Yeah. That'll be the day."

"Cheerios. Froot Loops. Yum!"

"Go on, before you're any later."

He kissed her and left for work.

Kelly frowned and adjusted the ice on her wrist. Now he was going to be late and the boss was already on his case for hunting ghosts in his spare time. How dare a serious accountant do something so silly? Well, people could make fun all they wanted, but their little ghost hunting operation had seen plenty of inexplicable things.

The cell phone rang again and this time she answered it.

"*Paranormal Seekers Society*. Hey, Jugs. No, he's gone to work. No new cases yet. Maybe after the broadcast tonight; that's when we usually get calls. I'll let you know."

She hung up and realized she had a voice mail. She checked it.

"Hi. My name is JoAnn Hernandez. Um . . . I know a place that might be good for one of your shows. Or, um, investigations. The Brahms Museum of Art has these noises . . ."

Chapter 7

Shortly after ten in the morning, Mickey arrived at the Brahms Museum of Art—a gleaming single story building of white granite and glass. From its center, wings shot to the north and south, elbowing at interesting angles. A wide series of low-rise steps led to a double-door, glass entrance. Trees and lush gardens disguised the fact that the museum was located in a dirty, bustling part of Los Angeles.

Mickey held the door for perhaps twenty—he didn't count—preteens entering the building, and wondered how many were actually interested in art. They chattered and teased and mostly seemed to be happy they weren't imprisoned in a classroom, tied to a desk, on such a bright, cool day. He followed them inside the cavernous foyer where their voices and footsteps bounced off marble floors and walls.

A woman sang out, "Over here. Luther Middle School students! Please stay together and gather over here."

The kids herded themselves in front of a smiling male guide who appeared to be barely out of his teens. Looking very official in his navy blue jacket with shiny gold buttons, he stood beside the statue of an attractive, seventy-something year-old woman whose bronze attire consisted of a simple sheath dress, high-heeled shoes, and pearls around her neck. Her smiling face had a beneficent air. The petite figure stood life-size on a three-foot high pedestal.

Mickey paid the six-buck price of admission and accepted a brochure that included a map of the exhibits. As was typical, exhibition galleries wove together like a maze. The layout made it easy to bypass a room if not careful. Mickey wasn't sure where he wanted to go. He didn't want to miss anything of importance by accident. Of course, at this point, he didn't know what was important and what was not.

"Welcome to the Brahms Museum of Art," Mickey heard the guide tell the children.

Their voices rang back, "Hi. Hello."

"I'm Mike. I'll be showing you around today. We are very pleased to have you here. Now there are a few rules I need to tell you about before we get started . . ."

Mickey listened as the guide told the children not to touch anything and to stay together. If they had questions they should raise their hand and he'd do his best to answer. After providing a few more museum regulations, he asked if everyone understood.

"Yes," came a chorus of young voices followed by a lone "no" and a snicker.

"Josh," one of the chaperons admonished.

A boy slapped his hands to his side and stood like a soldier. "Yes, ma'am!" he shouted. Some of the children giggled.

The guide began again. "We are standing beside a statue of Elizabeth Brahms Weldon, the museum's founder and benefactor. Mrs. Weldon lived to be ninety-seven years old."

"Whoa," the children responded.

"She loved art and collected it all of her life. She founded this museum in nineteen fifty-two . . ."

Mickey noticed that the brochure had a bio for Elizabeth Brahms Weldon and stopped listening to Mike. He could read about Elizabeth for himself.

He headed for the throughway that led to the exhibit halls, but first had to pass a six-foot-long security station. A guard, who appeared to be in his late sixties, sat behind the black console. It was possible he'd taken this job after retiring elsewhere, just for something to do. But Mickey got the impression he'd worked at the museum a long time. He had a friendly demeanor and bid everyone good morning.

"Good morning," Mickey said back, and stopped to chat. The guard's badge read Clarence. "You look like a veteran who knows his way around this place."

"Been here twenty-nine years. It's the best museum in town."

"So you like working here."

"I do and that's a fact. Got a little bit of everything for everybody. Not too much of the real way-out stuff, though. Gotta go to the MOCA for that."

"The MOCA?"

"Museum of Contemporary Art."

"Oh," said Mickey and it flashed through his mind that this was an opportunity to learn about John Carroll. "Tell me something, Clarence, if you can. I met a man who used to work here—"

"Well, I know everybody. Knew Mrs. Weldon, too. A real nice lady. Real nice. I was sorry when she passed. Although she didn't come in much the last few years of her life."

"Slowed down, did she?"

"That she did, that she did." Clarence looked sad for a moment and then smiled. "Fancy dresser, lots of money. A millionaire back in the day. Guess you have to be a billionaire now to really count and maybe she was; I don't know. No matter, I can tell you this. She wasn't stuck up. Not one iota. Not her. Never too busy to stop and say hello, ask how I was doing. Now, her daughter. I wouldn't give you a plugged nickel to have a conversation with her." Clarence frowned.

"A real pain in the ass, I take it."

"You said it; I didn't." His smile came back. "Now who is this fellow used to work here that you want to talk about?"

"John Carroll."

The guard guffawed. "Oh, him. Yeah, he's gone. Cooked his own goose with some very peculiar ideas about how things should be run." The guard looked seriously into Mickey's eyes. "Although he never interfered with me, mind you. I've been at this desk." He tapped it. "*Days*—for eighteen years. If he'd even suggested—"

"Excuse me. Can you tell me where the restrooms are?" A woman clutching the hand of a young boy stared anxiously at Clarence.

The veteran guard smiled warmly and directed the way.

"Thank you." The woman pulled the child along.

"Getting back to John Carroll," Mickey said. "He thinks someone is going to . . ." He hesitated, unsure how blunt he should be. "He thinks someone is going to get hurt now that he doesn't work here."

Clarence threw back his head and cackled, sighing when he finished. He took out a handkerchief and wiped his tear-filled eyes. "Told you about that, did he? He was something."

"I don't understand why he'd think that."

"I don't either."

"He said people didn't like the way he made the work schedule."

"That's right. He only scheduled *women* to work nightshift because nightshift works alone." Clarence chuckled once more, only this time with more control. "If a man worked alone, that man was gonna die; so said crazy John."

"Did he ever explain why he thought that?"

"Nope. Said we should just trust him." Clarence guffawed again. "Got away with it for a while. More months than I would have put up with, if I was in charge."

"Why did they?"

"He'd worked for Mrs. Weldon most of his life and I suppose the museum figured having him work here did something for her memory. But once the gals threatened to sue and he still wouldn't change his ways, management had to act. He was history. Didn't matter about Mrs. Weldon anymore."

Clarence's eyes caught sight of something on one of the console's security screens. He picked up a radio, pressed the button, and spoke. "Gallery six. Watch the gal in the pink sweater. She's got her nose up against that Sisley."

Clarence watched the screen and once he was satisfied, pointed to his ear. "They got a button receiver. No one else can hear."

Mickey nodded.

"Don't want to spoil the ambiance with a bunch of chattering help."

"No." Mickey smiled. "So, men are working nightshift and there's been no problem."

"Men aren't working nightshift. So happens two gals have the least seniority."

"Oh." Mickey was quiet a moment. "One more question. Has anything strange happened since John Carroll left?"

"*Niente di nuovo.*"

Mickey stared. Italian. From Clarence now.

"Excuse me?" Mickey said.

"Nothing new. Nothing worth mentioning."

"No?" He gazed at Clarence, hoping that would get him to say more.

"Oh, the gals get a little nervous at night. That comes with the territory."

"What do you mean?"

"They say they hear things. That new girl. That JoAnn. She's forever mentioning it."

"Mentioning what?"

"She hears *una donna.*"

Italian again. "*Una donna?*" Mickey repeated and Clarence looked at him like that was an odd response then rattled off sentences in a flurry of Italian.

"Thank you," Mickey said, backing away. He'd learned all he was going to learn from Clarence. And Italian was starting to give him a headache.

"*Benvenuto,*" Clarence said. "*Visitate la galleria diciassette.*"

"*Arrivederci.*" Mickey waved a hand in the air and strolled farther inside.

****

John Carroll sat on a white leather couch in the study of Heart House. Daylight barely made it through a bank of windows masked by drapes while a blazing fire in the large marble fireplace cast dancing shapes on fixtures and walls. He placed a large black book on his lap and pressed fingers of both hands upon it. With eyes closed, he spoke earnestly.

"Mother-power, Father-power, bring balance to this house. You are omniscient, omnipotent. With silver light cast your net wide, touching all who need you. I am connected to you, as are all. Because of this I can know the truth. No one may oppose you. You are the source of everything and, as such, can do all and protect all. You can break unjust and evil spells. You can destroy wicked—"

A breathy laugh broke his concentration. He opened his eyes and glowered.

"Oh, if you aren't the silly one," a sultry female voice said. "You've tried this so many times before. You must not be doing it right. I hear urgency in your tone. And fear. You know what they say. If you stand outside and pray for rain you'd best carry an umbrella, otherwise, you're showing you don't believe and your words are nothing but hot air."

He closed his eyes. She was right. He didn't know how to pray. He didn't know how to break spells. He was feeling urgent because time was running out. He needed someone more knowledgeable to help him because he didn't know what it was that needed to be done. Anxiety filled him and his chest heaved with concern.

"Leave me alone," he said. "This is your fault and I have to try."

"Don't you need candles, water blessed by the Pope, and magic dust or something?"

He had read "recipes" for spells, and yes, they called for candles and specialty items he didn't have. He'd brought people to the house many times, so-called spiritual practitioners who did own such things and claimed to know how to break spells. But nothing ever worked and here he sat, with the same problem, and the person who had caused the problem was needling him in his ear.

"Go away, Avery. I hate you," he said.

"Ewww. Hate? Such a strong word. Even when I attacked you, I don't think I hated you. But then again, maybe I did. Maybe I do. Why don't you give up? I mean, what is the problem really? I don't see one. I just don't think you should be so concerned."

There was a pause and then John spoke in a whisper. "Give up? Is that what I should do?"

****

The Brahms displayed paintings, drawings, and sculptures according to period—Byzantine, Gothic, Mannerist, Early Renaissance, and High Renaissance eras. Mickey looked for Italian pieces and recognized names of artists such as Michelangelo, Da Vinci, Raphael, Botticelli, and El Greco. Other names he did not know.

Staring at a painting—St. James Freeing Hermogenes—by Fra Angelico, on loan from another museum, he wondered if he was on the right track to learn anything about why he'd been drawn to Los Angeles. He was in the correct place; the museum was where death and destruction were supposed to happen, per John, but so far all he'd been given as a hint that he might learn anything at all was Clarence speaking a foreign language.

"Big clue," he said aloud. "Italian words I don't understand."

"*Scusatemi.* I speak Italian," a pretty young woman with an Italian accent said. She stood beside a young man, only a foot away from Mickey, and was staring at him. "Can I help translate something?"

Mickey smiled in surprise. The problem was he never knew when he would need a translator. "Thank you. But for the moment I'm fine."

She walked away with her companion.

Mickey checked the map in the brochure and decided to pay

gallery twelve a visit. It held Early Christian and Medieval Art.

Italian names jumped out at him, but Spanish, English and French artists' works were even more prevalent and he moved into an adjacent gallery. Paintings from the thirteenth and fourteenth centuries depicting Christ, Madonna and Child, and stories from the Bible covered the walls. Mickey watched people roam, reading plaques and closely examining the artist's brushwork, color palette, and drawing ability. He felt nothing for him here and walked into gallery fifteen. A large ottoman in the center of the room beckoned, and he sat and stared at a Raphael as he rested. It was amazing how tired he felt from just standing around.

The irregular cadence of marching feet drew his attention to the hall outside the entrance to the gallery and soon he saw the middle school youngsters traipsing past. Talking was hushed; they were whispering and giggling. Josh's voice rose above the din, "Hep, hep, middle school cadet. Teachers all got belly aches and can't keep in step."

Snickering.

"Shut up, Josh. Before we get in trouble."

"*Diciassette ragazzi —camminare, camminare, camminare.*"

Soon all of the kids chattered in Italian. Mickey pushed to his feet and quickly followed them into gallery seventeen. The space was rectangular and larger than most of the other exhibition halls Mickey had seen.

"Over here, please," Mike called and the children gathered around. Other visitors gave the guide their attention as well. Mickey noticed the pretty young woman who had offered him help. She stood only three feet away. They acknowledged each other with a smile.

"We are standing before an enigmatic example..." And suddenly Mike spewed forth his speech in Italian.

Mickey eased over to the woman and said, "Do you think you could translate for me now?"

"Now?" The woman looked astonished. "But he is speaking

English."

Mickey was certain his face turned purple but he pressed on. "If you could just tell me what he's saying, I'd appreciate it."

She eyed Mickey suspiciously and raised her brows. "He says this was the final painting to come to the museum from Elizabeth Brahms Weldon's personal collection. It was painted in sixteen thirty-seven by Lavinia Zanetti—a self-portrait. It is the only painting of Zanetti's here in the museum."

Mike began speaking English again and moved to another exhibit.

"Thank you," Mickey said.

The woman nodded, her expression wary.

As the crowd shifted, Mickey moved to Lavinia's self-portrait. Her lips curled upward in a dangerous, crazy smile. Her wild, confident eyes challenged him. They seemed to say: *How dare you look at me? I am not here for you. If you stay, you will be sorry.*

Mickey responded by thinking: *You made this painting intimate and seductive. It was meant for someone, wasn't it? Not for the general public. Your hair is loose, but not carefree. It is disturbed just as you are.*

As Mickey stared he heard an insane laugh in the recesses of his mind.

Is that you? Echoes of you? Were you insane?

Italian words swirled in his brain with no clue of what they meant. His right thumb began to ache and he rubbed it. Backing away, he nearly smacked into somebody, and in response heard a frightful chortle in his head. When he was nearly to the wall with the exit, his thumb stopped throbbing.

He observed the patrons in the gallery. Lavinia's intriguing stare seemed to call them. They paused longer before her portrait than before any other painting in the room. Some, however, moved away readily, almost as if they were afraid.

He watched and noticed a pattern. The men who gazed at her always began to rub their right thumb, just as he had. The women did not. Mickey watched for half an hour to be certain. The pattern held.

When there was a lull in the room he walked close to Lavinia again and his thumb began to ache.

"How do you do that?" he whispered. "And why?"

"You feel it, too?" the male security guard spoke from across the room. Mickey looked behind him. The guard was African-American, in his forties, tall and soft around the belly. "Acoustics. I heard what you said."

"Oh," said Mickey, walking toward the guard. A badge said his name was Pete. "Does your thumb ache?"

"Not from back here. I'm supposed to be standing over there." He motioned to a section of wall closer to Lavinia. "But I don't. My thumb never aches when I'm this far away. Guess her powers don't reach this far." He chuckled. "Listen to me. Never thought words like that would come out of this mouth."

Mickey smiled. His eyes drifted to the floor as he mulled over Pete's words and suddenly felt chilled to the core. The muscular corpse of a blond young man lying on his side materialized. Knees were bent and splayed. His head lay in the crook of his left arm, his right arm outstretched. He wore a t-shirt stained with blood. Pools of the stuff blighted the hardwood floor. A patriotic tattoo of an American flag entwined with the head of an eagle was partially visible on one arm. Mickey couldn't make out the large design on the front of the shirt because of the blood and position of the body, but he clearly saw the initials PSS and a skull on the right short sleeve.

"You okay, sir?" Pete asked.

Mickey looked up.

"You have a sick expression on your face."

Mickey tried to focus on the guard. "Umm." He looked back at the floor. The body was gone, but he stared. "I'm all right," he mumbled.

"You look sort of green around the gills."

Mickey managed to raise his eyes. "This may sound a little strange, but has anyone ever died in this room?"

"Don't think so. Not that I'm aware of."

Visitors entered the gallery and Mickey walked closer to Pete. "But someone might have?"

"The only death I know about in the Brahms was more than a year ago in receiving."

"What happened?"

"The police think it was a random act of violence. Some punk looking to kill someone for fun. Stabbed the clerk to death and took off. Didn't steal a thing."

"And they never solved it?"

"Didn't really try, at least not as far as us people at the museum are concerned. You know, most of this art is worth a fortune and there are cameras all over the place. The police took the security footage of receiving and got nothing. If you can believe that."

Mickey nodded. The police didn't always let the public in on what they knew. He wondered if John Carroll was aware of the murder in receiving. He glanced at the painting of Lavinia across the room. He decided he would walk through the rest of the museum before he drove back to the hotel, but he was sure he'd already found what he was supposed to find.

He would not be heading home to Tahoe any time soon. Most assuredly, a murder was going to take place. Who the victim was, how it would happen and when, he didn't know. Maybe there was nothing he could do to stop it. But that didn't mean he wouldn't try.

Chapter 8

Mickey was frustrated. He didn't know how he was going to learn the identity of the man on the floor in gallery seventeen. He told himself his psychic skills would come to his aid when they were supposed to. He told himself he was making progress, not to worry. Still his mind spun wildly. What if the answer didn't come? What if the headline in the morning paper read: *Patron Murdered in the Brahms—Psychic fails*?

What if? What if? What if!

He needed a distraction. Something to keep from going crazy. Grauman's Chinese Theatre was just across the street from his hotel. He'd be a tourist.

Mickey walked the short distance to the theatre and joined sightseers searching the forecourt cement for hand and footprints of famous movie stars. In particular, he looked for William Powell—a favorite. He soon realized the imprints were blurred except for names of Italian heritage: Al Pacino, Sophia Loren, Frank Sinatra, Jimmy Durante, John Travolta, Sylvester Stallone. Even when he came upon a name not of that lineage, it changed before his eyes. Marilyn Monroe became Gina Lollabrigida. Debbie Reynolds became Liza Minnelli.

I get it, he thought with some irritation. *I'm dealing with Italians or Italy, something like that. I already found the Zanetti self-portrait. Can we move on? Who is my victim? Are you saying he's Italian, because let me tell you, Universe, that's not enough to go on.*

He looked down and saw Susan Sarandon's immortalized autograph and prints. He happened to know she was half Italian and decided it was just more of the same. But then a melody he didn't recognize began going round and round in his brain. Was it from one of her movies? Whether it was or wasn't, what could it possibly mean?

He waited for something more precise—something he might actually understand. When it became apparent he would get nothing else, he left the forecourt and headed down the block. He'd had enough anyway. A walk might clear his mind.

The song continued to plague him.

Fifteen minutes later he found himself in front of a hole-in-the-wall bar and grill that seemed to summon him for dinner. He didn't like the look of the place, and he wasn't hungry. His intuition prodded him. He walked inside.

He found the restaurant as unappealing on the inside as it was on the outside.

The dim lighting isn't ambiance; it's a mask for dirt.

Stop it, Mickey told himself. *Since being married to Marjorie you've grown unaccustomed to greasy spoons, that's all.*

The only waitress in sight called to Mickey from a table where she was jotting down a customer's order. "Sit anywhere you like. Menu's on the wall." She motioned toward the bar. She was an overweight woman in her late fifties dressed in tight, unbecoming jeans and a loud, ill-fitting t-shirt.

Most of the tables were empty and he selected one near the bar where a television was attached to the wall. A balding man in his thirties tended a lone drinker.

Mickey began humming softly, very softly, the song he could not get out of his head. He looked at the menu items listed on a large green chalkboard and quickly settled on a bowl of clam chowder.

"I'm Going Home," a female voice said most decidedly and Mickey looked to his side. The waitress was standing ready, pencil and pad in hand.

The bartender responded: "Your shift's not over, Gent. You ain't going anywhere."

"Not that! The song this guy's humming." She began to sing the mysterious song in Mickey's head.

"You know it?" Mickey asked.

"You're the one humming; don't you?"

"No," Mickey said. "What is it?"

"It's Frank-n-furter's farewell song."

"Frank-n-furter."

"From Rocky Horror."

"Oh," said Mickey.

"I love that movie. Must have seen it a hundred times when it was playing at the Tiffany. Burned the lighter. Squirted the gun. Dressed up as Magenta. That's my name now. Legally changed it." She gave Mickey a satisfied grin.

"I think that movie was *after* my time."

The waitress looked smug. "Yeah? And yet here you are singing that song."

"Humming," Mickey corrected.

"Whatever. You didn't like it?"

"Never saw it."

"Oh, come on! Tim Curry. Susan Sarandon. Barry Bostwick. Meatloaf. You don't know what you're missing."

"Apparently not." Mickey had no desire to see the cult classic, but thought he might *have* to if the reason for the song didn't make itself known. "I'll have the clam chowder."

"We're out. I'll bring you the Thai chicken curry. It's the chef's specialty."

Before Mickey could protest, Magenta gave him a departing shot. "Netflix!"

The tune stopped playing inside Mickey's head and he relaxed. Mystery solved and curry it was. Good thing he had an iron stomach. He looked up at the television. The bartender was clicking through channels.

"There! Stop!" the guy at the bar commanded.

"This is what you want?" The bartender sounded surprised.

"Yeah. This is that ghost show where they found that dead body."

"Oh, yeah? We gonna see a dead body?"

Mickey began to watch too. He wouldn't have seen the episode if he hadn't stopped in to eat. He wondered if he was *supposed* to watch.

It didn't take long to get his dinner. "And Tim Curry's great!" Magenta said as she placed his meal on the table.

"Tim Curry's great. Got it," Mickey said.

The food looked surprisingly appetizing. He dipped his spoon, looked back at the TV, and caught his breath. The lead guy wore a t-shirt with the initials PSS on the sleeve. And he had a tattoo on his arm of an American flag entwined with an eagle head. Now Mickey couldn't look away. As the show progressed each ghost hunter was featured doing some ghost busting bit, their names captioned. The lead's full name: Dennis Curry.

Dennis was Mickey's dead man. He was also the one on the show with psychic abilities. Evidently those abilities weren't going to be enough to save his life.

Mickey watched as Dennis explained that he'd glimpsed a woman in the men's room mirror. It was the most exciting piece of ghost hunting in the entire program. But it didn't go far enough. Lollietta hadn't been able to get through to him. Was it because of the cameras? The other people? Or because Dennis wasn't receptive enough?

Mickey looked down at his meal. A curry dish. Tim Curry had sung the song stuck in his head. A guy named Curry was the murder victim. Mickey smiled. It would be so much easier if a voice just shouted in his ear: *The dead guy's name is Dennis Curry.*

Yeah, but not as fascinating.

He ate and watched the show as it wrapped. Dennis and Jugs went over evidence with Harvey Lack.

The barfly got excited. "This guy. This is the guy who killed his wife and he's so stupid, he calls in people who see ghosts to investigate. I saw it on the news." He laughed.

On the television Dennis said to Harvey, "We picked up this class 'A' EVP in the men's room. Didn't hear it at the time, but the recorder got it. Take a listen."

Jugs opened a laptop. The screen was black except for a purple bar. One section of the bar had up and down spikes, indicating voice phenomena. Jugs pressed a button and a thin white line traveled the bar. At the spikes a scratchy voice could be heard saying, "Find me here. Aquí." There was a modicum of static, but the words were clear. Harvey Lack looked confounded.

"Do you hear it?" Dennis asked.

"Not really." Harvey shook his head.

"It sounds like a woman's voice to us."

Jugs added, "She's saying, 'Find me here. *Aquí*.'"

Harvey shrugged. "I don't really hear it."

"Sure, you don't," Mickey muttered.

But he wasn't concerned with Harvey Lack. The police had arrested him and the law would have no trouble prosecuting. It was Dennis Curry Mickey was worried about. His body would end up on the floor in gallery seventeen if Mickey didn't take action to keep it from happening.

Using the number given at the end of the show, Mickey called the PSS while still in the restaurant. No one answered and he left a message.

****

Ray LaTour was one-hundred and sixty-two years old. And not because he had extraordinary genes. He'd worked at living that long. The kicker was he didn't look a day over fifty. His hair was white around the temples and thick with a healthy sheen. Because he spent most of his time indoors, his skin was pale. He didn't have the parchment-thin epidermis of an old person and he displayed no age spots. Wrinkles were present, but diminished, and the blush on his cheeks was natural. His lashes and brows were still brown.

As the keynote speaker at the Points of Light Spiritualist Church in Huntington Beach on this particular evening, he talked about the power of the human mind and how, when coupled with belief, it could bring about the most fantastic events in a person's life. Ray was seldom asked to speak. He was a brilliant scientist and an accomplished metaphysician, but laymen found him difficult to follow. He lacked passion when he spoke and used words that were too big.

He finished speaking and took a seat. Applause was light and brief.

Another member of the church stepped to the podium and began a guided meditation. Ray closed his eyes along with everyone else. Breathing evenly and feeling relaxed, he directed his spirit to leave his body and float to the side of the room. Achieving an out-of-body was easy for him—as easy as jogging was for a marathoner. From this chosen vantage point, he surreptitiously observed his recently-acquired protégée, Thomas Dibiasi. For five days they'd worked together and for five days Ray had the feeling Thomas had an agenda. But for all his extrasensory skills, he couldn't get a bead on what it was.

Thomas had an insincere smirk on his handsome face that he didn't display when people's eyes were open. Clearly he thought guided meditation was a joke. *Maybe he thinks his spirituality is more advanced than those around him.* Ray was guessing. He couldn't read Thomas' mind the way he could most people's. Not that invading another's privacy was something Ray did on a regular basis. But in Thomas' case he would have eavesdropped in an instant if he'd been able.

He watched Thomas open his eyes, look at those around him, then close his eyes again. Ray went back to his body.

He'd agreed to be Thomas' mentor for two reasons. One, Ray's former protégée had abruptly quit the day before Thomas introduced himself. And two, as Thomas explained that he'd heard of Ray's work, admired it, and wanted to learn from the best, a saying had run through Ray's brain: *Keep your friends close and your enemies closer.*

Ray didn't *know* that Thomas was an enemy, but he would keep him close until he did know.

The meditation ended, a collection was taken, and after a song was sung, people began to leave.

"That was an excellent talk," Thomas told Ray, having cornered him before he could leave. "Are we working any more tonight?"

"No," Ray said. "And I won't be working tomorrow."

"Oh?" Thomas' dark brows knit together.

Ray smiled inside. The desire to know why Ray wasn't working was written all over Thomas' face. That meant he couldn't read Ray's mind. Ray had put precautions in place to achieve just that, *in case* Thomas had the ability. It was nice to get confirmation.

"Yes," Ray said. "Tomorrow will be a day of prayer and study."

"What will you study?" Thomas asked.

"What I always study. Life. Spirit. Mind."

Thomas was about to ask another question when a knock-out blonde in her early twenties placed a hand on his arm and interrupted. She leaned in to speak to Ray.

"Thank you for the uplifting service tonight. It was just what I needed."

Ray smiled. He knew the blonde was really interested in Thomas. His protégée had to be twice her age, but he had the enticing good looks of a young Tony Curtis.

She turned her eyes on Thomas. "I haven't seen you here before."

"I'm working with Ray."

"That must be interesting. Perhaps you'd like to tell me about it over Starbucks. It's early and I have some time."

Thomas surprised Ray by turning down the invitation.

"Sorry. I don't." His tone was harsh, as if she annoyed him.

Ray decided Thomas must be used to invitations from pretty

Chapter 9

Feeling confident that the committee had dotted every "i" and crossed every "t," Marjorie closed the notebook on her lap and slid it onto the coffee table. She'd been a little nervous at first, taking on the role of committee chair, but now that the event was just around the corner, there was no doubt in her mind that the dinner-dance/silent auction was going to be a huge success. They had sold over three hundred tickets at seventy-five dollars a pop. The hotel was furnishing the meal at a reduced rate, its contribution to a worthy cause. And this year, donations for the auction were not only generous, but items sure to stir a bidding frenzy.

She smiled at the twelve people sitting in her living room. She appreciated every single one of them. There wasn't a lazy bone in the bunch. "Great work everybody. All that's left is to get to the hotel around four on Saturday to set up, make a nice display of our auction items, put out the center pieces, and I think we'll all have a terrific time at our own event."

Everyone nodded their heads and uttered words of agreement. Big Ed, the club's Commodore, stood. "I have to say, Marjorie, that you've done a masterful job leading this committee. Masterful. And I for one would join you on any committee you chose to lead in the future." Ed was often full of pomp; he gave her a salute before he began to clap. The rest of the committee members followed suit.

Marjorie's smile widened. "Ah, I hope you're clapping for yourselves, because this was a team effort. And, Ed. If you're buttering me up to be committee chair next year, if all of you are a part of it, I wouldn't mind a bit."

Everyone laughed.

"I have cake in the kitchen and coffee."

"Any bourbon?" Big Ed asked.

"That, too."

An hour later, almost everyone had hit the road. A couple of friends stuck around until close to midnight, making for an enjoyable, but long evening. Marjorie suspected they thought she was in need of company since Mickey was away.

After making sure the kitchen was clean and the house was closed up tight, she changed into her nightgown, cleansed her face, brushed her teeth, and climbed into bed. Suddenly, she wasn't sleepy. She did miss Mickey. Technically, because they'd been married for more than a year, she wasn't a newlywed, but she felt like one. Often, when they'd been apart for the day, for whatever reason, she could actually feel her heartbeat pick up at the sight of him. His dry wit made her smile. And, of course, she appreciated the mysterious abilities he had that seemed to go along with his caring heart. That's why he was in Los Angeles, after all: his caring heart. A stranger had asked for help.

It was difficult to understand why they hadn't met when they were younger. If the much-used term "soul mates" had any merit at all, it seemed to her they would have found each other a long time ago. Of course, wisdom said they wouldn't be the people they were today if that had happened and... She sighed. Analyzing things wouldn't get her anywhere. But a plane ticket to Los Angeles the day after the auction would.

And... and! When Mickey had finished with his business, wouldn't it be nice if they could fly to Italy for a second honeymoon? The possibility excited her. Now she really was awake.

She flung back the covers and scurried to the room that served as a library. Very quickly she found what she wanted: a book about Italy and another book that translated English to Italian. Taking the books with her, she went back to bed, and for the next two hours devoured their contents. She would just have to sleep late in the morning.

She turned off the lamp and rested her head on the pillow. Life was good. Better than good. Life was fantastic.

Chapter 10

"*Paranormal Seekers*. How may I help you?" Kelly's voice was chipper for nine in the morning.

Mickey knew immediately who had answered the phone. She was the cute one married to Dennis who didn't have a psychic bone in her body—her exact words on the show.

"Kelly," Mickey replied. "It's important that I speak to your husband."

"Everybody wants to speak to Dennis. What am I, chewed bubble gum?" She giggled with good humor. "He isn't available at the moment. Would you like to leave a message?"

"I left several messages last night and no one called me back."

"Like I said. Everybody wants to talk to Dennis. We got flooded after last night's show. Did you have a site that needs investigating?"

Mickey needed to win Kelly over, convince her that he wasn't a quack. He went with the words that jumped into his head. "How's your hand? Your wrist?"

He heard a gasp.

"How do you know about my hand? Oh, you saw last night's show. No wait. I hurt it after that episode was filmed. Who told you about my hand?"

"No one."

"No one told you. Okay. If you're so smart, how did I do it?"

"How did you hurt your hand?"

"That's what I asked."

Mickey smelled bacon. He heard sizzling. "Bacon grease," he said.

"Okay. You are definitely freaking me out. But you still have to leave a message."

Mickey wondered how blunt he should be. He needed Kelly to take him seriously. Maybe there was shock value in just coming out with it. "Tell your husband not to go to the Brahms Museum of Art."

There was a pause. No doubt Kelly was taken aback. Mickey hoped his words didn't sound like the threat of a mobster.

"Why?" she finally asked.

"You *are* going to investigate the place, correct?"

"Tonight. Oops. I'm not supposed to tell you that. Curiosity seekers, you know. Too many of them, and . . ."

"I get it."

How much to say? Mickey wasn't certain.

"Look. I sometimes know things," Mickey said. "You're in the paranormal business, you should understand. I know you won't stay away from the museum based on a phone call from a stranger, but at least stay away from gallery seventeen. It's important or your husband . . ."

Do I say it?

"What?" Kelly asked.

"Something will happen and Dennis will be killed."

Kelly didn't respond. He'd shocked her into silence.

"Tell your husband to call me. My number isn't blocked."

Mickey hung up. He waited. Dennis didn't call. Marjorie did.

"*Ciao. Ho rispolverato il mio italiano.*"

Mickey's stomach did a flip. "Are you speaking to me in English or Italian?" he asked.

"What did it sound like?"

"It sounded like Italian."

"That's because it was. I said, 'I have brushed up on my Italian.' *Sono pronta ad andare in Italia.* And that means, 'I'm ready to go to Italy.'"

Mickey laughed. "Oh, you are, huh? Right this minute?"

"No. I sort of wanted you to come with me. After the auction and after you're finished in Los Angeles, of course. How's it going?"

"I've made some progress. Not enough." He explained about the visit to the museum and the vision of the body on the floor and how he'd come to learn who the body was.

"Sounds like you're needed and you're going to be there awhile."

"Right now I feel like I'm putting out a fire. I still don't have the big picture of what it means. I'm hoping this Dennis fellow will call me so I can try to get through to him."

"Then I better let you go. I love you. Miss you."

"I love you, too."

After they'd hung up, Mickey checked for messages. There weren't any. He thought about calling Kelly again and decided against it. A visit in person would be more effective.

He signed onto the Internet to see if there was a listing with an address for the PSS and was glad to find one. They were close; the address was on Melrose. It was time to go for a drive.

With the help of the GPS, Mickey reached his destination without a problem and was able to park in front on the street. It appeared the paranormal team's headquarters was inside a trendy store called *Book the Place*. The deep-purple building had a large painted graphic of someone reading by candlelight. There were two good-sized picture windows, one to either side of the entrance.

Mickey went inside and found a desk with an unmanned cash register to the right. At least eight people were perusing the rows of books. Posted signs said: Hard to Find. History. Shakespeare. Classics. Used contemporary. Mysticism. Religion.

In one corner was a reading area with comfy couches and chairs. A woman in her twenties sat with a volume of poetry. A young man studied a book about the alternate universe.

In another part of the store Mickey spotted jewelry, clothing, and artisan items for sale: decorative wall art, statues, glasswork, dolls, pottery—nothing made in a factory.

A door in the back opened. Kelly walked out and headed for the desk. She hummed as she walked. Her hand was bandaged.

Cute as a button, thought Mickey. *She'd be cuter still without all the makeup.*

Kelly wore deep red lipstick. Her eyes were heavily bordered with black liner. The cheeks were indelicately rouged.

Mickey approached her at the desk. "Kelly?"

She smiled at him. She wore a black t-shirt advertising *The Paranormal Seekers Society*. It was illustrated with a woman's graceful hand holding a crystal ball. Mickey pointed at the illustration.

"You tell fortunes, too?"

"No. I just liked it. I don't have a psychic bone in my body, but I'm a total believer. My husband, if you watch the show, is very sensitive, but a total skeptic. If lightning struck him right between the eyes, you know what he'd say? 'It might have been my imagination. We need further investigation.'" She laughed.

"I see. Well, I'm Mickey McCoy. I talked to you on the phone earlier."

Kelly's smile vanished. "You! My husband is *not* going to die. I don't care what you say."

"Did you tell him what I said?"

"Yes, I called him. He said not to worry. That you're probably a crackpot."

"But you are worried. You believe me."

Kelly stared at Mickey. "I told you, he's a skeptic. He's not going to stop an investigation just because someone he doesn't know said to."

"Of course not. I wouldn't either." He sighed. "I came down here to impress upon you that you must watch out for him."

"And that'll keep him safe?"

"I think it might."

"Might!"

Mickey wished he could invite himself along on the investigation. It was not an option and he knew better than to ask.

Things were supposed to happen the way they happened, he reminded himself. You follow the leads that come to you and do your best. That's it.

"Just stay with him. And no matter what he says, don't leave him alone in gallery seventeen."

He saw fear in her eyes. He didn't like scaring her and part of him wanted to apologize. This was no time for soft words, he reminded himself. She had to be afraid or she wouldn't take precautions. "I guess that's all," he said. "Please, don't ignore what I've told you."

She stared at him, her lips pressed tightly together, chin quivering ever so slightly.

"I . . ." He stopped himself from saying he was sorry and left the shop. He climbed into his car and sat. What else could he do? He'd had to be frank with her—honest. It would have been nice to talk directly to Dennis, but Dennis had his wife on the front line. Then again, if Dennis had any sort of psychic perception, maybe Mickey could get through. He closed his eyes and rested his head against his fingertips. He took a few deep breaths and tried to relax.

Dennis, if you can sense me, if you can hear me, if you are in the least bit psychic—allow me to connect with you. It would be wiser to leave the Brahms museum alone. You could very easily be . . .

No time for soft words.

. . . killed. Please trust me. I'm serious. I want to save your life.

Mickey didn't know if Dennis heard him or not.

Chapter 11

"We are closing at four today," Mickey was told when he purchased his ticket to enter the Brahms. "A private party is scheduled for tonight." Noni at the register looked young, wore little makeup, had a sprinkling of freckles and light brown hair. Mickey accepted his ticket and stepped aside.

"Do we get a discount?" a peeved guy who was next asked. He was a slight man with thinning hair and wire rim glasses. He reminded Mickey of a worm. "It's already one o'clock. You're supposed to close at six."

"No discount, sorry," Noni said. "Do you still want to purchase a ticket?"

"Damn right I do. I drove all the way down here. Fought the traffic. Gas is expensive. You think I want to waste the trip?"

"I'm sorry, sir . . ."

"You should warn people."

"My understanding is it was a last minute thing."

"Last minute. Baugh. That's no excuse. What do you have, a bunch of imbeciles running the asylum?"

The guy wasn't going to stop and Mickey felt sorry for the ticket seller. He slipped a five out of his wallet and shoved it in the guy's hand. "Here," he said. "Better get moving before the place closes."

"Are you being smart with me?"

"No. But you're being smart with her. You only live five blocks from the place. You walked."

The man's face turned red. "How do you know that?"

"I took a wild guess, Norman."

Norman's eyes got big and this time the color drained. Mickey loved it when stray knowledge popped into his brain and he could play mind games with fools like Norman.

"How . . . how . . ."

"Time's a wasting," Mickey said.

Norman stared at him, deflated for the moment. Then he stuck out his small chest. "Oh, I see. People have been talking about me. Well, let me tell you, it's the principle of the thing!"

If it's the principle, thought Mickey, *you won't keep my money*. But Norman did. He bought his ticket without a word of thanks and stormed off.

"Thank you." Noni sighed.

"Have you been getting that all day?"

"Nope. He's the only jerk. Most people are nice."

"That's good to know." Mickey walked on.

"Thanks again," she called before she turned her attention to other arrivals.

Mickey stopped to speak with Clarence at the security console. "I hear you're closing early today. What's going on?" He knew it was because of the PSS; however, he was interested in what Clarence might say.

"Yep, yep. We're closing at four. Some TV show wants to film. Only a local cable thing. Good for business as they say. Gets our name out there."

"Been slow, has it?"

"Not really. Don't cost much to come in here. It's something people can still afford to do. Adults are eight. Seniors six. Children only three. It's a deal, I say."

"So how will it work while they're filming? Will someone be manning the station?"

"Oh, yes. Can't give up security. I volunteered, but they said no. It's JoAnn's shift. Well, Diane works six to midnight and JoAnn's graveyard. I think JoAnn is pulling a double. That's what I heard.

She's the one started the thing and the curator agreed."

Mickey bid the old-timer *adieu*.

****

Mickey smiled at the female guard watching over gallery seventeen. Her name was Evelyn and she looked to be in her late forties. She had platinum hair and wore the same navy-blue-jacket-with-white-shirt uniform that the other guards wore. He noticed that she stood where yesterday's guard had said he was supposed to stand.

It was a slow afternoon and Mickey counted only four visitors inside the gallery. He sat down on the large round ottoman in the center of the room and gazed at Lavinia's self-portrait.

She seemed different today. Calmer. The eyes were less challenging, the smile less Machiavellian. How could a painting change? And how could a painting speak to him in Italian as he'd experienced yesterday? Perhaps it was just his subconscious trying to communicate. Yes, perhaps. That was definitely a possibility.

Norman entered the gallery and planted himself before the self-portrait. Mickey sat up straight and watched him clasp his hands behind his back and glance at the guard as if to say, *My hands are appropriately away from the painting. See?* Mickey peered at Evelyn. She was vigilantly keeping her eyes on the strange little worm.

Norman turned his gaze to Lavinia. After a few seconds he began to rub his right thumb. "Hurt me," Norman said to the painting, his voice low at first, yet commanding, and then he repeated the request as a shout.

"Sir," said Evelyn. "You want to be asked to leave?"

Norman glared at her. "For that?"

"For anything."

Norman caught sight of Mickey, gave him a startled double-take that turned into a look of stunted annoyance, and promptly left.

People wandered in. People wandered out. Mickey stayed where he was. He gazed at the painting and it seemed to him that Lavinia's eyes had taken on a glint that hadn't been there a moment ago. Her smile looked dangerous now as if she was calculating something wicked. It seemed Norman had brought out the worst in her.

He whispered, "What are you up to, Lavinia?"

"Vai via. Non mi piaci," he heard in his mind.

Mickey sighed. "I don't understand a word you said."

"Does she speak to you?" Evelyn asked.

Mickey turned to the guard. She was smiling. "Ah, the acoustics. You heard me."

"It's my job to eavesdrop." She continued to smile. "It's funny the things people say."

There was no one in gallery seventeen except Mickey and the guard now.

"Like talking to Lavinia here?"

Evelyn cocked her head to the side. "A lot of people talk to Lavinia."

"Like that man who was just here?"

"He has a screw loose. I wouldn't base anything on him."

"He comes here a lot?"

"Used to. Used to come once a week. Hasn't been here in a while. About two months ago he tried to hide in the men's restroom so he could be here after hours. Like we don't check the restrooms." She shook her head with a lopsided frown.

"Did he say why?"

"Ha! Said he didn't realize the museum had closed. Didn't hear the announcement. It happens, but, um ... Let's just say he's odd. No one believed him. Guess he decided to lay low for a while. Now he's back."

"And he likes this painting."

"Yeah, that painting. I guess there's something about old Lavinia."

"You feel it?"

"Me? No. She's just a painting on the wall. I'll tell you a secret."

She looked about, cupped one hand to the side of her mouth and in a loud whisper told Mickey, "I don't give two hoots about art." She chuckled.

Mickey smiled. "Guess it's not a prerequisite for the job."

Grinning, she shook her head.

"What do you know about the painting?" he asked.

"Only what I hear the tour guides say. It belonged to Mrs. Weldon. Got delivered after she died. There's supposed to be a second painting that Lavinia painted. It never showed. There's a lawsuit going on."

"The museum is suing?"

"The Weldon estate or the insurance company. I'm not sure. The painting got lost. Supposedly."

"Hmm," said Mickey. "Interesting."

"Paintings worth millions don't get lost," Evelyn said. "They get stolen."

Mickey wanted to ask more questions, but half a dozen people entered the exhibit room and Evelyn turned her attention to them.

Mickey sat on the ottoman and faced Lavinia. He watched as patrons came near. Periodically he'd walk close and ask her a question. A couple of times he received an answer in his head, but never in English, and at some point, the expression on her face returned to one of complacency and stayed that way.

At three o'clock he left and sat in his car. Again he closed his eyes and tried to send messages to Dennis telepathically.

It isn't too late to cancel. But if you really must come, stay away from gallery seventeen. Dennis, please hear me—

I've got the message, now leave me alone.

Mickey's eyes flew open. Had that really been a communication from Dennis? He hoped so. Oh, how he hoped so.

Chapter 12

Kelly was miffed. She had tried, with no luck, to convince Dennis he should cancel the shoot at the Brahms, and her insistence had caused his moody side to surface. "I'm not worried about it," he told her. "Quit pestering me."

Part of her understood his stubbornness. He'd been a cop before becoming an accountant and he liked rational facts. He'd also been raised in a single-parent home by a father with extreme religious beliefs. When Dennis' propensity for knowing things psychically appeared at the age of five, he'd been beaten black and blue before receiving a lecture about sin and Satan. After that, he tried to stop his ability, but had little success, and so mostly he grew up hiding it. His father was actually a decent man, an honest man, but he was also self-righteous and unyielding. When Dennis reached adulthood, he rejected his father's religion. That caused a rift that kept them estranged to this day.

She got that Dennis was conflicted. He had experienced enough inexplicable things to believe in more than just the five senses, but he pooh-poohed it because he didn't want to know what he knew. He'd started the PSS to prove paranormal experiences had sensible explanations. Whenever he couldn't find one, he called the experience interesting and more often than not denied it. Denial showed loyalty to his father. The occasional acknowledgement showed he was his own man. However, anything like cleansing an environment with sage, chanting to reach another level of consciousness, or—as Kelly would have liked for him to do now—meditating and visualizing for protection were irrational acts and out of the question.

When Dennis refused to cancel the shoot, Kelly tried to contact Elyse. She wanted her to perform extra prayers of protection. Kelly thought that because she wasn't psychic, her own prayers had no power. Elyse had told her that was nonsense. Kelly wasn't convinced. She tried to visualize on her own without much confidence.

Finally Elyse called back.

"Where have you been?" Kelly asked anxiously.

"Out with a friend. I just checked my phone. What's up?"

"I'm bugged. Do you sense danger for us tonight? And by us, I mean Dennis."

Elyse didn't answer right away.

"Elyse?"

"No. I don't sense anything."

"You sure?"

"Kelly, I had two glasses of Chardonnay at lunch. Not smart, I know, especially when we have an investigation to do. It dulls the senses."

"So, what you're trying to tell me is, you don't really know."

"I don't really know."

"That's just great." Kelly was a ball of nerves.

****

"Miranda Evans, curator of the Brahms." She shook Dennis's hand and smiled sweetly, five gold bracelets jangling. She was a petite woman in her mid thirties, professionally dressed in brown tailored slacks and a form-fitting jacket. She had dark hair which didn't quite reach her shoulders, wore high-heels adding four inches of height, and was clearly attracted to expensive jewelry. Three chains around her neck glimmered and contrasted nicely against her russet, silk top.

Kelly offered her bandaged hand. "Kelly Curry. Mrs. Dennis."

"Oh, my. What happened here?"

"I was attacked by bacon grease."

Miranda grimaced. "Oh, no. Well, as long as it isn't contagious."

Kelly frowned, thinking that was an odd response.

"Here's how we work," Dennis said. "You give us a heads up on the place."

"Heads up?" Miranda looked puzzled.

"Tell us about the areas you are most concerned about."

"I don't have any concerns."

"Well, somebody did," Dennis countered. "Or we wouldn't be here."

Miranda clasped her hands before her and raised an eyebrow.

"We'll bring Jugs in."

"Jugs?" The curator raised the other eyebrow.

"That's the name of our lead tech."

Miranda's face said she disapproved of the name.

Stuck up, thought Kelly.

"He'll film us introducing ourselves, you mentioning the areas *somebody* thinks have activity, and then we'll take it from there. Now, you said we can't go dark."

"For security reasons."

"We respect that. But you also said the lights can be dimmed."

"That's right."

"And a security guard will be present while we're here."

"Yes. She'll stay at the console and monitor from there. Cameras are in every room. She will have her eye on you."

She thinks we're thieves, thought Kelly.

"Okay, that's fine. We'll still be setting up our own equipment in the hot spots you tell us about."

"I'll be frank with you. I only agreed to have you investigate because you have a television show and I thought—"

"The publicity would be good for business. To be frank with you, we get that a lot," Kelly said with a false smile.

"I'm just not a believer in the paranormal. I'll be very surprised if you find anything."

Dennis nodded. "Sometimes we don't."

"I hope we don't," Kelly said.

Everyone looked her way.

"I hope we don't. Sorry."

Dennis turned to Miranda. "Now we heard there was a murder here."

Miranda sighed. Her tone said she was annoyed. "Yes, but we've had no reports of ghostly sightings because of that."

"Tell us about it anyway."

Miranda gazed downward. "Oh, I guess it was a little more than a year ago. A receiving clerk, Doug, closed up for lunch and someone stabbed him to death."

"Someone he knew? Someone just came along? How?"

Miranda shrugged. "Nobody knows. He'd taken a delivery. The truck driver left and someone killed him. Security cameras didn't show anyone entering or leaving. The police claimed the camera in receiving malfunctioned and the tape was no good."

"Okay. So, when we get in there, you can show us where. What else?" Dennis asked.

"Gallery seventeen," Miranda said. "*That's* why JoAnn called you."

Kelly's eyes went to her husband and her heart fluttered. She put her hand on his arm. He ignored her.

"Let's go ahead and get Jugs in here," Dennis said. "He can film a quick intro. We'll go to receiving. You tell about the murder—our viewers will be interested. And then we'll move along to gallery seventeen."

You're so stubborn, thought Kelly. *Why do you have to be that way?*

****

Kelly frowned as she watched Jugs aim the camera at Miranda and Dennis and say, "Action." They were in gallery seventeen.

"So what can you tell us about this room," Dennis said.

Miranda smiled half-heartedly. "This is gallery seventeen where people have reported the sound of a woman weeping, humming, laughing, babbling, and calling out."

"Lots of people have heard this?" Dennis asked.

"Mostly the nighttime security staff." She motioned at JoAnn who was standing with Kelly out of camera range.

Dennis looked at the guard. "When was the last time you heard something?"

Jugs turned the camera on her for the reply.

"Last night. I always hear something. I come in. I check. And, there's nothing. Always nothing."

"What about the camera in the room? Do you see anything on it?"

"Sometimes the picture scrambles."

"When did all this start?" Dennis asked.

"As long as I've been here."

"And before you?"

"Actually, I think that's why the girl quit."

Dennis looked at Jugs and motioned for him to film Miranda. "Is that why the girl quit?"

"Oh, I don't know. Danielle had worked days. We hired a new supervisor and he put her on graveyard. She didn't like that. She claimed she heard things and quit."

"Okay, what else?"

"Well, some of our patrons complain," Miranda said. She walked to the Lavinia self-portrait and a fanatical look of admiration lit up her face.

This woman is bonkers, thought Kelly.

"First, let me tell you a little bit about Lavinia here. Isn't she lovely?"

Kelly stared at the painting and frowned. "She looks evil."

"Oh, no. You are confusing evil with a lack of passivity."

"Please. The eyes are vile and I'd like to wipe that smug smile right off her face."

Jugs chuckled. "Feeling a little hostile this evening, Kell?"

She was feeling a lot of things. Mostly she was worried about Dennis.

Miranda gave Kelly a look of blatant superiority. "Maybe there is some aggression in Lavinia's expression. If so, it is with good reason. In her day women were regarded as subordinates. They were expected to be bearers and rearers of children. They were *not* expected to be painters. Lavinia certainly never received the respect she deserved as a great artist. Still, she forged ahead and despite the times made a very good living doing what she was born to do."

Kelly would not be swayed. "She still looks crazy to me."

"You sense her strength. Her vigor. Her vitality. Notice the thumb?" Miranda pointed to Lavinia's right thumb. It was in a darkened corner of the painting, part of the hand holding the hilt of a dagger, only an inch of the blade in view.

Dennis walked a couple of steps closer. "It's not painted very well."

Miranda frowned. "One might think that if one had an untrained eye, and one would be wrong. She painted the thumb to look flat on purpose because she was tortured with a thumb screw which left her disfigured. You see, she accused a teacher of rape. He turned the tables and accused her of seduction. The court used the thumb screw as a crude form of lie detector. She lost the case and by all accounts—letters she wrote and her thumb in this painting—never got over it."

Miranda launched into an art history lesson about Lavinia and women in the arts. Dennis stopped her and brought her back on point.

"You said patrons complain."

Miranda grinned. "Yes." She took Dennis by the arm and placed him directly before Lavinia. "Now stay where you are." She walked eight feet away and motioned for everyone else to do the same. "Now be quiet. Give Lavinia a moment."

They waited for something to happen. Nothing did. Kelly crossed her arms and scowled at Miranda. The more she was around the woman, the more she disliked her.

Dennis shrugged. "What am I waiting for?"

Miranda lost her smile. "She's not going to do it."

"Do what?" Kelly asked.

"She likes to squeeze the right thumb of our male guests. Often to the point of pain. I guess not right now."

Dennis and Jugs exchanged glances.

"Thought you didn't believe in the paranormal," Kelly said.

Miranda gave Kelly an authoritative stare. "I don't. I believe in the power of art. I think Lavinia is beguiling."

Chapter 13

Dennis had had enough. It was after two a.m. and nothing—not so much as a mysterious footstep, an out-of-this-world knock, or freaky cold spot—had taken place. It was looking like the team was going to have a less-than-stellar episode on their hands.

Just as Miranda had said, there weren't any ghosts in receiving. Investigating two at a time, nobody felt, heard, or saw anything. Even with the lights out, the area wasn't a bit creepy. As for gallery seventeen, there hadn't been a peep. Electromagnetic field readings showed no inexplicable spikes. As for EVP work, they would review those recordings later.

"We've got nothing," Dennis said, everyone standing just outside the gallery displaying Lavinia's portrait. "It's time to stir things up. I want all of you to take your cameras and recorders and walk through the rest of the museum. Kell, you with Elyse. Jugs, you and Carl."

"You can't be alone," Kelly said. "Not in there." She took hold of his hand.

Dennis pulled away. He'd never seen Kelly so worried and it bothered him, but this was no time for weakness. "I'll be fine. You guys go on." He motioned with his head.

"You're the boss," Jugs said, and he and Carl headed out.

"My stomach is in my throat. My heart's pounding. You can't do this." Kelly's eyes pleaded as much as her words.

Dennis kept his face stony, but emitted a small sigh. "Would you just do as I ask?"

Elyse took Kelly by the arm. "Dennis runs the show. You know you can't stop him when he's made up his mind."

"I can try."

Elyse pulled Kelly down the hall the way a mother took control of a child. Kelly was strong, but Elyse was big.

"Dennis, no!"

"Stop acting like a baby," he said. Her desperation was getting to him. He was combating his own nervous feelings about gallery seventeen.

Kelly shouted, "This is exactly what I didn't want to happen! I'm telling JoAnn to keep her eyes on you!"

I have no problem with that, he thought.

Elyse kept pulling until they disappeared around a corner.

"Okay," Dennis muttered. "Let's get this ball rolling." He tucked a small communication radio in a pocket and slipped the EMF detector in his belt. He kept the digital recorder and thermal camera in his hands. Pausing at the entrance to the gallery, his eyes did a sweep.

It was a large rectangle of a room, about forty feet long by twenty-five feet wide. Lights softly glowed above each of the thirty paintings on the walls. All were of people, many Biblical scenes. There wasn't a landscape in the bunch. Lavinia's self-portrait was dead ahead. Dennis stared at her and felt like the sheriff in a western movie eyeing the gunslinger he's about to duel. *The Quick and the Dead*, he thought with a nervous chuckle. *But you look nothing like Sharon Stone.* As if to confirm what he was thinking, the lights in the room dimmed as the light illuminating Lavinia brightened.

"JoAnn, are you messing with me?" Dennis said under his breath. He stepped inside and walked as far as the ottoman. He placed the digital recorder and thermal imaging camera on the round, tufted seat. Keeping his eyes on Lavinia, he took the radio out of his pocket and pressed a button.

"Hey, Jugs. Do you hear me?"

"I hear you," Jugs answered.

"We all hear you," Kelly added.

"Jugs, I want you to head back to the security station and stay with JoAnn."

"Is something happening?"

"I'm not sure. I think we need to keep someone with her as a check."

"Sure. Sure. That's a good idea."

"Carl. You okay on your own?"

"I'm fine."

"Good. Dennis, out."

He put the radio back in his pocket. Looking at Lavinia he said, "We'll just give Jugs a little time to get with JoAnn."

He was apprehensive and he didn't like it. So what if the lights had changed; that was no big thing. He thought about Kelly and her adamant statement to Miranda that Lavinia looked evil.

"You do look a lot like a crazy person." The sound of his own voice lent little comfort and for some reason he kept the ottoman between himself and the painting.

Thump, thump, thump. He became aware of his own heartbeat and the rush of blood in his ears. He took a couple of deep breaths to calm down.

"Why do I get the feeling that you don't like me? Huh, can you tell me that? Of course not. And you know what? I'm the one who's crazy, talking to strokes and swirls of paint."

He froze. He could have sworn he saw her eyes change. She looked cunning now, and the smile on her lips had widened.

His heart started to beat too fast and he had a nagging suspicion something was about to go down. It was the same feeling he'd gotten as a patrol cop when he sensed he was about to catch up with a bad guy. The same as when he'd donned his bulletproof vest for no apparent reason and later that day gotten into a shootout with a suspect in a liquor store.

And what about the reason he'd quit the force? He'd had a vision. He'd seen his partner taking a bribe. Digging around on his own, he'd discovered a whole infestation of dirty cops. Turning them in to Internal Affairs had made him a lot of enemies. No longer able to trust that his fellow officers would have his back, he resigned.

The light on Lavinia brightened then dimmed.

"Just a power surge," he muttered. "Just a surge." He picked up the EMF detector and stretched out his arm. He wasn't ready to get close to Lavinia. The detector held steady at 0.3. He took a couple of steps in her direction and stopped, maintaining his proximity to the ottoman. The reading went up to 0.5.

I should walk right over there, he thought. *Right up to her and be done with it.*

He couldn't get his feet to move.

"Okay. Okay," he said and he put the EMF detector down. He was halfway inside the gallery, a good twenty feet away from her and he didn't feel safe. He picked up the digital recorder.

"Are you here, Lavinia?" Pause. "Are you in this room?" Pause. "Are you aware of me?" He waited several seconds. "Are you insane?"

He heard a woman's laugh. The muscles of his shoulders and the back of his neck immediately tightened. He swallowed. "Lavinia. Was that you?"

Another laugh. Louder this time. He took a step back when he should have been stepping forward. Maybe there was a speaker in the room. No. The laugh had come from the direction of the painting and he didn't see any speaker there.

"Lavinia. Say something."

This time there was no response.

His nerves were frayed. His knees felt like they might give way. His heart began to pound instead of thump.

"You're being ridiculous. You never get scared doing this."

Pound . . . pound . . . pound . . .

"You've done this a thousand times. Just what are you scared of?"

I don't know. I don't know. Something is wrong.

"Nothing's wrong," he whispered, squeezing the recorder so

tightly he realized it might break. He placed it on the ottoman. "Lavinia. If you want to communicate, this little device right here will hear you even if I can't."

Non parlo inglese.

"What?" Dennis swallowed again. He should have been ecstatic. He was getting a response. He was getting evidence. But he was scared. No, he was petrified. He closed his eyes a moment and breathed.

Venite.

His eyes flew open. He stared at the painting. She was staring at him.

No way.
She's staring at you.
No. You're crazy.
Look at her. She sees you.
You're out of your mind.

She laughed and he heard it. Had he seen her head move? Only slightly, but yes, he'd seen it.

Trick of the light. It's a painting. A painting! Four hundred years old. It can't move. Get some evidence. That's what you're here for. Quit playing mind games and get some evidence.

He looked behind him. The camera they'd set up was there. If her head had really moved, it would have been caught on video—he hoped. He reached for the thermal imaging camera.

Pound...pound...pound...

He pointed the camera at Lavinia and immediately felt his stomach spasm. She was there, a gray-green shadow. No face, no detail, yet the shape was undeniable. And she was moving. Her head, her hair, her body, were coming toward him.

Adrenaline shot through his veins. He dropped the camera. He couldn't see her now, but he knew she was coming for him. There was a static sound in the air and a...

Swoosh!

Dennis felt himself knocked backwards.

Swoosh!

Something hit his chest. He lost his footing and fell to the floor. His head smacked the marble. He flung his arms wildly when he felt her straddle him. He saw nothing.

Jugs' voice came on the radio, "Dennis! What just happened?"

"Help!"

Kelly's voice: "Dennis!"

Jugs voice: "I'm coming! Can you talk? Can you answer me?"

Dennis let out a scream. Something was striking his chest. Over and over.

"Hang in there, buddy. Hang on." Jugs' racing footsteps came from the radio and then from down the hall. "I'm coming, Dennis. Hang on."

"Dennis!" Kelly's voice was a shriek.

Dennis lay on his back, unable to fight his attacker. He closed his eyes. The blows to his body continued, but he had no reaction. The adrenaline rush had passed and he felt barely alive. The sounds coming through the radio were just that—unintelligible sounds. He lay there until the next thing he knew, Jugs was kneeling at his side.

"Is he alive?" Dennis heard a woman ask. It was JoAnn.

Jugs voice: "Yes. Yes, he's breathing. And he's bleeding."

"I'll call nine one one."

"No," Dennis managed to utter. His eyes fluttered open. His breathing sounded like a cry.

"Take it easy, buddy," Jugs said. "We're here for you."

"I think she cut my arm. It's not deep. She was going for my chest. My heart."

"Who was?" Jugs helped Dennis sit up. "There was no one on the monitor but you."

"Look." JoAnn pointed at Dennis's chest.

Jugs stretched Dennis' t-shirt taut.

"Those are stab holes," JoAnn said.

"Talk to me, buddy. How'd these get here?"

"I don't know." Dennis groaned.

"Look how many. How come he's not dead?" JoAnn's voice was full of awe.

Dennis mustered his strength and pulled up his shirt, revealing ultra-thin body armor. He was wearing a concealable, bulletproof vest.

Chapter 14

Mickey awoke at six in the morning. He sat up, rubbed his face to rid himself of the last vestiges of sleep, and yawned. He'd surfed the net until eleven, looking for any information he could find about Lavinia Rossi Zanetti, and had learned a few things. He'd dug up information about Elizabeth Weldon too.

He'd slept well. Had only one strange dream. Nothing earth-shattering. In the dream he'd seen Lavinia's self-portrait on an easel next to another painting propped upon a second easel in a dark, candlelit room. He wasn't able to see the image of the second painting, but presumed it was the one that had gotten lost or stolen on its way to the Brahms.

Someone placed the two paintings face to face, wrapped a cloth around them, and then carried them away. The next thing Mickey saw was a beautiful young lady dressed in a period gown from centuries ago accepting the wrapped gift. She removed the cloth and, looking perplexed, said something in Italian to the deliveryman. The man handed her a large book bound in black and the dream came to an end.

Mickey glanced at his cell phone lying on the nightstand. He'd left it on in case Kelly wanted to reach him. It hadn't rung and Mickey hoped that meant all had gone well during their investigation at the Brahms.

He went into the bathroom and, while in the shower, heard the cell ring. Kelly, he thought. It was too early for Marjorie. Something must have gone wrong after all. She certainly wouldn't call to tell him everything was fine. Although, she might if she wanted to gloat.

He rinsed the soap away, toweled off, and grabbed the phone. Caller ID showed PSS. Kelly had called and left a message. She wanted to meet at her book store.

****

"That Miranda woman is a bitch," Kelly said as she locked the door behind Mickey. He could see she'd had a rough night. Her eyes were puffy from lack of sleep, but at the same time they glinted with anger.

"I haven't had the pleasure." Mickey shifted the laptop in his possession from one arm to the other.

"Be glad. Follow me. We can talk in here."

She led Mickey to a cramped office in the back of the store and they sat at a table cluttered with papers. There was a desk, standard-issue file cabinets, and a computer. Cutesy knickknacks related to either books or ghosts were scattered here and there. On the walls were framed posters related to the same: a Ghost Busters movie poster; one that said "Got Ghosts?"; several posters of celebrities reading books.

Agitated, Kelly began her story. "She said no one would believe what we recorded wasn't staged and that we'd be branded as frauds. She said people would believe the museum was in on it and it would hurt their reputation. She wanted us to give her *our* recording or destroy it, and when we wouldn't, she said she'd sue us if we aired it, which she can't because of the release forms we all signed, but still! She didn't give a hoot about what happened to Dennis. He could have died for all she cared. I hate that woman. I'd like to punch her in the face."

Mickey nodded. Curiosity about last night's events pressed him, but he figured it best to let Kelly rant. She'd explain what happened when she was ready.

"Let me tell you, we don't fake anything." Kelly released a

growl. "It makes me so mad." She seemed to be as upset about the PSS's honesty being called into question as she was about whatever it was that had happened to Dennis.

"I believe you," Mickey said.

"Good. Because we don't fake anything. I don't even fake orgasms."

Mickey felt his face flush. The outspokenness of the young women of today never ceased to amaze him.

"So you ready to see it?" Kelly said. "You ready to see what happened to Dennis? How he almost got killed?"

"Please."

Kelly clicked the computer mouse and gallery seventeen appeared on the monitor. Mickey watched Dennis enter and move no further into the room than the ottoman. He used the EMF detector, then the infrared camera. Something startled him and he backed away, only to struggle with an attacker that couldn't be seen.

The fight does look staged, comical even, thought Mickey. *But it's real enough.* When the recording ended, he had Kelly play it again. This time he watched the painting of Lavinia on the back wall.

Her expression changes. It's slight, but it's there.

A light brightened on the painting and at some point, even though the image was in black and white, Mickey noted that the hue of the painting dulled. He watched. When the struggle ended, the brilliance of it returned and Lavinia's expression seemed one of a satisfied lunatic.

"Thank God, he wore that vest or he'd be mincemeat," Kelly said, rubbing her cheek.

"Is there sound?"

"Jugs has it. He'll line it up with the visual today. But I've listened to it. You can hear a woman talking in a foreign language and you can hear her laugh. It's scary as hell."

"I'd like a copy. I'd like to study it."

Kelly pursed her lips. "I can't give you one. At least, not now. It's still up in the air what we're going to do. And it's not because that bitch said she might sue us. Dennis thinks it looks phony too, even though it's not. He's the biggest skeptic I know and sometimes he drives me crazy. He says fear got the better of him and his imagination messed with his head." Kelly pulled Dennis's t-shirt out of a paper bag. She handed it to Mickey. "Well, his imagination did not make those holes."

Mickey examined the shirt. "Something sharp did."

Kelly nodded as if she had a bobble-head. "Exactly. Like a knife. His arm was cut. It bled. That didn't happen because he imagined it."

Mickey handed back the shirt.

"So, Mr. McCoy, can you tell me what happened? You warned me. You must be able to explain it."

Mickey shifted in his seat. "No, not really. But I can show you something I discovered." Mickey put his laptop on the messy table and turned it on. He logged onto the Internet and opened a site he had bookmarked. He turned the screen toward Kelly and she read the headline she saw aloud, "Avid Art Collector." Her eyes went to the photo of a petite smiling woman in her fifties standing before a display of fine art. It was captioned with *Elizabeth Brahms Weldon and her private art collection.*

Additional photos showed Mrs. Weldon as a wealthy philanthropist at different stages of her life, always impeccably dressed, dripping with platinum and fine gems, hair perfectly coiffed.

"She married twice," Mickey said. "The first, short-lived. Six weeks and it was over. Then she married a wealthy business tycoon named Howard Weldon. He was eighteen years older than her. That marriage ended when she was thirty-nine, with his death."

Kelly looked at Mickey and shrugged. "So?"

"There's more." He scrolled down and clicked on a link. A black and white photo of a rich man's study filled the screen. He showed Kelly.

"Someone murdered Howard Weldon," Mickey said. "Stabbed

him in this room, the doors locked from the inside. Their four-year-old daughter heard the whole thing."

Kelly stared at the photo, then looked at Mickey. "Who killed him?"

"It was never solved." Mickey let the scenario sink in before he said more. "Sounds a lot like the murder at the museum a guard told me about. I'm guessing you were told about it before you started your investigation."

"The receiving guy."

"And now your husband attacked the same way."

Kelly stood up, hands clasped behind her neck. She said nothing, walking a few steps away.

"There's more," Mickey said. "Look at the photo of the study where Weldon was killed and tell me what you see."

"Do I really want to?"

"If you want to get to the bottom of this."

She sat again and stared at the screen. "You want to give me a hint?"

"Those young eyes of yours should spot it right off."

Kelly's head rose in realization. "Above the fireplace. It's cut off, but—oh my God."

"You only see part of the painting, but it's definitely Lavinia. It's a known fact Elizabeth Weldon owned it. But for it to be in the same room where her husband was murdered. That means something."

Kelly stared at Mickey, afraid.

"That painting came to the museum right after Mrs. Weldon died." He pulled the laptop to him and clicked. "Now here's a short blip about the receiving clerk being murdered. Notice the date." He clicked again. "Here is Mrs. Weldon's obit. She died the week before. I bet if we checked into it, we'd find Lavinia had just been delivered to the museum. I bet her self-portrait was in receiving when the clerk died."

Kelly's face screwed itself into a question. "What are you trying to tell me?"

"I'm not telling you anything, because I don't know anything. I'm only sharing facts. That painting was in the study when Mr. Weldon was stabbed to death. It was in the gallery where your husband was stabbed. And, I think it was in receiving when the clerk was murdered."

Kelly didn't say a word. She entwined her hands, put them under her chin and flapped her fingers.

Mickey said, "Obviously, it would be good to know more about the painting. But everything on the web either mentions it in passing or tells me things I already know."

"This is too weird. I've always heard that ghosts are relatively harmless. I know people say they've been scratched and all that. But how does a ghost stab somebody to death? With a ghost knife? It's crazy."

"I don't think Lavinia is a ghost."

"Not a . . . What then?"

Mickey shook his head. "I don't know what. But somebody does. I think Mrs. Weldon knew what Lavinia was. And there's a man who knows something. He urged me to come to Los Angeles. But he isn't talking."

Mickey could see the wheels inside Kelly's head turning. Her eyes lowered and moved back and forth. "It's a long shot," she said, "but that is a second-hand book store out there. Let me see if one of the art books has anything. You could try searching the web some more."

She didn't wait for a reply, but moved swiftly out the door.

Mickey focused on the laptop. He'd already exhausted every key word he could think of to find something more in depth about Lavinia and had come up empty. "Yes," he mused. "John isn't talking."

"He will eventually," a woman's purring voice came from behind him.

Startled, Mickey sprang from his seat. The woman laughed.

"Sorry. Didn't mean to scare you. I sometimes have that effect on people." The thin, fortyish, auburn-haired beauty moved further inside the office. She wore a cowl-neck dress of light gray cashmere—short, form-fitting, and well suited for her body type. Heels were spikes. Mickey recognized her immediately.

"I saw you in Denny's," he said.

She roamed the office. "And I saw you in Denny's. This room is a disaster. I would never run a business like this." She threw Mickey a smile. "That is, if I ever ran a business."

"Are you a friend of John Carroll?"

The woman's face creased in several directions, expressing amusement. "Do I look like I'd be a friend of John Carroll? Please. He's my caretaker."

"Caretaker? You just hire him?"

"Oh, you're so off the mark." She sat in a chair at the table and crossed her legs. "I suppose there's no smoking in here."

"No."

She eyed the mess and raised a brow. "Yes. Something might catch fire."

"Do you always follow your caretaker to Denny's?"

"That was fun, wasn't it? I wanted to know what he was up to. Turns out, it was you. I've given up trying to fire him. He won't leave. I suppose, after working for Mommie for so many years, he's part of the woodwork and can't survive anywhere but at Heart House. He does well, looking after the place, I mean. And I am gone a lot. I love to travel. And, of course, I realize, Mommie did provide for him in her will. Her will. Ha! Why should she get to decide what happens after she's dead? I ask you, does that make any sense?"

"You're Elizabeth Weldon's daughter?"

"Who else would I be?"

"I . . . I don't know."

"I'm Avery. The daughter she loved best. And if you believe that, I've got some prime swampland in Florida I'd like to sell you. Actually, I'm her only offspring."

"What are you doing here?"

"I've been keeping an eye on you."

"Why?"

"I don't know. It looked to me like John was getting you involved in my business."

"What do you mean?"

"You tell me. Why did you come to Los Angeles? Why have you been hanging out at the Brahms?"

At the mention of the museum Mickey realized that Avery should know something about the Lavinia portrait. How strange for her to show up like this. He wondered if she was up to something, decided it didn't matter, and took a seat in the chair across the table from her.

"Lavinia Rossi Zanetti. Her self-portrait. I want to know about it."

"It was one of Mommie's favorites. Worth a lot of money. What else do you want to know?"

"How'd she come to own it?"

"I have no idea. She had it long before I was born."

"Does it kill people?"

Avery gave Mickey a wry smile. "John Carroll thinks so." She took a cigarette from a silver case in her purse, but didn't light it.

"But you don't," said Mickey.

"Do I think a painting can kill someone? No, of course not. I don't think paintings can kill. I don't think paintings can heal. I don't think paintings can do anything but boorishly hang on a wall and be stared at. The fact that people attribute qualities to them they don't possess . . ." She shrugged. "That only makes a painting worth more money, benefiting the person who owns it. Mommie killed Daddy, not Lavinia. I don't care what John Carroll told you."

"He didn't tell me that."

"No? Well, give him time. He'll tell you all sorts of fanciful things."

"You heard your father being killed, didn't you?"

"I was four. I don't know what I heard. Screaming mostly. Help.

Help. Help." Avery's eyes were glistening. "Poor Daddy. I loved my Daddy. He loved me."

She put the cigarette in her mouth, put two fingers around it, took it out of her mouth and exhaled. No smoke.

"There was another painting the museum was supposed to receive from your mother's estate."

Avery eyed Mickey. "You mean the portrait of Agostino?"

"What happened to it?"

She put the cigarette in her mouth again, did a pretend draw. "Nobody knows. It got lost in transit." She stood up and threw the never-lit cigarette in the trash. "Lost. Lost. Lost. Forever." She closed her eyes and gave a little shrug. "Too bad. It was Mommie's pride and joy." She moved around the room.

"She prized it more than Lavinia's self-portrait?"

"Oh, my, yes. She . . ." Avery smiled a crooked smile. "Don't you know? She thought it healed the sick. When I got a cold, she'd sit me in front of it. The flu, same story. A scrape on my knee. When I broke my arm."

"And did you get well?"

"Of course I got well. But not because of a painting. She always gave Agostino the credit though. She even conducted healing sessions for the unfortunate, as she called them, once a year. Sent out invitations to people she heard about or read about. She called herself benevolent. Now, I ask you, if she was really benevolent, wouldn't she have held those sessions more often? I mean, really? I asked her once and she slapped me." Avery's hand went to her cheek.

"Healings," Mickey said.

"Miraculous healings." There was sarcasm in Avery's voice as she raised one of her arms to the heavens. "She received piles of letters thanking her. 'Thank you, Mrs. Weldon, for generously allowing Michael to come into your home. My son no longer has epilepsy, chicken pox, leprosy, and cerebral palsy! Praise be to you, oh benevolent one.' Those paintings." Avery looked like she wanted to spit. "Such a big deal in our house. She talked to them, you know, more than she talked to me, and always kept them together. Never wanted them apart. Except, of course, briefly, when she conducted her healings. Now that Mommie's dead, I guess she doesn't get to have everything her way after all."

"Why not?"

Avery stopped roaming and looked Mickey in the eye. "Because I made sure."

The door flew open and Kelly spoke breathlessly. "I haven't found anything and I kind of forgot about the time. I have to open the store."

"Okay," Mickey said. "We'll go."

But when he looked, he saw no one in the room but Kelly and himself.

Chapter 15

Mickey sat behind the wheel of his rented Mercedes, still parked on Melrose in front of *Book the Place*. He had his cell phone to his ear. It was good to be on the line with his wife. Somehow it made him feel better to tell her everything that had taken place.

"A painting that kills and one that heals. Do you know how insane that sounds?" Marjorie gasped. "No wonder John Carroll didn't want to tell you about it. Does he realize Avery's spirit is hanging around him?"

"I have no idea. She doesn't seem to know she's dead. And if Kelly hadn't come back, I think she might have told me where the second painting is."

"So what's the plan now?" Marjorie asked.

"I think it's time to pay John Carroll an unexpected visit at Heart House. Now that I know about the paintings, he shouldn't worry that I'll think he's nuts."

"He shouldn't. He also shouldn't have kept silent about everything in the first place. Let me know how it goes."

"I will. Love you," Mickey said.

"Love you back. See you soon. The fundraiser is tonight."

"I'm sure it will be a success."

"Do I have that on *higher* authority?"

Mickey could sense her smile over the phone. He smiled in return. "The highest."

He started the engine and reached for the GPS to enter Heart House as a point of interest. But before he could press a button, it activated, and a man's voice said, "Pull away from the curb and drive one mile."

Mickey withdrew his hand and stared at the device. It spoke again. "Drive one mile."

He reached to see where the GPS wanted to take him.

"Drive one mile. Do not re-navigate."

Mickey pulled back his hand. He hesitated, then put the car in gear. After checking for a gap in the traffic, he eased into the street and followed the guidance system's directions. He drove one mile.

"After five-hundred yards, merge onto California 101, south."

Mickey did and was guided to the 2 freeway, north. After five minutes he transitioned to the 134, east. Five minutes after that he was told to exit. He found himself in Pasadena, threading a path he was told to take through neighborhood after neighborhood.

"Turn right."

He continued to drive as directed.

"After four-hundred yards, turn left."

Mickey turned onto a cul-de-sac canopied with camphor trees. He cruised slowly.

"You have arrived at your destination."

Mickey parked at the curb of a large, well-tended, Craftsman house. He stared. It had a cross-gabled roofline, olive-green wood siding, and a front porch with low stone pedestals. Stately palm trees rose somewhere from the rear and their leaves rustled in the breeze.

He stayed in the car, uncertain why he was here. If he brazenly went up to the door and knocked, what would he say? Of course, if he sat there long enough, a watchful neighbor might call the police and he'd be in another sort of pickle.

Or, maybe not. Cars crowded both the driveway and the street. Whoever lived here was having a party—a large one. Strangers should be tolerated.

He climbed out of the car and walked to the lawn. Cheerful chatter and the occasional laughter of a backyard get-together reached his ears. The jet stream had shifted and the weather was actually verging on hot. Someone had decided to take advantage and have an outdoor party in October. He eyed the driveway with its train of vehicles. Surely he'd been guided here for a reason. And hopefully, the reason would become apparent soon.

Go for it, he told himself. *Head to the back.*

No. Better knock on the door.

And then what?

He didn't know. Was he supposed to tell whoever answered what he knew about the Brahms Museum of Art? He'd sound ridiculous and he hated to sound ridiculous. It was surprising nowadays how often it happened.

He continued to stare at the house, stymied by his predicament.

He heard the growl of a dog. His line of sight shifted to the driveway where a tan and white boxer with a dark muzzle stood between a Lincoln Navigator and the house. Its teeth were bared and it was only thirty feet away. The growl grew menacing.

Mickey's heart began to hammer as if it wanted to leap from his chest. He took a step backward and the dog lunged forward, barking furiously.

Mickey extended his arms, palms toward the animal. "Easy there, fella. I'm gonna go, just like you want me to. Easy now." He took another step and the dog made a dash for him, paws tearing up the turf. Mickey turned for the car only to trip over his own feet. He fell on his side just as the dog pounced. Down on one elbow, Mickey threw up his right arm for protection. The boxer's powerful jaws clamped on. Teeth punctured flesh and Mickey let out a yelp.

"Nipsy! Nipsy Rose Lee! Heel. Heel girl!"

Instantly the dog obeyed. Nipsy sat, tongue extended, and panted away. Running feet padded the lawn, quickly bringing a man in his early fifties to Mickey's aid. "Oh, boy. I'm so sorry. She never acts like that. I don't know what got into her. Get back there," he told the boxer. "Now." He snapped his fingers and with a sweeping motion directed the dog to the backyard. Nipsy pranced across the yard and disappeared down the driveway.

"Nipsy?" Mickey questioned. "Nipsy doesn't nip?"

"She did as a puppy, not..." He saw blood oozing from Mickey's wounded forearm. "Oh, man. She's never bit anyone. I swear."

"Fat lot of good that does me," Mickey answered, holding his arm so he could see how bad it was. The man helped him to his feet.

"She's had all her shots, I promise you. Come in the house. Let me take care of that bite and I'll show you the paperwork. I'm Jay, by the way."

"Mickey."

Mickey rested his injured right arm on his left hand and followed Jay down the driveway to the back of the house. The sounds of a pool party grew louder. "Cannonball!" a boy shouted, followed by a loud splash.

They entered the yard and Mickey kept his eyes peeled for Nipsy. He spotted the boxer lying on her tummy, happily having her head scratched by a young man.

"My turn. My turn. Get out of the way." A sprite of a girl stood on the diving board, waving an arm at the boy who'd just jumped.

"Move it, Steven!" A pretty teenager in a pink two-piece bathing suit shouted from the sidelines. "You're in her way."

"Come in and make me, Shari." The boy's taunt was more of a flirt than a refusal. "Or don't you want to get your hair wet?"

Mickey saw the pretty teen jump in the water.

Jay paused and smiled at the activity in the pool.

"Amazing." A woman seated at one of the round patio tables was watching Shari swim after the boy. She took a sip of iced tea and leaned toward the woman next to her. "It's like the accident never happened."

"I know. For a while there I didn't think she would make it to fourteen. I thought we were going to lose her just because she was so depressed."

"I remember. What a difference a year makes."

"It's a miracle. It truly is." The woman noticed Jay with Mickey cradling his arm. "Hon. Everything all right?"

Jay opened the slider. "Just need to take care of something." He and Mickey slipped into the kitchen. "I am really sorry. I don't know what made Nipsy do that. All of a sudden I saw her take off like there was no tomorrow. I thought she was after a bird or something."

"No. Just me."

The man grimaced. He turned to a cabinet and rummaged for a first aid kit, stopping almost immediately. "Oh, wait. The bathroom. Don't you just love it when you try to get organized? This way."

Jay led Mickey through a dining room followed by a living room.

"Nice house," Mickey said.

"We like it. Been doing some remodeling recently, changing things around."

They walked down a hall. Family photos covered the walls. Mickey stopped to have a look.

"You doing all right there, Mickey? Bathroom's over here."

Mickey moved forward. "Big family."

"Family's what it's all about."

The bathroom had white tile, a claw-foot tub and pedestal sink. Everything looked new, but period to the home. An attractive chest of drawers served as a vanity. Jay located the first aid kit and went to work on Mickey.

"It's still bleeding." He moistened a washcloth and wiped away the blood, then pressed another cloth against the wound and held it. "Nasty looking. Hurt much?"

"Some," Mickey downplayed. It was throbbing.

"Go ahead and wash it."

Mickey moved to the sink and grabbed the soap. He ran the water. "How long have you lived here?"

"All my life. Well, except for thirty-some years." Jay smiled. "It was my parents' home. They've passed. Twelve years for Dad. Six for Mom. I bought out my sibs and moved my family in. It's a little small with three kids, but we added a separate all-purpose room in the back. Figured out additional closet space." He tossed Mickey a hand towel.

Mickey dried the wound. "Lots of photos in the hall." He extended his arm for more nursing.

"Yes, all over the house." Jay squeezed Neosporin from a tube and coated the breaks in Mickey's skin. He taped a large bandage over the bite. "Okay, now. I don't think you're going to lose an appendage or anything like that."

The sound of giggling and running feet drew their attention.

"I'm first."

"No, I am."

A boy of eleven and girl of eight tore into the bathroom and came to an abrupt halt. Both wore bathing suits, dripping wet.

"Oops."

"Yep. Oops."

"What are you doing in here? Use the toilet in the back."

"Kris stunk it up."

"Yeah. Stinky." The girl pinched her nose.

"You got water all over the floor."

"Sor-ry," she sing-songed, clasping her arms against her chest, feet marching up and down, taking her nowhere.

"Sorry," the boy echoed.

"Well, you're here now. Dry off before you go back."

"Okay, Uncle Jay."

"Okay."

Jay whipped a towel from a rack before he and Mickey left the boy in the room and closed the door. The girl waited in the hall. Jay handed her the towel and she wiped herself off. She gave the towel back and Jay used it to mop water from the hardwood floor. Mickey examined the photos on the wall as they moved down the hall, Jay erasing the kids' telltale trail of pool.

The photos were a mix of old and new. A 1950s wedding picture of Jay's parents, no doubt. Pictures of Jay and his wife throughout the decades. An assortment of children from the fifties 'til now.

"Hurry up!" the girl shouted at the door.

The boy came out and the girl went in, giving him a small shove. He ran down the hall shouting, "Cannonball!"

"Walk," commanded Jay and the boy slowed to fifty.

"What's this?" Mickey asked, staring at a six-by-nine black and white picture. So this was why he'd been led to this house.

"What? Ugh." Jay put a hand to the small of his back as he stood erect. "I should have had the kids mop up after themselves. What are you asking about?"

"This one here."

Jay took a look. "Oh, that. That's me."

In the photo, a nice-looking lad of seven grinned from ear to ear. He stood beside a stately, middle-aged woman, her arm on his shoulder. A Christmas tree glowed behind them.

"Next to you. Is that who I think it is?"

Jay glanced at Mickey. "I guess that depends on who you think it is."

"Elizabeth Weldon."

Jay nodded slightly. "Then that would be yes."

"She a relative?"

"Hardly."

"A friend of the family?"

"More along the line of an acquaintance."

"Are you one of the children she invited to her house for what she called her healing sessions?"

Jay's smile completely vanished. "You know about that?"

"I do."

He stared with suspicion. "Really? Because most people don't."

Mickey nodded and tried to appear nonchalant, although he wanted Jay to keep talking. He rested his hurt arm on his good one and held it at the elbow. "Didn't mean to sound nosey. Is there a reason I shouldn't ask?"

Jay's eyes went to Mickey's bandaged arm and he smiled suddenly. "No, of course not. Just surprised you knew about her. I had a rare bone disorder when I was a kid. Fibrous dysplasia. Affected my skull and my legs. Fibrous tissue replaces the bone. In the case of my skull, the bone expanded. It was very, very painful."

"Sounds painful." Mickey examined the man's face. "You wouldn't know it to look at you now."

"I know." Jay searched the wall for a photo. "There aren't too many pictures of me when I was affected. I wouldn't let them take any if I could help it. Kids liked to call me a monster and I suppose I felt like one. Here."

He grabbed a picture from the wall. "I keep this on display to remind me to be grateful." He handed the photo to Mickey. "I'm six there."

One of Jay's eyes was a full inch higher than the other, his forehead lopsided.

"This is you?"

"That is me. Before Mrs. Weldon and her miracle cure."

"So she *did* cure you?"

Jay's head moved from side to side as if on a spring. "The doctors don't believe it and I don't try to convince anyone." He shrugged. "But, facts are facts. I was one of the fortunate few who were invited into her home and . . ." He paused, carefully selecting his words. "And I was told to stand in this room and face this certain direction. And I got well. I left the house with no pain. It took a month. Maybe more. But the disease not only went into remission, it reversed itself. Call it the power of belief. Call it God's will. Call it a miracle. That's what happened."

"You were told to face a certain direction. That's it? You weren't told to face something? A painting maybe?"

Jay's expression grew wary again. "There was a painting in the room."

"Agostino?"

Jay narrowed his eyes.

"By-ie." The girl was out of the bathroom, running down the hall. Jay didn't bother to tell her to slow down. His focus was on

Mickey.

"I'll tell you something. I only learned about Mrs. Weldon's healing sessions this morning," Mickey said, hoping honesty would loosen Jay's tongue.

"And now you're here? That can't be a coincidence." Jay almost sounded angry.

Mickey gave the picture back. What could he say? That a rogue GPS system led him to his house? Then again, maybe that wasn't any less fantastic than the claim that a painting could heal. "Call it a fluke."

"No way," Jay said, tapping the frame against his hand, appearing to analyze Mickey. He turned and hung the picture back in place. "I don't believe it. What do you want?"

"It's the truth. I never heard of you before now. I'm as surprised as you are to find myself in your house catching sight of an old photo of Mrs. Weldon."

"Uh-huh. You a reporter or something? We've had our fill of those."

It was a revealing statement. Something must have happened to bring the press around. Mickey hesitated, but he had to ask. "Why? Did something happen?"

They stared at each other.

"You really don't know?" Jay said.

"Maybe I shouldn't mention this, because it seems to be a sore spot, but I was a reporter. I'm retired now. I'm not here to write a story about you. I didn't know there was a story. I followed the directions of my one-tracked-mind GPS and happened upon your street. I parked my car and got out and you know the rest."

Jay chuckled unexpectedly. "One-tracked-mind GPS. I know how that goes."

"But because I do know about Mrs. Weldon, I would love to hear more about your experience and about the Agostino painting. Do you know where it came from? How she came to own it?"

Mickey waited for a response, wishing this was one of those

times he could read minds.

Jay took a deep breath, then said, "Come with me." He led Mickey to the other end of the hall. "I don't know why I'm going to show you this. Maybe I think I owe you because my dog bit you."

"That's as good a reason as any." The wound continued to throb, but now Mickey was glad he'd been bitten.

They entered a good-sized office with darkly stained wooden wainscot. Large windows allowed the room to flood with sunlight. All furniture was in keeping with the home's Craftsman style.

Jay slid behind a desk. "Have a seat."

Mickey sat in a wooden chair opposite his host.

"My parents kept tabs on Mrs. Weldon. They always feared a relapse which, thank God, never happened." He opened the bottom-most drawer and withdrew a brown folder. "She wasn't as paparazzied as Princess Diana, but still . . ."

"Good fodder for the press?"

Jay nodded. "Charitable work aside, she did like to . . ." He thinned his lips looking for just the right words. "Rub elbows with a certain breed of man. Younger than her, good-looking, often a little dangerous."

"You're saying she liked to walk on the wild side. I didn't realize that."

"She sought a good time. She had the money. She could afford to do what she wanted with whom she wanted."

Jay handed the folder to Mickey.

"You won't find any mention of her healing sessions in that mess, which I can understand. If it had been publicized, too many people might have beaten a path to her door."

Mickey leafed through the newspaper stories. They weren't sensationalized. A few had a titillating edge, but mostly there were photos of her hobnobbing with the rich and famous, or the extremely attractive and not-so-famous. "How did she learn about you?" he asked.

"She had feelers out with certain doctors. I was a special case."

"Is there anything here about the murder of her husband?"

"No. That happened before I met her, before my parents started gathering clippings. But there is an article about the murder of her boyfriend, Eddie Torregrossa."

"Another murder? I don't know about that." Mickey searched for the story.

"Ten years after her husband was killed."

Mickey found a clipping with a photo of Elizabeth entwined with Eddie, grins on both faces. He read, stifling a gasp when he noted that Eddie was stabbed in the same room as Elizabeth's husband. The article said Avery, 14, had a schoolgirl crush on Torregrossa and was blamed for the homicide, jealousy the motive. She was never tried, the murder weapon never found. Avery claimed to have heard a ruckus, came into the room and found Mr. Torregrossa flailing about on the floor. He stopped moving when she arrived. He had thirteen stab wounds but survived long enough to be taken to the hospital. Weldon and Torregrossa had gotten into a heated argument. She'd left the house to cool off. Her alibi was confirmed by a number of people who saw her gallivanting around town.

Mickey read the final sentences aloud. "Police said Torregrossa talked gibberish about who had stabbed him until he expired in the hospital emergency room. He never named Avery Weldon as his killer."

Mickey closed the folder. "There's nothing here about the Agostino painting or its companion piece. You know about Lavinia Zanetti's self-portrait?"

"Heard of it."

"But you don't have information on where they came from or how Mrs. Weldon came to own them?"

Jay softly knocked fisted hands upon the desk. "I don't know how Mrs. Weldon came to own the paintings."

He's being cautious, Mickey thought. But he's already told me how he came to be healed. He decided to press him. "Meaning you do know where they came from?"

Jay reached for a second folder. He placed it on the desk blotter. "I know a little. Naturally, after I was healed, the Agostino portrait fascinated me. So when I was old enough I tried to find out everything I could."

"Understandable."

"I know it sounds strange, but when I was a kid, staring at his face alone in that room, I swear he moved. He smiled. I would have been scared to death, except Mrs. Weldon gave me something strong to drink before I went in."

"She drugged you?"

"She said it would relax me. It did. But I think it made me hallucinate too."

This time, instead of handing the entire folder to Mickey for his perusal, Jay pulled papers out and searched for the items he would allow Mickey to see. One article dropped free and was quickly recovered, but not before Mickey caught a glimpse of a headline, GIRL SURVIVES. There was a picture of a car wreck.

"First off, I've never found a photo of the Agostino painting. I never flew to Italy either to dig around and find what might be there, but I don't think a photo of it exists. Just a drawing of him." He placed a photocopy of a page from an art history book before Mickey. Included with the text was a small black and white sketch of Agostino by Lavinia Rossi Zanetti. He was a handsome Italian with dark hair and a beard.

"There isn't much known about the man. Nobody knows who his parents were or the year he was born. His name first appeared in the diaries of women—mostly from prominent and powerful families, including the Medici family. He was considered a natural healer by some and a con artist by others, men in particular. He had a lot of benefactors because of the miracles he was said to have performed. He also had lovers, including the artist who drew this sketch."

Jay stopped talking so Mickey could read. Agostino was a healer. He and Lavinia were lovers. They'd disappeared together in sixteen thirty-seven. Although there was no evidence, some historians theorized a jealous husband might have wanted Agostino's head and he convinced Lavinia to give up her art for love. Others suggested the Roman Inquisition had gotten wind of his claims to affect miracle cures and were ready to arrest him on grounds of witchcraft so he and Lavinia went underground.

When Mickey finished, he looked up. "Interesting."

Jay pulled the papers from beneath Mickey's hand and secured them in the folder. He placed everything back in the bottom drawer of the desk. Mickey wondered what the pages he hadn't shown him were about, but didn't ask.

"Now you know everything I know and that will have to be the end of the tour. I need to get back to my family and guests." He made a move for the door.

"Right," Mickey said, and his wounded arm suddenly pained, reminding him that he'd been bitten, that there had been a second reason for entering the house. "What about the dog?"

Jay looked at him, perplexed.

"The rabies paperwork." Mickey rose to his feet.

"Oh." Jay moved to a door to the left of the desk and opened it to reveal a walk-in closet. Mickey came closer. He rested against the doorjamb and his eyes did a sweep as Jay searched the drawer of a tall file cabinet. The closet was big, filled with boxes containing who-knew-what that rose practically to the ceiling. Must have been part of the remodel, Mickey thought. Old houses didn't come with closets of much size. Jay quickly grabbed the health records on Nipsy.

"Found it. I'll make you a copy." Mickey moved aside and Jay closed the door.

****

Mickey drove back to the Roosevelt, his mind on what he had learned. There was nothing in either of Jay's folders that said how the paintings came to belong to Elizabeth Weldon. Mickey would have liked to know that. But perhaps it didn't matter. Perhaps all that mattered was that she had owned the paintings and it appeared that one healed while the other killed. Interesting pair.

Mickey lay down on his hotel bed to rest. His arm no longer ached, but still, he thought, how nice for the paranormal powers-that-be to lead him to Jay's house and arrange for a dog bite to get him inside where he could learn about Agostino. Couldn't the universe have been just as creative and less drastic? He looked at the bandage. Jay had done a good job. Mickey would check the wound in the morning. Hopefully it would be fine and he wouldn't need to seek medical attention.

He called Marjorie around eight in the evening. When he reached her voice mail he remembered the charity event was being held that night and wished he'd called sooner. He left a message about the dog bite, meeting Jay Serling, and Jay's connection to Elizabeth Weldon. Then he got ready for bed. It was early, but he was tired, and his arm had begun to throb again. When he closed his eyes, all he could hope for was a good night's sleep.

Chapter 16

Norman stifled a chuckle, but allowed a grin. He was so clever—so very, very clever. This was his moment-of-a-lifetime and he had set it in motion well. Such ninnies. Such fools. All those staff members watching him like a hawk during the day. Well, not exactly like a hawk. They weren't that eagle-eyed. They were more like near-sighted turkeys—pompous, chest-strutting, thinking what they did was so important. Tell him what to do? Ha! No way. He had their number; they didn't have his. He covered his mouth and smothered another laugh.

His eyes went skyward. From inside the giant urn all he saw was the ceiling. He strained for sounds and heard nothing but the rush of blood in his ears. He smiled.

The building was as silent as a mausoleum. When the museum was open you heard the constant click of heeled shoes upon the marble floors. Or you heard soft-soled patrons shuffling from one art piece to another. But now there was none of that. No hushed conversations took place. No secretive whispers or unexpected giggles reverberated amid the sectioned rooms. The place was a tomb.

It had taken weeks to case the layout, observe the security cameras, and watch the action at closing time. He'd tried to rush it once and they'd found him after hours hiding in the men's room. The men's room of all places! He hit himself in the head. What a simpleton's plan. He told security he'd gotten sick and lost track of the hour. Security merely escorted him out. But after that fiasco, he took his time. He figured out where no one would look for an after-hours stowaway. He devised the perfect plan. He spent two uneventful nights inside his hiding place, listening to the movement of the guard, timing everything well, emerging in the morning after opening hours. Oh, the things one does for love.

Now the time had come. He was exactly where he needed to be—inside the six-foot-high, cast-concrete urn that was virtually ignored by employee and visitor alike. The narrow rope ladder he'd made himself served him well.

He let six hours pass. It wasn't his nature to be patient, but for something as important as this, he would allow nothing to go wrong. He had one shot. If he was caught this time, they would never allow him inside the museum again.

He heard the expected footsteps. Security was on schedule. He listened as the guard passed and then he waited an additional ten minutes. He felt like a teenager ready to escape to a forbidden party. Mom had just done a bed check and he had skillfully led her to believe he was asleep. Giddy with excitement, he giggled. The coast was clear. He could emerge. Soon he would be alone with *her*.

He placed the hooks of the rope ladder on the lip of the urn and stepped onto the first rung. Carefully, he poked his head out the mouth. As expected, the guard was nowhere in sight. It would take her a good forty minutes to get back to her post, to the security monitors. All systems were go. He climbed another rung, grabbed hold of the lip, and swung a leg over the side. He pulled the rope ladder out of the urn and dropped it to the floor for later use. The dowels clattered, but he wasn't worried. The security guard was too far away to hear. He hopped to the ground with a thud and made sure the ladder was well hidden behind the urn.

Now he was poised for the meeting of a lifetime. He would not have to share her tonight. No. This time there would be no one else around. No interruptions. No one watching his every move. Part of him wanted to shout, *Hold on. I'm coming.* But he didn't dare. Instead, he lifted his arms to waltz position, closed his eyes, and danced to *Cheek to Cheek*, sung in his head.

Heaven . . .

A silly laugh emerged from his throat and he slapped both hands over his mouth. This was happiness. This was joy. This was pure ecstasy! Gallery seventeen was only five rooms away. The guard should be in the next wing. His heartbeat quickened. His eyes moistened. True love was something he'd never experienced before. All previous encounters with the opposite sex had ended in disaster. That wouldn't be the case this time. Granted, he'd never read any of the classics; only heard of lovers linked for all time. Romeo and Juliet. Antony and Cleopatra. Lancelot and Guinevere. And now, Norman and Lavinia.

He'd heard her speak to him. In Italian, yes, but instinctively he knew she wanted him. Theirs was the language of love. She'd told him to come to her because she wanted him for herself. Him. Him! No one else, but him. He even saw her smile. And it was not a flimsy Mona Lisa-type thing, but a beaming, seductive come-hither grin. If he were a wolf, he would be howling at the moon.

Now he had to be careful. He slipped a latex, James Bond mask from a pocket and pulled it over his head. Precautions were necessary. No one was manning the security desk at the moment, but he wouldn't be able to skirt the cameras covering all the passages to his destination. If, for some reason, they reviewed footage later, he didn't want them to know who he was.

Identity obscured, he danced on his toes from gallery to gallery, spinning as if holding a woman in his arms. When he reached gallery seventeen he paused at the entrance.

There she was, across the length of the room, centered upon the back wall. Lovely Lavinia. His Lavinia. He stared at her like a love-sick pup, desperate longing sucking his breath away. This was his moment of a lifetime. He would take it slowly. He would savor every second.

"My love. My love. My love."

He took a step inside, still out of view of the security camera.

"I'm here. I've come just as you asked."

He waited for an answer, but got none. He frowned before he remembered. He had a mask on his face. He was such an idiot! Also, mesmerized by Lavinia's charms, he'd forgotten that the camera needed to be covered or their tryst would be discovered. He'd planned for this. He had attached a camera to the eve of his mother's garage, ten feet up in the air, as high as the camera was in gallery seventeen, and he'd practiced and practiced and practiced.

He pulled a Ziplock bag from his waistband and opened it. Inside was a moistened terrycloth towel attached to a length of string. The moisture weighted the towel and made it possible for him to toss it with accuracy—accuracy because he'd practiced.

"Dammit," he said as he missed the first toss and the cloth slipped from the camera to the floor. How could he miss? Nerves, that was it. When he'd practiced, there'd been no pressure. He hadn't been under the gun. He glanced over his shoulder at Lavinia.

"I'll be only a moment, my love. Be patient with me."

He tossed the towel again and this time it draped nicely. He perfected its position with the attached piece of string. Now things were set. With so many locations to watch on the monitors, even an alert guard would take a while to notice surveillance in gallery seventeen had gone awry.

He removed the latex mask and turned to face Lavinia.

"My love, we are alone at last."

He expected an immediate transformation of her image and Italian lyrics of love. What he received was no reaction.

"Hello."

No response.

"Answer me."

No answer.

Norman scowled as his short fuse sparked. He walked toward the painting. "Are you deaf?"

Still nothing happened. His puny chest heaved with anger.

"Don't tell me you're a tease. Don't tell me you're like all the other self-centered, blood-sucking females I've known in my life.

After all I did to be here. After all my planning and worrying and risking."

No answer.

"Bitch."

The small light above Lavinia brightened and dimmed.

Norman smiled. His anger disappeared. She was beckoning him.

"Oh, my love. How could I have doubted you?"

He practically floated across the room, stopping a foot away.

"My love. My dearest one. Forgive me?"

His eyes swept every inch of the painting. Dare he touch it? Dare he touch her? No. It should be the other way around. He raised his hands, palms upward, and stood completely still. He felt his heart race. He heard his measured breath.

"Tell me you love me. Take my hands. Rub my thumbs. Press them soundly. Squeeze. Hard. Harder. Hardest. Allow me to feel that glorious pain."

He closed his eyes. "Ohhh," he moaned as the anticipation of her touch caused a delicious sensation to excite the most personal parts of his anatomy.

Fifteen seconds passed. Thirty. A full minute. She did not touch him and the feelings he'd created for himself vanished.

He opened his eyes and what he saw startled him. Her face had changed. She displayed a beaming, jack-o-lantern grin, teeth exposed, mouth too wide for her face. Her eyes were black and predatory. She frightened and repulsed him. This was not the look of someone about to provide orgasmic pain. She was a fiend—a wild, malformed thing, bent on his destruction. Her mouth opened fully. The head tilted back. He heard a malevolent laugh.

Norman took several steps backward, then turned, hoping to run. Would his legs carry him? Bone and muscle had transformed to pulp. He wanted to scream for help, but his vocal cords had vaporized. What had happened? What had gone wrong? Every nerve fired a high alert flight impulse.

Walk, walk, faster, faster. Yes, run if you can.

Pad. Pad. Pad. He heard the soft soles of his shoes. His legs were holding, although not very well. He was crouched like Groucho Marx.

Walk this way.

Not funny. Not at all. Just get the hell out of here. That bitch had tricked him.

His shoulders felt tight. He had shortness of breath. When his stomach lurched into his chest he feared he might vomit.

Keep moving. Keep going. Maintain control. You are more than halfway there.

He felt a hand on his shoulder. It was strong. Commanding.

His voice squeaked when he spoke. "Security? Is that you, security?"

Yes, of course it was. Oh, thank God. Relief washed over him. He was safe. But what had taken so long? If security had been doing its job, he wouldn't be in this predicament in the first place. Anger replaced relief. His vocal prowess returned.

"Where the hell have you been? Finally, you do your job." He started to turn around, but the pressure on his shoulder told him not to move. The nerve! "Do you know how long I've been here? How easy it was for me to hide? No, you don't. Because you're incompetent. Do you know how scared I was? How terrified? I could have had a heart attack alone in this place with her. This is the museum's fault. It's your fault, and I'm going to sue."

He felt the hand leave his shoulder and something sharp pricked his back.

"What the hell is that? A knife? Since when are you allowed to carry weapons? Look, I'm no thief."

He spun around, ready to let whoever was there have it.

No one stood before him. Why was no one there?

He tried to step back, but before he could, a razor-sharp blade plunged into his belly. He gasped, hands to his midsection. Another pierce. Then another and another. The thud-sucking sound of the dagger entering flesh filled his ears, soon joined by the plop of the terrycloth towel hitting the floor.

   Norman wheezed ever so slightly. His eyes went upward and his world went black.

Chapter 17

Fear ripped Mickey out of a deep sleep. His chest heaved like a bellowing accordion and sweat soaked the sheets. He sat up and worked to catch his breath. The clock on the nightstand glowed: 2:14 A.M.

He had no idea what he was afraid of. He hadn't been dreaming, so it wasn't a nightmare. He snapped on the light. The room looked fine.

He got out of bed and went into the bathroom for a drink of water. Standing before the mirror, lifting the glass to his mouth, he noticed that the bandage was no longer on his arm. And he noticed something else. The bite wound had healed.

He stared. The wound had been deep, but now there wasn't a trace of it, not even the dent of a tooth mark. And no pain. He stroked the place where the injury had been. The skin was smooth. There wasn't a blemish. No way could it have healed in such a short amount of time. Something extraordinary had happened.

Agostino.

Mickey thought of Jay coolly offering information he'd gathered, saying, "I've never seen a picture of the Agostino portrait. I don't think one exists."

Who needs a picture when you have the real thing?

Mickey spoke aloud as he stared at his arm. "A painting that heals when you come near? It's in that closet."

How would a man like Jay get his hands on the Agostino? And why did he feel the need to own it now? Or was it just that with the death of Mrs. Weldon, the opportunity had presented itself?

Or was Mickey jumping to conclusions? He rubbed his arm. No. He didn't think so.

He shut off the bathroom light, went back to bed, and lay still for a moment, thinking. It wasn't likely that Jay hijacked the painting—stole it outright. He must have paid someone somewhere along the line. Avery, perhaps? Jay needed some looking into.

He reached to turn off the table lamp when laughter pierced the room. Mickey jolted with fear. He flipped to the seat of his pants, braced himself against the headboard, and stared. Lavinia's self-portrait hung midair, several feet from the bed.

I'm dreaming, or this is a vision. There's nothing to fear.

But he was afraid. Lavinia floated free of the oil on board, eyes glassy, grin insane. She appeared to be focused on Mickey, a dagger held low to her side. Her laughter vibrated the air again.

An inch at a time, she eased closer to the bed. Mickey crossed his arms, a hand on each shoulder, and for a moment he stopped breathing.

"You're an image. A picture," he managed to whisper.

She raised the dagger, ten inches long, and pointed it straight ahead. She looked as solid as any person in the flesh. Her hair was dark and free-flowing, her smile diseased. She halted her advance.

Mickey heard a man's voice. "Look, I'm no thief."

Lavinia thrust the weapon with zest. Once, twice. On and on. Mickey heard the sound of steel plunging into flesh and he saw blood drip from the blade.

She lowered her arm, her face expressing dazed delight. Back she moved, fading with every centimeter until there was no trace of her or the portrait.

The room held the disturbing smell of blood. It grew stronger and Mickey felt nauseous. He managed to step from the bed and his bare feet sensed a cold, exposed surface. He looked down. The hotel carpet was gone. In its place was the museum floor. Mickey moved to the foot of the bed. The marble was covered with red liquid trails of spatter and tiddlywink pools of a red substance that certainly wasn't paint. He lowered himself to the floor and extended an arm to touch it. Before he could, the horrific sight vanished and the hotel's carpet reappeared.

Who had Lavinia attacked now? Dennis wouldn't have gone back to the gallery, but Mickey couldn't be sure. Visions were speculative. They could be revelations of things about to happen or warnings of events that needed to be changed. Sometimes they were factual accounts of something that had already taken place.

Mickey threw a robe over his pajamas and slid on sturdy shoes. There was no time to dress. He had to know. He left the hotel and drove to the museum. He pulled into the Brahms parking lot and saw what he feared. Police cars lit the night with strobes of red and blue.

Chapter 18

In order to get to Heart House, someone had to buzz open the gate. Mickey pressed the intercom button once again. "John! I know you live here. I need to talk to you."

He got no reply.

It was morning. Mickey had waited until light to visit. He'd stayed in the museum parking lot until the activity had stopped and all he'd managed to learn was that a man had been killed. Who, how, why? The police didn't know or weren't saying yet. The news had picked it up and while getting dressed, he'd caught a short blurb on a morning newscast. It said there was a mysterious death at the Brahms and more information would follow.

Mickey pressed the intercom button again. "John. This is important."

The iron gate slowly began to move. When there was enough space, Mickey drove past, up the curved, red-paver drive, to the mansion. It was two stories high, sprawling, and Mediterranean in style. It looked like it had been built decades ago, but was well maintained.

He parked and as he stepped out of the car he noticed a man with large clippers watching him from a distance. Mickey waved hello and received no acknowledgment. The man went back to trimming shrubbery.

Mickey walked to the front door. Hopefully, since John had opened the gate, he would talk to him. He rang the bell, rang it several times. Ultimately he knocked.

"He's not going to answer," a woman said. Mickey recognized

the voice.

"Avery."

"In the flesh."

Mickey refrained from commenting. She stood only three feet away. She was dressed as she'd been dressed both times he'd seen her before. "*You* opened the gate."

"Well, someone had to. You were making such a ruckus. I tried to tear John away from what he's doing, but he never listens. Never hears a thing I say. It's like I'm invisible."

"What's he doing?"

"Breaking spells. If you can believe that. Or, I should say, he's trying to teach himself to break spells. Got himself a book."

"Can you let me in? I need to talk to him."

"Why talk to him when you can talk to me? He's a bore."

"All right. I do have a question for you. How much did Jay pay you for the Agostino painting?"

Avery's mouth stayed closed, but held a hint of a smile. She hugged herself with one arm and put a finger to her chin. "I don't know what you're talking about."

"You as much as told me you sold the painting the last time I saw you."

"Did I?"

"The head of the museum would be very interested in knowing where it is."

Avery's smile widened. "Really? I think she—"

The door swung open and Mickey turned his head.

"What are you doing here?" John asked.

Standing behind John, several feet back, Mickey could see Avery in the house smoking a cigarette. "I'm here to talk to you. May I come in?"

"I'm very busy."

"Learning to break spells?"

John froze. He didn't answer. He also didn't let Mickey come in.

"Look," Mickey said. "I'm not going to laugh or think you're crazy. Mrs. Weldon owned two paintings. They were sent to the museum when she died, probably with the stipulation that they stay together. *And*, I'm thinking, she made you their guardian. Only Avery managed to shanghai the portrait of Agostino and, for some reason I don't understand, that causes the portrait of Lavinia Rossi Zanetti to become very dangerous to men. Am I right?"

John still didn't answer. Mickey saw Avery throw her hands up in a gesture of disgust. He returned his attention to John.

"I'll take your silence as a confirmation."

"Lavinia killed Mr. Weldon," John said.

Avery stormed toward the door, glaring, and stopped just behind John. "That is a bold-faced lie. Mommie killed Daddy."

"It was my fault," John said. "Avery was four or five, but I believed her when she told me her mother wanted Agostino moved to another room. I didn't know about the paintings then—what Lavinia could do. Mrs. Weldon had only said the paintings should always stay together."

Avery looked at Mickey. "I told John to move the painting. So what? It was just because I knew Mommie never wanted them apart. I wanted to upset her. She was always upsetting me. What's the big deal? Why does he always have to bring it up?"

John said, "I should have checked with Mrs. Weldon before I moved it."

"Yes, you should have," Avery said. "I'm tired of this." She vanished.

"Mr. Weldon came home. He went in the study, closed the door, locked it like he always did, and was mysteriously stabbed to death. Mrs. Weldon made certain the Lavinia portrait was returned to the study before the police were called. And she shared her secret with me so that I would be certain never to separate the paintings again."

"She didn't blame you?"

"She blamed her daughter."

Mickey shook his head. "A four-year-old."

John didn't elaborate, but his expression said there was

something more to be learned about that.

"I think Lavinia killed a man last night at the Brahms," Mickey said.

"What?"

"You haven't seen the news?"

"I've been occupied." John closed his eyes and looked completely distraught. He started to shut the door.

"Wait," Mickey said, not understanding John's reticence now that he knew Mickey believed him about the paintings. "You asked for my help."

"Do you know how to cast a spell for protection? Cast spells that break spells? Do spells of any kind?"

"I know nothing about spells, but—"

John closed the door.

Mickey knocked and even tried the doorknob. Finally, he walked back to the car. Whatever John's plan was, it didn't include Mickey. He climbed behind the wheel and found Avery sitting in the passenger seat. Through the window, he watched the man working in the yard.

"I think John's going to try to steal the painting from the museum," Avery said. "Won't work. He'll probably get himself arrested. I'd hate for that to happen, but at least I'd get the house to myself."

She disappeared again, and Mickey thought, *She's right. Only it's just as likely he'll get himself killed.*

Chapter 19

"Surprise!" Marjorie said when Mickey walked into his hotel room. She loved the joyful, astonished expression on his face, threw her arms around him, and hugged. He laughed and held her tight. "I didn't tell you I was coming today because... Oh, I don't know why. I just wanted to surprise you. I missed you. The fundraiser was great. We made lots of money. Everyone's floating on cloud nine, me included. But I said, 'I'm out of here. I need to see my husband.'"

They kissed each other tenderly. She put her hands on his cheeks and slid them to his arms. "Hi." She kissed him one more time. "How is that dog bite—" She saw that there wasn't one. "What happened?"

Mickey displayed his arm. "All better."

"Really?"

"I think I came across Agostino."

"What? Where? How?"

"At Jay Serling's. Maybe. I'm pretty sure. It's a theory that needs further tests."

"Okay. We'll add that to the list."

"Marjorie. I don't know. This time things seem a little more dangerous."

"I get that. I'll be careful. But if I'm here, I'm going to help. Besides. It's men she hates, correct? Maybe you should send me out to do your dirty work." She gave him a teasing smile.

"Marjorie..."

She moved to another corner of the room. "I like this. It's a little smaller than I expected, but very modern and quite nice. An extra little sitting area here. A comfortable chair and lamp over there. Very nice indeed."

She looked at him and saw that he was staring at the floor. For the first time she realized he appeared to be drained and preoccupied.

"I would tell you about my plane ride, but it was uneventful, and you look exhausted."

"I'm fine. And I feel energized just looking at you."

She moved to him. "That's sweet, but I don't think so. You've got that where-do-I-go-from-here look."

"I guess I did have a rough night. There was a murder in the museum."

"I hadn't heard," Marjorie said.

"Because it happened in the middle of the night and I haven't talked to you. And the cops appear to be keeping a lid on it. Details anyway. It did make the news."

"Lavinia?"

"If my vision was anywhere near accurate."

"You had a vision?"

He told her about it. Then he told her about his short visit with John Carroll.

"Well, I'm here to help. So I may as well start right now. You get some sleep."

"You just arrived." He glanced at the clock. "And it's only a little after ten in the morning."

"Sleep and I'll be back before you know it." She kissed him and picked up her pocketbook. She held out her hand. "Keys."

Mickey furrowed his brow. "What are you going to do?"

Marjorie laughed at the expression on his face. "Newspaper archive diving. Cleaner than dumpster. You want to know about Jay, right? And the painting of Agostino? And whatever else I find."

Mickey yawned. "Of course." He handed over the keys to the rental.

"Now lie down."

He sat on the bed and pulled off his shoes. He dropped his head on the pillow and closed his eyes.

"That's a good boy." She leaned over, gave him a kiss, and heard the rhythmic breathing of someone already on the verge of a sound sleep. She went out the door, made her way to the valet, and as she waited for the car, came to a decision. She needed to see the painting—this Lavinia who killed. She would visit the newspaper office after a stop at the Brahms.

****

"Oh, wow," Marjorie murmured as she cruised the packed museum parking lot. It was a decent size lot. However, not only were all the spaces taken, but several cars were circling for a spot just as she was. She could come back later, she supposed, but she really wanted to see this painting, this Lavinia, and there were no assurances it wouldn't be just as crowded when she returned.

One more time around the lot and she struck gold. A Chevy sedan pulled out and she whipped the Mercedes in. Entering the lobby, she found a long line of people waiting to buy admission tickets. Oh, well. She'd found a parking spot; she would stay. She joined the line.

The man in front of her glanced over his shoulder and said, "They should have a murder every night."

"That's why it's so crowded?" Marjorie replied, glancing at all the people. It had never occurred to her, although maybe it should have. She was there to see a painting. Others, it seemed, were interested in staring at the space where a murder victim had lost his life.

Fifteen minutes later she went in search of gallery seventeen and found its line was even longer. For safety reasons, security let visitors trickle in only as people left. No more than sixty viewers were permitted in the one-thousand square foot gallery at any one time. As she edged closer to the entry, a twenty-something goth, dripping with chains, exited with a pal, and complained as he walked past her. "That was kick ass. Eight bucks down the drain."

"Wha'd you expect?" the companion responded. "Want to gander at some art as long as we're here?"

He received a shrug for an answer.

Five minutes later Marjorie was inside. She saw nothing out of the ordinary and couldn't tell where the body had been found. The crime scene had been thoroughly sanitized. She decided the museum must have pushed for the hazmat team to do their job quickly in order to stay open. Or maybe there hadn't been too bad of a mess. None of the paintings were missing, so the blood must not have flown far. With so much priceless art, they couldn't afford to be sloppy.

She stopped being analytical about the cleanup and perused for Lavinia. Mickey had mentioned she was located straight ahead. She glimpsed her when a handful of people parted for other paintings before new viewers closed ranks. Marjorie joined them. She didn't know what she'd expected. An emotionless face, stiffly posed. Certainly not something as dramatic as what she saw before her. Lavinia's expression was enigmatic and mesmerizing. It was almost as if the woman was thinking. Marjorie realized, after a moment, that her mouth had gaped. She closed it.

Are you pleased with yourself? Marjorie asked with her mind. She didn't see any sort of satisfied smile. *My husband told me about you. He's going to make certain you are a good girl and I'm going to help him.*

She stared, waiting for a reaction. The portrait drew her in. "You are magnificent."

A college-age girl looked at Marjorie. "There is something different about her. I don't know what it is."

The girl's female companion said, "She looks like she walks on the dark side."

"A wild, dark side," the first girl responded. They stared a moment longer before they moved to another piece.

Marjorie continued to view the painting, looking for signs of life. When she had a moment without others nearby, she whispered, "Well, Lavinia. I've got other things to do. If you—"

"She fascinates you," a man said.

Marjorie smiled. She'd been caught talking to a painting and kept her eyes on the portrait as she answered. "Yes, she does."

"I've been sitting on the divan and you haven't moved. You've looked longer than anyone."

Marjorie wondered what his point was and felt prickly. It was none of his business. Why did he feel the need to comment?

"I suppose that's true." She turned to look at who was addressing her and was startled by his Tony Curtis-esque good looks.

"I too am fascinated." He looked at the painting and Marjorie saw admiration in his eyes. His hands were clasped before him. He didn't rub his thumb, as Mickey had told her men did. Perhaps Lavinia was sated from her night of mayhem.

He put a finger to his mouth and looked at Marjorie with a smile. "Dare I give you a compliment?"

Marjorie was leery. She didn't trust strange men when they tried to charm. She decided to keep her guard up and allow him to say whatever he wanted to say. "Compliment away," she said.

"You would make a lovely portrait."

"You see me hanging on a wall, do you?"

"No. I did not mean that way."

Marjorie realized he had a bit of an Italian accent. "Thank you," she said, turning her eyes to Lavinia. She could feel him staring at her and didn't like it.

"You remind me of a princess. That beautiful old-time movie star."

The ice-princess, Marjorie thought. She'd been told this before. Especially when she was younger.

"Oh, but you are not cold."

Marjorie snapped her head toward him. Why had he said that?

"Princess Grace," he said. "You know this?"

She looked at him. Why was she feeling defensive? She'd thought he looked like Tony Curtis, after all. It didn't mean anything. It was just that there was something about him she found objectionable.

"I do. Although no one has said it in a while."

"Oh, a beautiful woman should be told every day that she is beautiful."

Okay. That was enough. He was laying it on way too thick. She needed to end the conversation. "It was nice to meet you. Enjoy—"

"But we have not yet met. I am Thomas Dibiasi." He boldly took her hand and kissed it as if he were a European nobleman. She was so shocked it took her a moment to pull her hand away. She hadn't met anyone so forward, not in recent memory.

"We don't do that here. Not to strangers," she said sternly.

"You did not seem like a stranger to me."

She stared at him. His eyes seemed dangerous and, at the same time, amused about something. Her body felt weak for some reason. Fear? They were in a large room filled with scores of people, for heaven's sake. Still, she felt like a frail bird facing a predatory cat about to pounce and feed his hunger. Every part of her wanted to flee. She glanced at Lavinia and noted a change in her expression now. She seemed to be staring at her with delight. Instinctively, Marjorie took several steps back. She looked at Thomas. He'd turned his back to her and was staring at the portrait. Other patrons crowded around. Strange how no one had joined them while they were talking.

Marjorie looked down at her hand, the one he had kissed. She could still feel his lips upon it. She rubbed her skin. The sensation did not go away.

****

From the ceiling, the spirit of Ray looked down. He watched Marjorie rubbing her hand, walking toward the exit. He saw Thomas continue to stare at the painting that was before him. He wondered what had just happened. He didn't have a clue, but something told him it wasn't good.

Chapter 20

Mickey slept. And while he slept, he dreamed. He dreamed a jumble of dreams with Italian narration he didn't understand.

He saw a man's thick hand holding a small key. The key unlocked a desk and two hands lifted a book—a very old book with black binding, eleven inches by nine inches, an inch and a quarter thick. On the cover were the words: *Accordo*. The hands opened the book. The words on the page looked Italian. There were illustrations of the moon in woodblock print. The hands turned the page. There was another illustration. A woman this time. She looked like Lavinia. The next illustration was that of a man. He looked like the sketch of Agostino Mickey'd seen at Jay's. The next page displayed the picture of a second man. His appearance was masculine even with the long dark hair that began with a widow's peak and flowed down his back. His face was strong, malevolent, and devilishly handsome.

The book morphed into raven wings and flew into a night sky blanketed with stars. The wings became a passenger jet and Mickey heard the roar of the engines. The roar softened as if Mickey were on the ground and the jet far away. It cruised for several seconds, but then the engines abruptly sputtered and the plane fell from the sky.

Mickey didn't see the crash; he saw the aftermath. A jet split apart, smoke spiraling. He saw no bodies except for one. Avery lay on the ground. Mickey saw himself, standing, watching, several feet away. Avery rose to her hands and knees and crawled toward him. Then she picked herself up and walked. Her clothes were torn and burned, her face blackened with soot. Facing Mickey, she spoke, "*Tutti quei soldi. Per niente. Spero che Miranda se li goda.*"

And then something unexpected happened. Mickey knew the English translation of Avery's words. "All that money. For nothing. I hope Miranda enjoys hers." The tone was anything but sincere.

She turned and walked toward the plane, becoming more invisible with every step. The plane became whole and morphed back into raven wings, darting through the air. They landed in the hands from the beginning of the dream and once again became the open book. As if Mickey'd been watching through the eye of a camera, he pulled back, and now he could see that John was holding the book. He stretched his hands toward Mickey and said, "Time's almost up."

Mickey opened his eyes. The drapes had been drawn and the room was dark, but he could hear breathing and it wasn't his own. A glow formed and brightened around a large man in the chair in the corner. At first his features weren't discernable. But as the glow balanced and settled, the man radiated an inner light and his features became clear.

"John?"

"Yes."

The book from Mickey's dream lay in his lap.

"I couldn't explain at the house with Avery there," John said.

"You know she's there?"

"Of course I know she's there. I ignore her. I felt sorry for her when she was a child, but grown up, she became quite the self-centered pain-in-the-ass. She's the reason everything is in such a mess."

The light emanating from John dimmed sharply then brightened again.

"I shouldn't do that."

"Do what?" Mickey asked.

"Feel hate. It messes with the energy and not in a good way. I probably shortened the time I have here by several seconds. Besides.

It is also Mrs. Weldon's fault. If she hadn't despised Avery so, if she had treated her like a daughter... Perhaps I should start at the beginning."

John remained in the chair. As Mickey stared at him he wondered if he was still dreaming or if this could possibly be real in some sort of surreal way.

"Mrs. Weldon was a good person. She had her faults, but we all do."

He paused for a reply, but Mickey didn't give one.

"She was first drawn to magic in the fifties when her husband started cheating on her. She thought the right prayer, the fervent-enough wish, would make him be faithful. When that didn't work, she sought help outside herself. People who claimed they could perform magic and had potions and things like that. She also wanted a baby, but she had trouble conceiving. When she got pregnant, she thought things were looking up. She thought the potions and spells she'd been paying for were beginning to work. But then the baby died when she was only a month old. And, adding insult to injury, three months after the death, Mr. Weldon brought Avery into the home. He thought replacing their baby with the bastard infant of one of his mistresses would cheer his wife up. Now you know why Mrs. Weldon hated Avery. And you know why she left the house to me instead of her daughter, even though I was only an employee."

Mickey nodded.

"One day, two paintings showed up special delivery, along with this book. This *Accordo*." He lifted the book from his lap and put it back down. "It means agreement or contract in Italian.

"The paintings were from Italy. Mr. Weldon sent them while he was there on business. He'd brought a mistress on the trip, and thinking money and gifts made up for everything, he'd bought the paintings for Mrs. Weldon. He said he'd come across a small art gallery run by a little old married couple and when he told them he needed something special for his wife and he described her interests, they said they knew just what she needed.

"Knowing what I know now, I can say they were the caretakers of the paintings. They were getting old and must have been desperate for someone to take over their duties. I say that because they didn't know Mrs. Weldon and couldn't have really known if she would do a proper job or not. As it turned out, Mrs. Weldon was an excellent choice.

"Now. Soon after the paintings arrived a stranger came. I didn't see him; he met with Mrs. Weldon in private. He explained the book to her."

John touched the book in his lap. It brightened like a supernova and dimmed again.

"It is a book of dark magic. It isn't in English and only some of it is in Italian. The majority of the book is in a language all its own. Mrs. Weldon followed its instructions faithfully, as explained to her by the stranger. I, unfortunately, was not provided a teacher. I only know the things I gathered from Mrs. Weldon's actions while I was her employee. And since it is time for me to move on . . ."

John paused and Mickey felt the nerves in his body tingle. "What do you mean?" he asked.

"I'm dead, Mr. McCoy. When you didn't know that, didn't sense that, I thought you weren't the one to help me. But now I think you've proven yourself. Seeing Avery, figuring out about the paintings. That was well done."

"You want me to help you get the paintings back together."

"I did. I want much more than that now. Like that elderly couple, I am running out of time. I'm very sorry things are in the state they are in. Avery had no right to sell the portrait of Agostino. When her mother left her with nothing, she thought it only right she get something. So she stole it for the money it would bring. I confronted her about it. I demanded to know who had it and where it was and how she had accomplished it. But I underestimated her feelings about being disinherited. She wouldn't tell and the last time I demanded she explain, I chose the wrong place and the wrong time. She had a bat in her hand. She smashed in my skull."

John smiled.

"That's funny to you?" Mickey asked.

"Funny? Not really. It was just so stupid of me to make a demand when she was in such a frenzied state and armed. And it doesn't hurt now." His smile remained. "Unlike some other spirits, I've been earthbound by choice, trying to figure a way to get the paintings back together while I found a replacement for myself."

"A guardian for the paintings." Mickey felt his stomach churn. It was very clear what was coming and he had no desire to babysit the murderous Lavinia Rossi Zanetti for the rest of his life.

"It's been over a year since Mrs. Weldon died and several months for me. I'm exhausted. I want to move on. I am leaving the task to you."

"No. No, no, no—"

"I'll do what I can from the other side. I haven't actually been there yet, so I don't know how that will work. But if there is something I can do to help you I will."

"I don't want this responsibility."

John placed the book on the table next to him along with two keys. A large one and a small one.

"You will need to find someone to help you decipher the book. The stranger who came to see Mrs. Weldon never came to help me. Perhaps because I died too soon. I thought all I needed to do was keep the paintings together. They still belong to the estate that was willed to me, you understand."

"No. I didn't realize that. But I don't—"

"However, it was stipulated in the will that the paintings be displayed at the Brahms and always together."

"A dangerous stipulation, considering." Mickey realized there was no use protesting his new role as guardian. He'd be arguing with a ghost, one ready to cross to the other side. He'd have to figure a way out of it later.

"I asked to have Lavinia returned since the caveat of keeping the paintings together couldn't be fulfilled. Miranda . . ." John's face said he found her distasteful."

"The curator of the Brahms."

"Yes. That woman. She has a strange fascination with Lavinia and refused. I think she gave me the job at the museum to appease me. I still filed a lawsuit to have the painting returned to Heart House."

"And?"

"I died before the matter was settled. With the portrait of Agostino lost, I fear there is more coming down the pike. Perhaps the stranger will know that you are the new guardian and will visit you and tell you what to do."

"And perhaps not. Listen—"

"I'm sorry. I don't know what else to do. I'm leaving you a key to Heart House so you may come and go as you need. The other key is to a desk in the study. The code to the gate is seven four nine nine."

"John." Mickey reached for the light beside the bed. When he looked back at the chair, John was gone. The book and keys lay on the table like elephants in a room.

"You're awake."

Mickey turned his head. Marjorie sat at the table in the opposite corner of the room. She had a small flashlight in one hand and a book in the other. She'd been reading and keeping the room dark.

"It's three in the afternoon. I'd say you needed to rest." Marjorie got up and threw open the drapes. The room flooded with light. "Feel better?"

"I don't know," Mickey said, still trying to comprehend what just happened. He looked at the table next to the chair where John had been. It still held the book and keys.

"I found some good information. I think you'll be pleased."

Mickey threw his legs over the side of the bed and sat a moment to clear his head. He wanted to see what Marjorie had found, but he was still reeling from John's visit and the responsibility that had been thrust upon his shoulders. He would tell Marjorie about it in good time. He didn't want to frighten her, and needed to take it slow. She wasn't psychic, but she would believe him. She knew of, and believed in, Mickey's abilities.

She didn't speak and Mickey appreciated the fact that Marjorie knew when to push and when not to. He got up and joined her at the table. She handed him copies of the newspaper articles she'd found and he silently read. The first was dated fourteen months ago.

Red Light Runner Kills Two. Local Teen Survives. Shari Serling is lucky to be alive following a horrendous crash that took place just two miles from her home . . .

Jay's daughter Shari had been in a car accident. Driving an estimated sixty miles an hour, a drunk had plowed his pickup into the driver's side of the Chevy Impala in which Shari was a passenger. The drunk died at the scene along with Shari's nineteen-year-old cousin. In a rare case of survival because of not wearing a seatbelt, Shari had been thrown from the car. She suffered two broken arms, a broken leg, a broken ankle, deep lacerations to her face and body, and several fractured vertebrae which left her paralyzed from the waist down. For a while it was touch and go if she would live.

Mickey pictured the young Shari jumping into the pool at her home. Obviously she'd not only survived, she had regained the use of her lower limbs. And as far as Mickey had been able to see, there wasn't a scar on her. She'd made a complete and miraculous recovery.

Agostino.

Mickey put the article down and read the second one. It concerned the theft of the Agostino painting. Actually, the story called it "a loss." Two months after the accident that had left Shari a paraplegic, Mrs. Weldon died. Most of her extensive private art collection was auctioned off except for two paintings. The Lavinia Rossi Zanetti self-portrait and the painting of her lover, Agostino, were to be placed on loan in Weldon's Brahms Museum of Art. The self-portrait arrived safe and sound. The Agostino painting never arrived. It was thought that one of the bidders for another art piece had received the painting by mistake. An investigation determined that wasn't the case and the painting was never found.

Jay must have made a deal to divert the painting to his home, Mickey thought. *He must have paid Avery.* And if the dream with the plane crash had any merit, Miranda also got paid. An audit of Jay, Avery, and Miranda's bank accounts should surface a connection. But how would Mickey get the police to do that? Surely the painting was insured and the insurance company would have done some snooping before paying out any sum. He wondered if they had scrutinized the matter thoroughly.

"I have one more," Marjorie said.

She handed Mickey another article. It was a brief story about John Carroll's death. He had indeed been beaten with a baseball bat, just as he'd said. The article didn't mention Avery. "He's dead," Marjorie said.

"I know." And he carefully explained to Marjorie about John's visit.

Chapter 21

Mickey decided he should give Stern a call. His cop-friend obviously didn't know his cousin was dead.

It wasn't the sort of phone call anyone liked to make, but at least Stern hadn't felt close to John Carroll. The thing that would freak him out, though, was the fact that he'd spoken to John *after* his demise.

"When?" Stern said after Mickey broke the news. "What happened?"

"Months ago. He was murdered. Hit in the head with a bat."

"Is the killer in custody?"

"No, because she's dead too. Killed in a plane crash. While on the run, possibly."

Stern was quiet.

"I know you're stunned. I was too," Mickey said.

"You know what this means. When I was talking to him . . ."

"You were communicating with his spirit."

"Crap. You know how I hate that stuff. It freaks me out."

"I'm sorry. And I'm sorry about his death." He allowed Stern a moment to process. "It's probably indelicate of me to mention, but I don't know if John had time to make a trust or a will. He was killed so unexpectedly. I believe the house may be intestate. Mrs. Weldon only had Avery and she's dead. The estate did belong to your cousin. You could have a claim."

"I don't care about that. Besides, it sounds like a can of worms."

"I know. But if the estate is yours, then the paintings are yours and . . ."

"What paintings?"

Mickey'd forgotten that Stern knew nothing about Lavinia and Agostino. And he wasn't sure how much he should say. Stern only believed in the paranormal as much as he did because of past experiences with Mickey. He debated telling him that John had come to him and made him the guardian of two paintings—one that stabbed men to death while the other healed dog bites as well as paraplegics. He decided to wait.

"Did John have relatives closer than you who would want to fight about the estate?" Mickey asked.

"I don't know. His parents are dead. He never married. He had a younger brother who was mentally slow. Something was wrong. He had the mental capacity of a first grader. Something like that. He may have died a long time ago. No one ever talked about him."

Stern was silent again.

"Well, I'm sorry. And I'm sorry to bring this up now, but I may be calling on you to vouch for me with the police. A police lieutenant named Mars. I haven't actually met her yet."

"But you know you're about to."

"That's right. I'm going to need her to do something for me."

Mickey decided the only thing he could do was update Stern about what was going on. The paintings, the murders, even John's visit. Stern made no sarcastic remarks to undercut Mickey's veracity. He'd reached the point where he knew better.

"I really got you involved in something this time," Stern said. "And it sounds weirder than the case we worked together. More dangerous too."

Mickey didn't disagree.

****

Police lieutenant Mona Mars had steely gray eyes and blondish gray hair that was cut short at the neck and styled longer at the crown. Sometimes a lock of it fell into her stony face and she would lift it back and put it in place. She didn't mind. She liked to fiddle with her hands when busy processing thoughts. She wore little makeup—a touch of blush and a little mascara, no foundation. She kept the eyebrows well arched. She thought it gave her an intimidating air. And she always wore red lipstick because red was bold and she liked bold.

Another action she took to keep her hands occupied was the removal of one of her clip-on earrings. Her ears were pierced, but she wore clip-ons while on the job just so she could easily perform this task. She would roll the piece of jewelry over and over in her hand.

Mars was in a quandary. She had a very strange murder on her hands. Two, if you counted the one that had taken place a year before in the Brahm's receiving area. And she did count it, even if her superior had told her to relegate it to the cold file and forget about it. She never did. It was always there, lurking in the back of her mind. And now she had a new murder to deal with in the same facility and this one was just as puzzling, just as mind-blowing, as the first—murder by invisible intruder.

It was her birthday, her fiftieth, and for some reason she couldn't help thinking about that. Not because there would be any sort of celebration. She didn't have close friends. But because the murder victim, Norman, was thirty-five and had breathed his last early in the morning on her day. Happy birthday to her. Happy death-day to him. Life was bizarre.

Dennis and Kelly Curry entered her office and she invited them to sit in the chairs on the other side of her desk. The other members of the so-called paranormal investigation team were being questioned in separate rooms. Mars didn't think they'd killed anyone. She didn't want cross-contamination of their stories by having witnesses questioned in the same room. Dennis and Kelly were married and she figured they would already have their story straight. Or, if they were like the married couples she knew, wouldn't be afraid to disagree with each other.

"Someone was murdered in the museum early this morning," Mars said, removing an earring. She rolled it over in her hand.

Kelly spoke for the two of them. "We heard it on the news."

"And you were there the night before."

"That's right."

"Tell me what happened."

"Didn't the museum curator tell you?"

"She told me something. I want the story from you."

"You don't look like someone who will believe us," Dennis said.

Mars looked at him. If there was one thing wrong with her approach to police work, it was that sometimes people didn't trust her. She had a hard face and she wasn't good at pretending she was anything but a cop digging for the truth.

"People lie. I like proof," Mars said.

"How about you just watch for yourself. We made you a copy." Kelly pulled a DVD from a book bag.

Mars was surprised. The guard had said the museum curator had made her destroy the security footage to protect the Brahm's reputation. Mars had assumed—stupidly—that the ghost hunters had done the same. But they wouldn't have, would they? Bizarre occurrences were their bread and butter. And the curator couldn't make them destroy their own property. She took the DVD from Kelly. The three of them walked down the hall to another room to watch.

****

Mickey heard footsteps approaching Mars' office. Lt. Mars, Dennis, and Kelly were on their way. He had to admit, it gave him a certain amount of satisfaction when he was able to pull the sort of stunt he was pulling now. He'd come on his own, without having been summoned, because he knew, without having been told, that Dennis and Kelly were there to have a chat with Mars. He knew, without having been told, that Mars would be shown the recording of what happened to Dennis. He knew, without having been told, that Kelly would explain to Mars that this strange man named Mickey McCoy had warned her something life-threatening would happen to Dennis and, even though Dennis still wouldn't admit it, that's the reason he wore the bulletproof vest. Therefore, Mickey knew that Mars would want to see him.

"Who are you?" Mars asked as she entered her office. Another chair had been brought in so there was one for everyone in the room. Mickey sat nearest the door.

"Mickey McCoy."

Mars glanced at Kelly and Dennis, who were just taking their seats.

"That's him," Kelly said with a toss of her head and a smile.

Mickey reached across Kelly to Dennis, extending his hand. "Dennis, I am relieved to meet you."

"Because you aren't dead," Kelly said to her husband.

"I know what he means," Dennis quickly replied. He took Mickey's hand and shook it once. His eyes were hostile. Mickey wasn't sure why.

"Well, fine. Saves me a phone call," Mars said.

Mickey eyed Kelly's bandage. "How's the hand?"

"Not good. I'm going to have to break down and go to the doctor. That won't be cheap."

"May I have a look?"

Kelly removed the bandage and stuck out her hand. It was blistered, red, and swollen. "It still hurts."

"I told you I'd take you," Dennis said. "I told you I wanted you to go."

Guilt, thought Mickey. *This man is riddled with guilt for things that aren't his fault.*

Mars broke up the circle of concern. "How did you know Dennis was in danger, Mr. McCoy?"

"You won't believe me, but I'll tell you anyway." Mickey proceeded to explain how he had certain abilities that allowed him to know things without having been told. He told her he knew she was in a pickle because she had a job to do and nothing but peculiar, inexplicable data to work with. The tapes of the two murders, including the one from a year ago with the receiving clerk, indicated people were being attacked by an invisible killer. He told her she would never solve the killings without his help and without opening her mind. Then, at the risk of sounding insane, Mickey explained about the paintings. He paused so she could express her disdain about what he'd just said.

She smiled the kind of smile that let him know she thought he was up to something devious. "That's quite the tale." She reached for an earring, but it wasn't clipped to her ear. Her eyes strayed to the top of her desk in case she had dropped it there.

"I think you'll find it about seven feet down the hall," Mickey said.

She stared at him, the look piercing, as if they were discussing something more important than a lost earring.

"Shall I get it for you?" he asked.

"No," Mars said, clearly annoyed. "And don't play games."

"Are you saying I took your earring?" Mickey asked.

"No, I'm saying you're guessing and . . ."

"Oh, for heaven's sake." Kelly sprang from the chair and went down the hall. She returned with the missing earring in no time. "He was right." She placed the bauble on the desk in front of Mars.

"Bravo," Mars said sarcastically. "But it hardly matters." She clipped the earring to her ear even though a moment ago she had been reaching to remove it.

"But you are relieved. They were your grandmother's," Mickey said.

Mars tried to cut Mickey with a glare. "Am I supposed to be impressed with your powers of observation? Clip-on earrings would more likely have been owned by a woman of her generation, now wouldn't they?"

"Your sister got the good stuff," Mickey said.

"Are you insinuating my earrings aren't good?"

"Not at all. It's just, your sister is married and she has daughters so she got the diamond ring."

Mars didn't comment.

"But, I think you'll be pleasantly surprised if you have those earrings appraised."

"We're off the subject," Mars said.

"By all means. Let's get back on the subject. I was telling you about the paintings. I believe if you will take the time to . . . well, I don't know which department you need to speak with exactly. But the painting of Agostino went missing. It was supposed to be delivered to the Brahms and never was. I believe it was stolen. I'm not certain who had it insured. Certainly the Weldon estate who owned it, but I would think the museum might have also since it was to be in their care. Either way, the insurance company should have paid a hefty sum of money to someone. It would be quite a coup if you were to come up with the painting, wouldn't it?"

"I don't work robbery or fraud."

"It's related to this. Track the money, find Agostino, return it to the museum, and the murders will stop."

Mars eyes grew steelier. "I don't know what you're up to, or who you think you're talking to—"

"If you were to do a forensic financial accounting of the bank accounts of Avery Weldon, Jay Serling, and Miranda Evans—"

Kelly hit her thigh with her good hand. "The curator! I knew she was evil."

"Not evil," Mickey said. "Just greedy."

"Why are we talking about this?" Dennis snapped. "This man . . ." He waved an arm at Mickey. "He's a whack case."

For some reason he'd made a detractor of Dennis when he'd only tried to help. It had something to do with Dennis' psychological makeup and nothing to do with him.

"He knows what he's talking about," Kelly said.

"I can't order an investigation, get warrants, without proof. I don't care about this Agostino painting anyway," Mars said.

"Two murders in an art museum where it was supposed to be displayed—and you don't care."

He could feel anger rising in Mars, but she spoke with restraint. "I need probable cause, not incredible theories."

"The Agostino painting is in Jay Serling's house. In a closet in his office. And there is a way to prove it. Go with Kelly. Get inside. Get to the office, to the closet. If it's there, even if it's hidden and you don't see it, Kelly's hand will heal within hours."

"Bullshit!" Dennis shouted.

All eyes turned toward him.

"She's going to a doctor." He glared at Mickey.

"Take her to one. Then go to Jay's," Mickey answered evenly.

"No," Kelly said. "Jay's first. And I'll go alone. I'll ask to use the phone. I'll let him see my bandaged hand."

"And maybe he'll want to help. Smart girl," Mickey said.

Kelly grinned.

"You're not buying this," Dennis said to Mars.

"Not at all," she said. "But it can't hurt to let him make a fool of himself."

Mickey didn't blame her. He wouldn't have believed it either if he hadn't experienced it with his own skin. He was lucky Kelly was so open-minded.

The interview ended and despite being the farthest from the door, Dennis left first, then Kelly. As Mickey rose from his seat he said to Mars, "Oh, by the way. Happy birthday."

Chapter 22

"Thanks, Mickey," Kelly said as she watched him write down Jay's address for her. They were still inside the lobby of the police station. She ignored Dennis who stood by glowering. He was being a real pain in the ass. "I'll let you know what happens." She accepted the paper from Mickey, put it in her pocket, and watched him leave.

"This is stupid," Dennis said.

"No, it's not."

"It won't work."

"I think you're worried that it will."

"That's ridiculous."

"There's still some daylight; I'm going *now*." Kelly walked toward the door.

"I'm coming along," Dennis said.

"You can't. Jay won't trust me unless I'm alone. I won't make it inside the house."

"You believe in this Mickey McCoy so much you'll go inside some stranger's home—"

She stopped in her tracks. "As far as I'm concerned, Mickey McCoy saved your life."

"A bulletproof vest saved my life. I'm following in my car. I'll park out of sight. But I'm coming along. And the only reason I'm agreeing to this is, the sooner we do it, the sooner you'll know this character you admire so much is nothing but a phony."

****

Just in case someone was watching, Kelly turned the ignition key one click and allowed the car to coast to the curb. Once in front of the right address, she stepped on the brake, put the car in park, and turned the key all the way. She got out. Still wanting anyone who might be watching to believe she was in need of help because her car had died, she slammed the door and gave the vehicle an angry look. Then she took out her cell phone and punched in a number. She stared at the phone as if it wasn't working and tossed the "offending" device into her purse. She scanned the neighborhood before she set her course for Jay's front door.

She rang the bell and waited. The barking of a dog. Footsteps. A kid answered. She could just make out his face through the security screen.

"Hi," Kelly said, wishing it was Jay standing before her. "Um, is your mom home or your dad? I'd like to use the phone. My car . . ." She motioned toward it.

"What's wrong with it?"

"I don't know. It just stopped running."

"Don't you have a cell phone?"

So he hadn't been watching. All her acting skills had been for naught. "It's not working either."

"Shari!" the boy shouted as he ran somewhere inside the house. "That lady from that show you like is at the door."

Kelly grinned. A fan of the show. How fortunate.

A pretty teenager's face appeared behind the screen. She smiled the moment she saw who it was. "OMG. I watch all the time!"

"I'm so glad." Kelly said, smiling and shrugging. "Do you think I could come in and use the phone?"

"Of course! OMG." She unlocked the screen door and pushed it open. "I'm Shari. This is my house. Welcome to my house." She squealed. "What are you doing here?"

"The phone." Kelly pressed her bandaged hand to her chest, placing it on display. "I, um—"

"Oh! What happened? You didn't have that on your last episode."

"No. I didn't. I—"

Shari's eyes went from the bandage to Kelly's face. "When will there be a new one?"

"Episode?"

"Uh-huh."

"I don't know." Kelly wished they'd remain on the subject of her injured hand. "We filmed, but I can't say for sure."

"Oh. That sucks." Shari looked pained. "Big time bummer. Our whole family watches. Well, me and my mom and sometimes my dad. You know, we—" She stopped herself and laughed, seeming embarrassed. "Never mind."

"What?" Kelly asked.

"Family secret. So. The phone. The kitchen's this way." She turned toward it.

Damn! Kelly thought. *The office. I need the office.* She thought fast and dropped her purse, spilling its contents. If she could just draw Shari's attention back to her hand. "Oops." She knelt beside the mess. "Oh, man. I carry so much junk. You'd think I'd lighten the load with this hand of mine." She lifted it and scooped with her good one. "It just won't heal and I've been to the doctor twice."

"What happened? You didn't say."

"Burned it. Cooking bacon. It's been a few days and it still hurts. Bad. Radical bad. Keeps me awake at night, throbbing, you know." She hoped she wasn't being too obvious as she finished picking up the contents of her purse. "There." She stood.

Shari hesitated, glancing at Kelly's hand. Her face, then her hand again. "You know . . ." She paused, thinking. "The kitchen phone isn't all that clear sometimes. Let's use the one in the office."

"Great," Kelly said, trying not to appear too anxious. "Whatever works."

She followed Shari into Jay's office. A cordless phone was on the desk. Shari picked it up and handed it to Kelly.

"This is your dad's office?"

"Yeah."

"Okay. Thanks."

"You should probably stand over there." Shari pointed. "Reception's better."

Kelly moved toward the only other door in the room. It had to be the closet. "Here?"

"Uh-huh."

Kelly punched in Dennis' cell number as she leaned against the door and then hung up before the call went through. "Misdial or something. I'll try again."

"Open the door," Shari said. "Lean against the jamb. That helps."

"It does?" Kelly felt her heart racing and had to work to contain her excitement. She opened the door and punched in Dennis' number again. This time she let it ring. Dennis picked up.

"Honey. You'll never guess. The car conked out again. What is it you said to do when that happened?" She listened. "Uh-huh. Uh-huh." She wondered how long she needed to be exposed to the painting. She took a risk and glanced inside the closet. There was no painting to be seen. Just a lot of junk in the darkness. She turned and smiled at Shari. "Okay. I'll try that."

She walked to the desk and hung up the phone. "Everything should be fine now." She hadn't felt a thing and wondered briefly if Mickey was off his rocker. "Thanks, Shari."

"You're welcome."

Shari had an impish smile on her face as she walked Kelly to the door.

****

Marjorie stared at the red smears of lipstick scrawled upon the bathroom mirror and a shiver climbed her spine. Five spent tubes of the lip rouge lay scattered on the counter. A bag from a drug store was in the trash. The receipt for the purchase was clutched in her hand. Clearly someone had tried to draw the face of a man and a woman on the glass.

Tried? Had she used the word "tried?" Considering the medium was lipstick, the person had actually done a damn fine job. She stared. Below the drawing in Italian were the words: *Un piccolo sacrificio per amore.*

When had this marring been done? Who had done it? And why? She'd gone to the pool for a short stroll, a bit miffed that Mickey didn't want her to go to the police station with him. That in itself was strange, because she completely understood that there was no reason for her to go. When she'd returned to the room, everything was fine. She'd been here the entire time after that.

She looked at the receipt. The purchase had been made with a credit card—her credit card! And she had red stuff on her fingers. Could she have...? Her hand began to tremble. She didn't remember doing it. Not walking to the store. Not buying the lipstick. Not drawing on the mirror. She certainly didn't know enough Italian to write a sentence. Her legs suddenly felt like jelly and she sat on the shelf of the tub.

Think. Think! What did she remember?

She had been thumbing through that black book, that *Accordo*, finding none of it comprehensible, and been overwhelmed by a headache. She'd taken a couple of Excedrin and rested in a chair. Had she blacked out and done this in her sleep? She'd never done anything like that before. But maybe knowing all that Mickey was going through, visiting the museum, seeing Lavinia for the first time, and encountering that despicable man... maybe all that had inflamed her imagination and she'd acted out.

It was possible, she supposed. And really, the only explanation. She would have heard noise and woken up if someone had entered the room, stolen her credit card, and returned to scrawl on the mirror. Sleepwalking made more sense.

Now she was irritated and she stood. How could she fall apart when Mickey needed her help?

Wait a minute. You're not falling apart. This is a fluke and not something he needs to see.

She didn't keep secrets from Mickey, but she didn't want to worry him. He didn't need something else to fret about. She called housekeeping and asked if they could bring her a bottle of Windex and a roll of paper towels. And could they do it right now before her husband got back? She didn't want him to see the mess she'd "accidentally" made.

A few minutes later there was a knock on the door and she had her cleaning supplies. As she sprayed the mirror and wiped, she felt increased tension instead of relief. Part of her wanted to leave the drawing. It felt like she was erasing a part of herself. That made no sense and she rubbed more furiously. A thought in Italian she didn't understand rolled through her mind and she massaged her forehead.

Get control of yourself! Clean this up. Go out to a nice dinner with your husband and forget it.

First you could go to that bar you heard about while at the pool.

Bar? She wasn't one to frequent bars.

Go. Live a little. Meet people. Go now if you like.

I don't like.

She wiped and wiped and soon the mirror gleamed. She stared at herself. This argument, this war, she was having with herself was exhausting. And it made her even more irritable.

As she stared, she softened. Reflected back at her was a woman who was still lovely. Still vital. Still attractive to men.

An unintelligible whisper traveled through her brain.

What? What was that?

She stopped fighting the feelings she was having and dug her fingers into her hair. She lifted the locks so that her hair fell loose and wild. She unbuttoned her blouse low enough to be provocative. A sense of excitement filled her and she smiled at herself.

****

When Mickey got back to the hotel room, he found Marjorie standing before the mirror in the bathroom. He immediately went in to give her a kiss.

"Sorry it took me a while to get back. There was an accident and I was delayed." He pecked her cheek. "The meeting at the station didn't take that long. And I may be making headway with this Lieutenant Mars. I don't think she's written me off as a complete loon."

Marjorie didn't comment and he noticed her odd appearance. Her hair was disheveled, as if she'd slept on it and then made it all poofy with her fingers. If it was a style, it wasn't hers. And the blouse she was wearing was unbuttoned low enough to display her cleavage. Also, not something Marjorie did.

"How are you?" he asked.

"I'm fine." She shrugged.

He spotted the Windex bottle on the counter and crumpled paper towels smeared red overflowing the trash bucket.

"Did something happen?"

"Went down to the pool for a while, just to see it, and heard people talking about a bar inside the hotel. The bartender is a master mixologist. He buys fresh ingredients from the Farmers Market. Fruits. Herbs. Makes his own syrups. Sounds delicious. I need to get out of this room."

She moved past him, into the room.

Mickey nodded, following. He had figured they would go to dinner, but then he wanted to stay in and study the black book, see if he could discern something, anything. He needed to figure out who might be able to help him translate it. But if Marjorie needed to get out now and see a unique bar, he was game. She came first.

He watched her snatch her purse. "Don't you want to freshen up?" he asked.

"No. What do you mean?"

He wasn't about to challenge her. He never told her how to dress or groom herself. Then again, he'd never had to. She'd always been fastidious about her appearance—clothes and makeup impeccable.

"All right," he said, holding out his arm for her to walk with him.

They found the bar tucked away in a corner of the expansive lobby. There was no sign, just an open door. The room was cozy, dimly lit, with few places to sit. Since they'd arrived early they found open seating on a couch. Marjorie insisted Mickey order something exotic, not his usual beer. In this place it was best to tell the bartender—mixologist—what sort of taste you favored and he created something unique for you.

Marjorie ended up with something called *The Last Tango* made with gin, strawberries and other fresh ingredients. Mickey's drink was called *The Roquette*, a kind of gin gimlet with wild arugula. Mickey was impressed. He'd never had a cocktail so flavorful and fresh. He struck up a conversation with the mixologist and learned about how he made the drinks and of his aspirations to own his own bar. Marjorie was attentive at first, but then her eyes began to stray. Mickey saw her give a "come hither" look to a handsome businessman at the bar. The man smiled back. When he caught Mickey watching, the smile grew to a grin. He lifted his glass in a salute and turned his back.

Marjorie finished her drink. "I'll have another."

Mickey frowned. Marjorie was petite. The drinks were strong and she'd already displayed behavior that was unlike her. "Really? Are you sure you can handle—"

She gave him a look that could have scalded water and rose to her feet. "I'll get it myself."

He watched her strut to the bar and order. Instead of returning to the couch while she waited for her drink, she moved beside the handsome businessman and said something Mickey couldn't hear. The two laughed and continued to talk. The drink came and Marjorie sipped at it, still glued to the stranger at the bar. Mickey felt his heart leap into his throat when he saw his wife take the man's hand and begin to gently rub his thumb.

Mickey decided it was time they leave. He moved to the bar.

"I'm hungry. Let's go to dinner."

"You go," she said. "Bill and I haven't finished our conversation."

"We're going now."

The businessman sprung into action. "Hey, bub. The lady doesn't want to—"

"The lady is tipsy, in case you haven't noticed. And, she's my wife."

"Ohhh." Bill looked amused. "Better keep her on a leash." He turned away.

"Hey!" Marjorie slapped Bill's shoulder. Not hard, but it made her seem like a fool. He eyed Mickey and said nothing, putting his drink to his mouth.

Mickey paid the bill. "Coming?" He looked directly into Marjorie's eyes. Her expression was disturbing. She didn't look like the wife he knew. He glimpsed anger and ridicule. He glanced to the side and saw people watching. This made Marjorie look, too.

"Fine," she said. Holding her head high, she marched from the room.

Mickey took a deep breath and followed. He caught her at the elevators. "We need to get some food in you."

"Forget dinner. I don't want to eat with you." The elevator doors slid open and she stepped in. "You can take the next one." She laughed as the doors closed.

Mickey caught the next ride. Walking toward their room, he was almost afraid to go inside. Afraid she wouldn't be there and, at the same time, afraid she would be, afraid of what she might do. Through shear will, he maintained a steady hand as he placed the key in the slot.

Marjorie stood in the center of the room, both hands over her face. "I'm sorry," she said through her fingers.

Mickey walked to her, took her by the wrists and pulled her hands down. Her eyes were closed.

"I'm so embarrassed." He hugged her and she threw her arms

around him. "I don't know what got into me."

He held her. He didn't know either, not for sure. But the aggressiveness she'd displayed, the thumb-rubbing ... it made him think of Lavinia. As far as he knew, Marjorie had yet to see the portrait, but could her vile spirit somehow be influencing his wife?

"Maybe I have a brain tumor." She chuckled and he knew she was joking.

"Do you want to go home and see your doctor?"

"No." She tapped his chest lightly and pulled back. "I don't have a brain tumor." Her face held a pout. "And tomorrow, I want you to take me with you wherever you go. Let's go to dinner. But first, I *will* get cleaned up."

She walked into the bathroom and when she emerged she was the Marjorie he was used to: hair and makeup perfect, the blouse buttoned more appropriately.

"Wait a minute." She held up a finger. "In case we run into someone from the bar." She quickly changed clothes and then stood before him with a grin. He was glad she was once again aware of decorum.

Enjoying a meal in the hotel's steakhouse, Mickey felt like things had returned to normal. "What do you think happened to you back there in the bar?"

"I guess I had too much to drink."

That was the simple explanation, of course. Except she'd acted strange before they'd even gotten to the bar. He could tell that she didn't want to talk about it. Still, he said, "That's why you rubbed that man's thumb?"

"What?" Marjorie looked frightened. "I don't remember doing that."

He believed her, pausing a moment before he said, "Do you think you should go home?"

"Do you want me to go home?"

"Only if this situation, the murder, this puzzle I'm trying to sort out, only if it's getting to you."

"It's not. I don't want you to worry about me. I'm fine."

Mickey quit pushing. He'd watch her. That's all he could do right now.

After dinner, they went straight back to the room. Mickey changed into his pajamas before he settled into a chair with the *Accordo*.

Marjorie took a bath before she climbed into bed. "I love you," she said.

Mickey's heart brimmed with affection as he looked at her. "And you are the best thing that ever happened to me."

She closed her eyes. He put the book down and rubbed his face. He was bushed. The day had been a full one. He'd awakened in the middle of the night to find his arm had healed. He'd had a vision of Lavinia committing murder and rushed to the museum to verify whether or not it was true. He'd visited John at Heart House, returning to the hotel to find Marjorie. Then, while she ran errands, he'd taken a nap filled with informative dreams and a visit from John Carroll. John had brought him the *Accordo* and keys, and revealed that he was dead. He'd reviewed the articles Marjorie found at the newspaper office. He'd called Stern and informed him of his cousin's death. He'd gone to the police station and tangled with Mars. And finally, he'd gone to the bar with Marjorie and experienced her strange behavior.

He peered at her. She looked like an angel.

It was time for sleep. He checked his cell phone and placed it on the nightstand. Kelly had said she was going to Jay Serling's house. If she'd maneuvered her way in and gotten near the office closet, if her experience was anything like his, that burn on her hand would be history come the middle of the night. She might call.

Mickey heard his cell phone blip at three in the morning. He picked it up and found a text message from Kelly. It simply read:

Thnq

Chapter 23

"This is Heart House," Mickey said, sitting in the driver's seat of the Mercedes, staring at what could be seen of the home through the lace of trees that grew large beyond the gate. He punched in the security code and the iron bars began to open. He cruised up the driveway and more of the house came into view.

"It's big. And lovely," Marjorie replied. "I guess I was expecting something a little bit on the spooky side. You know. Old Los Angeles mansion high in the hills with an unsolved murder in its history."

"Two. But I wouldn't call them unsolved."

"Lavinia."

"Mmm."

"Gives me the shivers just to think about her."

"Don't forget that good things happened in this house too. Mrs. Weldon helped a lot of kids."

"I'll keep that in mind."

Mickey parked the car and they stepped out. "I'm little surprised at how well things look," he said. "Although I did see a worker the last time I was here, so I shouldn't be. Taxpayer dollars at work."

He unlocked the front door and they stepped inside a large foyer. The first thing to draw the eye was an ornate crystal chandelier. The second, a grand, winding staircase with a wrought iron railing. Subtle hearts were visible in the railing's design.

"This is nice," Marjorie said. "Although a little dark."

"Older house. Doesn't have an open plan."

"It could use some updates, but then it would lose a lot of its charm." She spotted the light switch and turned the dial. The chandelier brightened and sparkled. "Electricity's on and the crystals have been cleaned."

They moved into a hallway. It was dark until Marjorie found the switch for it.

"I'm guessing the study where Mr. Weldon died and where the children were healed is this way," Mickey said. The hallway elbowed toward the rear of the house and continued. Closed double doors on the right caused Mickey to stop. "Here," he said, reaching for one of the knobs. Because there was a keyhole in the plate below the knob, he knew it might be locked, but it wasn't. They went in.

This time Mickey located the light switch. Two lamps came on, maybe forty watts each. Other lamps remained dark. In the soft light, furniture, fixtures, and closed drapes could be seen.

Marjorie immediately crossed her arms. "I know I'm not the one who's psychic, but there is something about this room I don't like."

Mickey lifted his arms slightly from his side, palms facing out to sense the energy.

"I don't know why," she continued. "It's lovely really. I'm surprised it was a man's study."

She moved to the west wall with its bank of windows hidden behind floor-length, flower print drapes and swiftly pulled the cord that opened them. "That's better." She stayed in the warmth of the sun.

"Mrs. Weldon used this room more than her husband ever did," Mickey said. "I'd say that's why it's feminine."

He stood as close to the center as he could and allowed his eyes to do the walking. The space was rectangular with off-white walls and a high ceiling. To the west a marble fireplace rose four-and-a-half feet high. It was the same color as the walls. Fleur-de-lis and scrolling on its face included small tasteful hearts. Two thick, brass candlesticks, each eighteen inches high, supported squat amber candles. They were spaced perfectly for a painting to hang between them; however, the wall was blank. A clock sat on the mantel.

In front of the fireplace was a seating arrangement consisting of a six-foot couch and two matching chairs, a footstool before each. In the center was a glass coffee table.

Along the wall opposite the fireplace was a desk flanked by tall bookcases filled with books. The space above the desk, also perfect for a painting, was bare.

Mickey closed his eyes, extended his arms a more few inches from his side, and sensed a strange combination of energy. The push-pull of a healer and a murderer having been kept for decades in the same room had left their mark. It came in waves: A sense of peace came from one direction; then a sense of retribution from the other. When they combined Mickey felt a sense of well being and calm.

He thought: *Put darkness with light and light always wins.*

Mickey opened his eyes and looked back and forth from west wall to east. "I'd say Lavinia hung above the fireplace and Agostino hung over here. That way they could gaze at each other."

"Gaze at each other, with paint for eyes?" Marjorie looked grim. "You are so far out on this one. I'm sorry, but I don't like it."

"Can't say I like it much either. There's been one death since John drew me on board and an attempted murder. One way or another we need to get both paintings back here, if only temporarily until I know what else to do."

Marjorie's nod was barely discernable.

He walked to the desk, slipped the small key John had provided from a pocket and unlocked it. Opening the bottom drawer first, he found folders with papers that held no interest. Then he discovered a three-ring notebook wedged in the back. He pulled it out, placed it on the desk, and began a review.

"Ah. The children Mother claimed to have healed," Avery said.

Mickey recognized the voice immediately. He glanced to his side. Avery was leaning over his shoulder watching his every move. He didn't answer, but went back to his review.

The notebook held the names of children, their ailments, and the dates they'd come to visit Heart House. Behind the list of entries were photographs. He did a quick count and found there were twenty names, which meant if she did this only once a year, she did it for twenty years. He went back to the list and reviewed each one. The eighth healing was for Jay Sterling. He turned to the picture and looked at it. Avery made no comment. He went back to the list and found something interesting. The last entry was for someone named Morris Carroll. The layman diagnosis Mrs. Weldon had written said *Mental Retardation – abilities that of a child*. Mickey flipped pages to his picture. It was of a man in his thirties. This had to be John's brother. Mickey wondered if the treatment had been successful and if he was alive.

Mickey didn't want to speak aloud and alert Marjorie to the fact that there was a spirit present. He could sense she was on edge. Normally she'd be right beside him, interested in everything that was going on. He glanced at Avery and wondered if he had to speak out loud for her to know what he was thinking.

Is this John's brother?

Avery didn't reply. He flipped to Jay Sterling's picture and tapped his finger upon it.

Jay Sterling?

He looked at Avery. She merely looked back. Her expression told him nothing.

Appears you're smart enough not to say something that makes it perfectly clear you know this child.

Avery didn't respond. Evidently she didn't read minds.

Mickey glanced behind him. Marjorie had moved to the couch and was sitting, staring into space. The energy in the room appeared to be too much for her. And now the spirit of Avery was present. The air was charged with electricity.

"You okay?" he said.

"Hmmm," Marjorie responded. "Okay."

Mickey opened another drawer and found several photo albums.

He heard Avery snort. "You won't find one shot of me in those," she said. "Not one!"

Mickey looked through the first album. It began with pictures of young Elizabeth enjoying happy days with her handsome, wealthy husband. It progressed, chronicling their marriage, documenting its decline with the expressions on their faces, ending with an actual death photo of Edward Weldon in his casket.

The next album was more of a scrapbook. It had newspaper clippings of her exploits as a socialite running the social circuit and photos of her with the men whose company she most enjoyed after the death of Edward.

"Mother was a tramp," Avery said.

Mickey opened a small album with very few photos. All were of a baby. The final shots were of the baby posed in death.

"She kept photos of *her*," Avery said with distaste.

Mickey went to another drawer. It held stationery and pens. It was shallower than the others and Mickey suspected it had a false back. He hit his fingers against the wood and it fell loose. He pulled three diaries from their hiding space and Avery gasped.

"Those are Mother's private thoughts. Let's read!" She sounded giddy.

Mickey heard Marjorie sigh.

"Would you feel better somewhere else?" Mickey asked.

"This is my house," Avery said. "And I don't recall inviting you inside. You have a lot of nerve—"

"I would," Marjorie said, rising from the sofa. "My stomach is in a knot."

"Oh. Her," Avery said.

"I think I'll wait in the foyer." Marjorie joined Mickey at the desk. "And if that becomes a bit much, I'll take a walk and look around outside." She spotted the leather bound books on top of the desk. "What did you find?"

"Mrs. Weldon's diaries. Would you mind taking them to the car? I'll read them later."

"Are you sure it's okay?"

"No," Avery said. But before she could touch them, Mickey scooped them up and handed them to Marjorie.

"I'm sure."

"That's my property," Avery complained.

Marjorie kissed Mickey and left the study. She seemed so listless. Mickey determined to hurry. He continued to search the desk, but did it quickly.

"I'm going to want those diaries back," Avery said.

"What for?"

"Because I do."

He opened the last drawer and stopped cold when the distant cry of a baby reached his ears.

"What's that?" Mickey said.

"I don't hear anything," Avery said.

Mickey looked at her. "Yes, you do. Where's it coming from?"

Avery shrugged but then she rushed from the room. Mickey pushed out of the chair and followed. When he got to the hall, she'd vanished.

Whaaaa. Whaaaa!

A baby was screaming. He followed the sound down the hall to a back stairway. Without hesitation he climbed. The crying grew louder with every step. When he reached the second floor, he saw a door only a few feet away. It was ajar. He approached and slowly pushed it open.

Whaaaa! Whaaaa!

The cry was now a scream. Mickey saw a young Elizabeth Weldon holding an infant in her arms, pacing to and fro.

"She's burning up. My darling's burning up. When's the doctor going to get here?"

Mickey watched with fascination. He was always amazed when a picture from the past projected itself into the present and replayed.

Whaaaa!

"Hush, hush. Oh, my darling. What's wrong with you?"

She held the baby to her and continued to pace.

The crying subsided and she gently placed her daughter in a fancy cradle with ruffles and bows, sat down beside it, and began to weep.

Mickey felt his heart break for the distraught mother, knowing she would lose this child. Then once again he heard Avery's voice. This time it was piercing.

"Enough is enough! No more. I've had it!"

Avery ran to the baby's cradle swinging a baseball bat. Mickey nearly rushed to stop her, but then realized it was all a picture. And besides, the baby was no longer in the cradle and Elizabeth Weldon was gone.

Whack!

Avery set to work battering the cradle to pieces. "You're dead," she screamed. "Long ago dead. I hate you. I hate you!"

Whack! Whack! Whack!

The cradle splintered and fell to pieces. Still, Avery swung. Then she looked up as if someone had come in and stopped. She held the bat midair as her image vanished.

Mickey looked about the room. This had been the first baby's nursery. Elizabeth Weldon had left it as it was in the baby's memory, never using it for Avery. The destroyed cradle had never been swept away.

John had walked in on Avery, Mickey realized, when she was swinging her bat.

Wrong place. Wrong time.

This was where John had died.

"What are you doing in here?" a man's voice said.

"Mickey," Marjorie's voice trembled.

Mickey turned from the rubble that had once been a cradle to see a man standing just inside the door with Marjorie at his side. The man held Mrs. Weldon's diaries in his hands. He was the gardener Mickey had seen on his last trip to Heart House when John had refused to allow him in. Perhaps he worked for the state as a sort of day watchman too. Apparently he spent hours outside rather than in. His face was deeply lined and tanned, and the word craggy came to mind. Stubble grew on his jaw and chin. He looked to be about sixty, wore khaki pants with a matching button-up shirt, and the cap on his head was khaki-colored as well.

Mickey saw alarm in Marjorie's face and quickly calculated how to best inform the man, who held no weapon of any kind, that they were not a threat.

He fumbled for the key to the house and held it aloft. "John gave me this. Said I could come and go as I needed."

The man's serious expression only grew more solemn. "My brother's dead."

"I—" Mickey froze. "You're John's brother. Is this your house now?"

"It's mine. I live here."

Mickey motioned to the destroyed cradle that was now bits and pieces of wood on the floor. "I didn't do that, by the way."

"I know that. Been that way since the day she killed him. At first I wanted the police to see it and then . . ." He looked at the mess. His mouth began to quiver and his eyes suddenly gleamed. He looked back at Mickey. "I couldn't."

Mickey nodded. "I understand."

John's brother regained control of his emotions. "What's your name?"

"Mickey McCoy and this is my wife, Marjorie."

Instead of saying hello, Marjorie moved away and that small action worried Mickey. Yes, the man had frightened her, but the Marjorie he knew would have been cordial, friendly even, now that she knew the man meant them no harm. But she didn't say a word.

"My name's Morris. I saw you when you came the other day. If John gave you that key, he must have wanted you here. Want you here." He corrected his tense.

Mickey eyed Marjorie, measuring how strong her state of mind might be. She knew about ghosts. He decided the topic shouldn't bother her.

"Do you see him?"

"No. Feel him sometimes. And sometimes when I dream he talks to me. He was a good brother. Got me cured from how I was. He and Mrs. Weldon. I used to be slow. Real slow. I'm still slow, but not so much."

"And how did they do that?"

"Had me sit in the study."

Without Lavinia and only the portrait of Agostino.

"I suppose you're doing something John asked you to do," Morris said.

"I am."

Morris looked at the crumbled cradle, eyes moving back and forth. "For the last few months my brother was always trying to figure something out. Didn't want to burden me with it. Wouldn't explain. But I know it had something to do with those paintings."

Morris suddenly turned and gave the diaries to Marjorie. "You can return them or not. You know better than me."

He walked out of the room and his footsteps could be heard treading down the hall.

Chapter 24

As they drove away from Heart House, Mickey squeezed the steering wheel to relieve some tension and glanced at Marjorie. "I'm worried about you. I think you should go back home to Tahoe and call the doctor."

Marjorie smiled. "No. I don't need a doctor. And I want to help. I'm sorry about my lethargy back there. I feel fine now."

Mickey frowned, skeptical. She laughed.

"Really. I am. I'm staying. But do you think we could take a break? Do something together to enjoy the day? Lunch somewhere would be fine."

"I hope you're not just putting up a good front," Mickey said. "If this investigation is too much for you, I want you to tell me."

"I promise."

They turned off their cell phones and drove to Montrose where they found a Chinese restaurant and enjoyed lunch. They didn't talk about anything remotely connected with murder, paintings, or ghosts. They talked about Marjorie taking the rental car to visit her daughter Luce in Brookdale, a little more than an hour away. They talked about what sights she might like to see in Los Angeles. Mickey mentioned flying to Italy once they were home, which made Marjorie smile. Only after they had returned to the hotel, and Marjorie had slipped away to enjoy the hotel pool, did Mickey check for messages. There were three.

Lt. Mars wanted to talk to him. Kelly wanted to see him. And Dennis was pissed. He wanted Mickey to stay away from his wife. Didn't care that her hand had healed. Things were getting too gnarly.

"And you're putting Kelly's life in danger. I can feel it! Leave her out of this from now on. I'm not kidding."

Mickey wanted to respect Dennis' wishes; he didn't call Kelly back. He did call Lt. Mars.

"Your little stunt worked, Mr. McCoy. Congratulations. Kelly's hand apparently healed overnight. She came in to show me. How'd you manage to accomplish that miraculous feat?"

She was testing him, just to see what he'd say. And all sorts of information about Mars swarmed to him over the phone. He needed Mars on his side and any information he could gather and mysteriously throw back at her would work to his advantage.

"The painting is for real," Mickey said. "I think you're beginning to realize that."

She wasn't, but it didn't hurt to plant the seed that would send her in that direction.

Mickey continued. "I know you need more proof and you can't get a warrant to search Jay Serling's house based on Kelly's hand. But you could start investigating the financial records of Avery Weldon. She's dead and can't very well object. That should lead you to Miranda Evans as well as Jay and then you should be able to get a warrant."

"I'm—"

"A homicide detective, not fraud. I understand that. I also know that you're keeping your superiors in the dark when it comes to the security footage you have on Norman's murder as well as Dennis Curry's attempted murder. You know that if you allow them to see it they'll have the same reaction they had to Doug's murder video and they'll deep six everything because they'll think these crimes are unsolvable. You don't."

He paused. Mars didn't say anything for a while. Then she said, "Go on."

"If you want to look into the reputation of the painting, how it was used in the past, then I'll drop off some information I have about children who were exposed to it and got well. There are twenty names. Jay Serling is one of them. And if you want to know more about me, more than you've already checked into, then contact a homicide detective in Brookdale. Detective Stern. He started out as opposed to me as you are."

He gave her time to say something.

"How'd you know it was my birthday yesterday?"

"It popped into my head."

"So you believe anything that just shows up in your brain."

"Not everything. But I knew that was true. And you were thinking how weird it was that your birthday should be Norman's death day."

There was a long pause.

"I make no promises," Mars said. "But bring me the information you have on the painting and the children."

It was less than twenty miles round trip to the police station, but it took Mickey an hour to accomplish the task of dropping off the information for Mars and getting back to the Roosevelt. Traffic. Traffic. Traffic. He was glad he didn't live in Los Angeles.

Finally he was back in his room and felt he could settle in and review Mrs. Weldon's diaries. He hoped they would be the link in the chain that would lead him to someone who could translate the *Accordo*. According to John, she'd had the benefit of a stranger who came to explain things to her. Someone knowledgeable about the paintings and how they were to be maintained. Maybe that stranger was named in one of the diaries.

Mickey began to read. He found that Mrs. Weldon did not make daily entries. She wrote when significant thoughts occurred to her or when events worth recording took place. He tried not to become too absorbed in the prose and felt most of what he read was none of his business. He deemed it necessary and until he found what he needed, he would keep reading.

At last he came to the period of time where the paintings had entered her life. She adored them and instinctively knew they belonged together. That instinct was driven home when the stranger—The Practitioner, he called himself—appeared on her doorstep and told her they had to be kept together. Bad things would happen to anyone who separated them and bad things would happen to innocent bystanders as well. He didn't elaborate on what he meant by bad things except to say Lavinia was capable of murder.

John was wrong about The Practitioner. He'd visited Mrs. Weldon more than once. In fact, there were numerous entries about their encounters. They met often and in secret. And sometimes they rendezvoused outside the confines of Heart House. She grew enamored of him and the diary was filled with phrases expressing her undying gratitude. He taught her a few basic incantations concerning love and she'd used them on her husband to no avail. "Don't worry," the Practitioner told her. "It takes time and practice."

And then Mr. Weldon was murdered and the Practitioner made a mistake. He told her he believed she had used Lavinia to kill her husband.

Not true! She had furiously penned in the diary. *I loved him no matter what. His own bastard daughter killed him. She's young, but she knows about the paintings because she's forever lurking, eavesdropping...*

Elizabeth Weldon went on to write about her grief at the loss of her husband and how she hated that outsiders thought she had killed him. The Practitioner seemed to relish the idea that she had committed murder and wanted to school her in the art of dark spells. This made her end her relationship with The Practitioner. At her core she was kindhearted. Except toward Avery. She was able to see past everyone's foibles, except for a child's whose only sin was the fact that she had been born to another woman. Any animosity and hatred Elizabeth felt, she collected and directed at Avery.

Entries about The Practitioner stopped and Mickey waded through page after page of things that weren't useful. He came to a passage about the healing of John's brother Morris through exposure to Agostino. John had approached Mrs. Weldon. "Does that painting only work on children?"

So that was how that had come about.

Mrs. Weldon wrote a lot about John. He was her right-hand man. Her rock. Through all her trials and tribulations, John was the one she confided in. The person in whom she found strength. Perhaps, at first, she'd thought of him as a son, but she developed an attraction of a sexual nature which they carried out. She loved him in her own way. And he loved her. But John was not in her social strata and she still ran wild with whomever she pleased. He tried to break away. Found a girlfriend and was going to make a life with her. Mrs. Weldon lured him back and John never strayed after that.

Mickey heard the door open and he put the diary down. Marjorie entered the room. She smelled like suntan lotion and sweat from the sun. She looked wilted. She placed her straw pool bag on the bed and stared at it.

"Too much sun?" Mickey asked.

She glanced at him. "Don't think so. Stayed in the shade and read the whole time."

It didn't look like that was the case to Mickey. Her skin had some color to it that it didn't have before. "The heat can still take a lot out of you," he said.

"I guess I shouldn't have stayed so long. I'm not sure, but I think I fell asleep."

"You're not sure?"

"I was suddenly on page one-forty-nine in my book when I'd been on page one-twenty. I didn't remember a thing of what I'd read."

Mickey frowned.

"I guess I was sleep reading." She smiled, took his hand and led him to the bed. They sat beside each other. She draped an arm around him and rested her head on his shoulder. "I need to sit with you like this," she murmured.

Mickey put an arm around her and placed a hand upon her cheek. He couldn't read her thoughts, not like he could with Mars. But he could sense her energy and it was lagging. She was on empty, as if something more than the sun had come along and drained it. Mickey held her close and tried to share his energy with her. After ten minutes of just sitting still and not saying a word he could tell she'd fallen asleep. He didn't move for another twenty minutes, but let her sleep. Finally she stirred and he could see from the gleam in her eye that she was her old self. She kissed him and said, "I feel better. I think I'll take a shower."

She stood up and headed for the bathroom.

"I love you," Mickey told her.

"And I love you." She closed the door. Soon, Mickey heard the water running.

*****

"John's turned the guardianship of the paintings over to me, but I'm not certain he can really do that," Mickey told Marjorie. They were seated in the hotel's restaurant. Mickey was enjoying a steak, Marjorie a light pasta dish.

"Why not?"

"Because I don't own them. His brother does."

"There are rules?"

"I'm assuming so. That black book he gave me. I'm sure it's the contract that specifies all. But I can't read it and so far Mrs. Weldon's diaries haven't illuminated me on who can."

"I'd help you if I could."

"I know . . ." He put his knife and fork down. He reached across the table and took her hand so she would look at him. "I need to be honest with you. There's something about this whole situation that seems to affect you negatively. It worries me. I was thinking of taking you to the museum tomorrow so you could see Lavinia's painting. But I don't think I want that to happen."

He saw Marjorie stiffen. "I forgot to tell you something," she said.

"What?"

"I've already been to the museum and ... I saw Lavinia's portrait."

"When?"

"Before I went to the newspaper office, I stopped by the museum. It was crowded because of the murder."

Slowly, Mickey withdrew his hand. "So, you made her acquaintance."

"Acquaintance." Marjorie took a deep breath and her gaze went off to one side. "I guess you could put it that way. I did talk to her."

Mickey's heart began to pound zealously. He wished she hadn't done that. Lavinia's consciousness, her being, was attached to that painting, and now she was aware of Marjorie.

"What did you say?" Mickey asked.

"I told her you were my husband and were in town to make sure she was a good girl. She was silent on the matter." Marjorie smiled.

No, thought Mickey. She hasn't been silent on the matter. She's been messing with you. This certainly explained a lot. Lavinia was playing games, tapping into Marjorie's energy and causing lapses of memory. He didn't want to frighten his wife and didn't tell her what he was thinking. Instead, he decided, he would push for her to leave Los Angeles. It was the only thing he could think of that might put an end to Lavinia's manipulation.

"Well. No harm done, I guess." Mickey did his best to sound nonchalant. "I was thinking, though. I saw how Heart House affected you and I think you should sit this deal of mine out. Take a drive to Brookdale. See Luce."

Marjorie nodded. "I'd like to see her." She began to eat.

****

Mickey finished reading the diaries as Marjorie slept. The name of The Practitioner was never mentioned and he felt disappointed. He had no clue who could help him interpret the book and took some time to surf the net for translators of obscure languages. Trouble was, he didn't have a name for the idiom in the *Accordo*. At two in the morning he gave up, turned off the light and climbed into bed. For a while his mind kept busy with thoughts about what he should do. Nothing resolved itself and he finally fell asleep. But it wasn't a peaceful slumber. His mind spun a disturbing dream. It was short and repeated itself as if caught in a loop.

It was night. Marjorie was driving the rental car on a winding mountain road. She drove it over a cliff.

Chapter 25

Thomas Dibiasi was pleased with himself. Sitting in the barber's chair, getting a trim and a shave, he mused about his "mentor" Ray La Tour. If the man had been brilliant at one time, there was no evidence of it now. He was a scatterbrained fool. A doddering blemish upon the earth. Whenever he glimpsed Ray's mind, he heard gibberish—looped random thoughts that circled and landed nowhere. The experiments he and Ray labored over were rehashed tests of things Ray had discovered in his prime. Today would be no different; Thomas was certain of that. Although Ray had told him to be ready for something more interesting today—

Thomas interrupted his own thoughts with a laugh.

"Excuse me?" the barber asked, pausing with his clippers held aloft.

"Continue. Continue," Thomas ordered.

There would certainly be something more interesting going on today. But it wouldn't be Ray's experiment. The *Accordo* that had been breached and needed his attention. It would be in his possession by the end of the day. He'd been lax in his oversight of the compact. For decades the Guardians in charge of keeping the paintings together had performed the task without incident. He should have paid closer attention when Elizabeth Weldon died.

He almost sighed at the thought of her. He'd enjoyed that woman. If only she'd been a little more open to his view of life, they could have spent more years together, and she would have had the time of her life. He'd offered to construct an *Accordo* just for her. She could have looked twenty-five again and maintained her beauty for the rest of her life, however many years she'd wished to bargain for. Unfortunately, she wasn't willing to bargain. And that, as the saying went, was that.

Today, only a handful of *Accordos* were in operation the world over. Those that didn't involve centuries of maintenance ended when the person contracting died. Sometimes there was an escape clause for a person who found his heart's desire not so desirable after all. And sometimes a Practitioner, like himself, forgot to pay attention and the compact got breached, as had happened here. There were dire consequences for the Practitioner if he didn't remedy the situation with whatever option had been built into the agreement. Thomas was well on his way to restoring this *Accordo*. *Well* on his way. He smiled inwardly.

Thomas had sought an alliance with Ray because Ray lived in the vicinity of the compact and was one of a handful of people who had the knowhow to interpret the compact if it were to be placed in his hands. How fortunate Ray had turned out to be a dried-up has been. Ray's ineptness made things much easier. Thomas didn't need to keep his guard up, and there he saw no obstacles to his plan.

He'd sent out a call for the current Guardian to bring the compact to him. He would offer to translate, which of course, the Guardian would be only too grateful to accept. At that point Thomas would be in a position to tell the Guardian whatever he wanted. He could tell the truth or not. He could take the book and vamoose! It wouldn't matter. Things had progressed to the point where there was little the Guardian could do about anything. But, to be on the safe side, Thomas planned to lie. He would soothe the Guardian's worried mind so that he would attempt no interference and the *Accordo* would enter its next phase.

The barber placed a hot towel upon Thomas' face and feelings of ecstasy traveled his body. He was delighted with his choice. He felt there was great symmetry to it—a tasty irony he found delicious. His choice was the Guardian's wife.

Great suffering lay ahead for many and he loved it. He savored it. Aside from living the good life and always having things his way, orchestrating the suffering of others was one of his favorite things. It never got old.

He laughed.

****

"Now you don't want me to go?" Marjorie said, standing before the bathroom mirror, finishing with her hair. There was the slightest hint of irritation in her voice that wasn't like her.

Mickey stood in the doorway. "It's not that. I'm worried."

"That I'll drive off a cliff."

"That was the dream and you were in the Mercedes."

"I'm pretty sure there are no cliffs between here and Brookdale. The 10 freeway is on flat terrain."

"I know. I know. Just promise me, you'll be safe."

"I promise."

"Don't decide to take a drive to Big Bear."

"Luce isn't much of a mountain girl, and I'm going to be right where she is, so put your mind at ease."

The matter was settled and Marjorie edged past Mickey, grabbed her pocketbook, gave him a perfunctory kiss, and blew out of the room.

Mickey had almost grabbed her, told her he was going with her to Brookdale and that he was ready to forget this whole thing. But he'd maintained his composure. He reasoned that by leaving town, she was out of the negative influence that had been affecting her. She was safe.

But what about the dream?

He stood in the middle of the hotel suite, hands on hips, and stared at the diaries he'd left stacked on the table. Mrs. Weldon's life was summed up in those five small volumes. He found her to be an interesting woman, a complex woman. Many insights into her character had come to him. But she'd left no clue as to the name of the person who could translate the *Accordo*. It was frustrating.

What now? he wondered, fully aware of what needed to happen, but helpless as to how he could bring it about. Lt. Mars was working on the financial audit, but sometimes the wheels of justice turned slowly and there was no telling when the Agostino painting would be returned to its rightful owner. And if Jay got wind of the fact that he was being investigated, he might even hide the painting somewhere out of reach.

Beside the diaries lay the *Accordo*, looking very much like a small Bible. Mickey had skimmed it, but had yet to examine it, his intuition telling him every time he looked at it that he needed an expert.

He picked it up and sat on the bed. He opened to the first page. Amid the Italian scrawl was Lavinia's signature, neat and easy to read, and then the signature of the person she'd compacted with. That person's signature was indecipherable. Big, flashy, with ambitious loops and ambiguous squiggles. Mickey placed a finger on the signature and closed his eyes. He waited to see if an image—anything—would come to him. He heard a sound in his head. It went: Tap. Tap. Tap. A short pause followed by two quick taps.

Nothing else came to him and he opened his eyes.

Turning the page, he almost missed that it was stuck to the page behind it. Very carefully he placed a finger between the two and slid upward. The pages came apart without ripping.

At the top of the page he recognized the word *Custode*. It didn't take a genius to figure it meant custodian or guardian. Below was a list of names. The first: Catherine De Rosa. He put his finger on the name to see if something would happen. He decided this was the young woman he'd seen in a dream accepting the paintings from a delivery man. He received no other information about her and opened his eyes.

Mickey kicked off his shoes and made himself comfortable on the bed. He leaned against the headboard and looked at the other names on the list. Over the centuries all of these people had been guardians of the paintings. Twenty-three names in all and the last three gave him chills: Elizabeth Brahms Weldon, John Carroll, Mickey McCoy. John had written in Mickey's name—from beyond the grave.

Mickey almost put the book aside. It made him nervous. But he knew he didn't have that option. He turned the pages, one by one, slowly, deliberately, hoping something would happen that would allow him to understand or direct him in some way. But the radio didn't come on, nor did the television. The words in the book didn't morph into English. John's spirit didn't mysteriously appear. Nothing happened to tell him what to do. He was worried about Lavinia's presence in the museum, and still bothered by the way Marjorie had been acting. And now this last dream he'd had. He hoped it was merely a vehicle for his mind to express his worry about her and not a premonition.

When he reached the final page, he stared. It contained only a number. A large handwritten one. He could have sworn the number was a two the day before. His heart fluttered. He felt fear, but he didn't know why. He stared at the digit. It was just a number. Nothing about it changed. He went back to the beginning of the book and began again. This time, when he reached the final page and it still showed the number one, he closed the book, rested his hands upon it, and closed his eyes in meditation. Maybe he could coax the unknowable powers of the universe into sending him information.

His cell phone rang. He picked it up. The caller had a 714 area code and a number he didn't recognize. He answered and was surprised to discover Kelly on the line.

"You didn't call me back," she said without saying hello.

"I didn't think I should. Dennis is afraid for you and I don't want to cause trouble."

"He's my husband, not my keeper."

"Of course. But he's spooked and I don't blame him. I also don't want to get in the middle—"

"You are in the middle whether you like it or not. He told me he left you a strong message to leave me alone. I reminded him that you saved his life and you helped me heal my hand, so his fear is all wrong."

"And what did he say?"

"He grunted which is his way of backing down while saving face."

Mickey chuckled. "I guess we all have our own method."

"Well, that's his. I just wanted to talk to you. You obviously made a lot of progress since your visit to my store. I want to know what's going on."

"Right now, not much. My wife took the car—"

"Your wife's in town."

"Just left town, as a matter of fact, to visit her daughter. I'm . . ." His brow creased. "Did you change your phone number?"

"No."

"Are you phoning from a seven one four area code?"

"No. I'm using my regular Blackberry."

"Kelly. I need to go."

"What happened?"

Mickey smiled. "I don't know. Maybe nothing. But, if I need a ride somewhere, are you available?"

"Yes. I can have someone look after the store."

"Good."

After they hung up, he found the 714 number on the list of received calls and punched it.

A woman answered, *"Potere della luce."*

Italian. He felt his skin ripple with expectation. "Ah, what was that?"

"Power of Light."

"Oh, Power of Light. You're a church?"

"We do hold Sunday services. We are nondenominational and everyone is welcome. We also offer a variety of classes for development of personal consciousness and spiritual growth. Past life regression, psychic development, healing through one's own consciousness. A host of metaphysical trainings."

"That sounds intriguing," Mickey said.

"What area of development are you interested in?"

"I'm in possession of something called an *Accordo*. I need to know more about it."

"That's a new one on me. Maybe someone here knows something. For a small fee, you could join our organization and post on our cyber bulletin board."

Posting on a bulletin board would take too long. He needed answers now. The phone number appearing on his cell was a lead. He needed to visit the Power of Light in person and ask around.

"Where are you located?"

"Huntington Beach."

Mickey called Kelly and she agreed to give him a ride. But when she arrived to pick him up, Dennis was driving.

Chapter 26

"I decided to come along," Dennis told Mickey. "You got a problem with that?"

"Not at all," Mickey said, knowing full well Dennis didn't care how he felt about the matter. His aura was blazing red with gray. He was angry and frightened at the same time. Dennis was a walking contradiction. He believed enough in the paranormal to hunt for it, but hunted it so he could deny it. His skepticism had taken a beating because of Lavinia. He was scared and not because he was afraid of death. He was afraid of life. His world was out of whack. Dennis wanted to close the door on all he'd been doing. He was no longer willing to be a seeker. He'd even disbanded the PSS and cancelled his show.

"You disbanded your group," Mickey said.

"I told Kelly not to tell you." There was anger in Dennis' tone.

"I didn't tell him," Kelly piped up from the back seat.

Mickey was sorry he'd mentioned it. The ride to Huntington Beach took forty minutes and Dennis was driving. He was already on edge. Mickey didn't want to upset him any more than he already was.

So you're a mind reader, Dennis' words were filled with disdain.

"Occasionally I know what people are thinking."

"Who asked you?" Dennis said.

Mickey realized that when he'd heard Dennis say, *so you're a mind reader*, he had been reading his mind. It had come through that clear. Mickey only read minds when there was a reason for him to do so. Otherwise he felt it a complete invasion of privacy and blocked them. Not everyone's thoughts came through to him and he couldn't make someone's thoughts come to him at will. But he could always block them. He decided that right now, in Dennis' case, it would be good to know what the man was thinking.

"Sorry," Mickey said. "I thought you said something."

"I didn't."

You son of a bitch. I don't know what your game is, but I'm here to make certain everything is on the up and up. And I swear, if you do anything I don't like while we are at this Power of Light whatever-it-is place, I will leave you there. I have no qualms about doing that. Did you read that Svengali?

"I'm no Svengali," Mickey said. "And please don't leave me there."

Mickey felt a punch in his stomach. No one had hit him. It was an energy synapse. Dennis felt like striking Mickey and had done so mentally.

Dennis' eyes strayed from the road to his passenger.

"Let's try this," Mickey said, closing his eyes, ignoring the jumble of words Dennis now spewed forth. He envisioned a ball of blue light. He envisioned its energy flowing to Dennis, filling the man's entire body with a calming current of secure and relaxed feelings. He kept this up for several minutes before he stopped. He didn't want to go too far. Complete relaxation would mean sleep and Dennis was, after all, driving.

It worked.

"I'm sorry," Dennis said sincerely. "I don't know what's wrong with me. Ever since what happened in the museum, I've been a little crazy."

"I'll attest to that," Kelly said.

"Don't fight it," Mickey said. "Accept what happened. I think you're on edge because you are not only denying what happened to you, but you are denying your own power. And, I'm going to tell you this."

He didn't say the next sentence, but thought it. *I think you're capable of reading other people's thoughts. At least mine because I'm open to it and I know for a fact you answered me once already.*

"I can't read people's thoughts," Dennis said.

"Why did you say that?" Mickey asked.

"Because you just said—"

"He didn't say anything about reading people's thoughts," Kelly interrupted.

Mickey saw Dennis' throat move. He was swallowing his feelings.

Mickey thought: *Let's leave it at that and see what the rest of the trip brings.*

Dennis gave Mickey a completely perplexed look.

****

The Power of Light was a small church that had a large two-story building connected to its rear. Mickey knew it was a building addition because not only didn't the architecture match, it was a different color. The church portion, which also served as an auditorium for guest speakers, was white sideboard with emerald green trim. The subsequent building which was boxy and without charm, was covered with pale peach stucco and trim. Windows were too small for the size of the building and reminded Mickey of pock marks. So much for synergy of style.

This learning center for development of higher human consciousness meant well, Mickey felt, but he was certain a lot of quacks came through its doors. He supposed that couldn't be helped. Every area of human endeavor had its shysters. It didn't matter what it was. But metaphysics, oh, that was ripe for the traipsing.

With the black book tucked under his arm, Mickey led Dennis and Kelly through a rear door that allowed entry from the parking lot. There was no one posted at this entrance to act as security. It appeared the organization was truly open to visitors and had no fear of its detractors because, certainly, any organization dedicated to parapsychology and the paranormal had its detractors.

They stood in a dimly-lit hallway, unsure which way to go. Bulletin boards hung on the walls with an assortment of flyers haphazardly tacked to them. None of the information offered interested Mickey. The walls were pasty white and the industrial grade carpet a nondescript color.

"What do you think, Dennis?" Mickey said.

"What? I don't know." Irritation had returned to his tone. Mickey knew he was feeling anxious again. He'd had a shock to the system realizing how psychically gifted he really was and he was still fighting it.

"Why don't you ask me?" Kelly said.

"You know where we should go?" Mickey said.

"No. I don't even know why we're here."

Mickey smiled. He enjoyed Kelly's sense of humor.

"Why are we here?" she asked.

"Because of a book. I need it interpreted."

Kelly put her hands on her hips, rolled her head to one side, and gave Mickey a stare that could have scorched wood.

"What's the matter?" Mickey asked.

Kelly tapped her chest. "Hello. I run a book store. I've seen it all. You didn't show it to me? Think that maybe I could help?"

"It's a very unusual book."

Kelly's scorching stare remained. She motioned toward herself. "This isn't just a pretty face."

Mickey had no choice but to hold up the *Accordo*.

"Ever see anything like this?" He kept it out of reach.

Kelly snatched it from him. "Shees. I'm not going to hurt it."

Mickey wasn't worried about that. He was worried about her, although he didn't have a particular reason why.

Kelly looked at what she had in her hands and lightly stroked the cover. "I love books," she said. "You'll never catch me with one of those electronic readers." She opened it and began to read.

"On this day August thirty-one, in this year sixteen thirty-seven."

She glanced at Mickey and commented, "This is old. This is so cool."

"I don't know about cool," Mickey said.

Kelly continued to read. "We are in accord. Lavinia Rossi Zanetti and Practitioner Three. All benefits and conditions follow. Sanctified by he who has the power to do so. Custodians to follow in sequence." She looked up. "Then there's Lavinia's name and another I can't read."

"You know Italian," Mickey said.

"Don't look so surprised. Languages are my thing." She returned her attention to the book and began turning pages. "Oops. I spoke too soon. The first page is in Italian; the rest isn't in any language I've ever seen. Except. Did I see your name?" She tried to return to the right page, but Mickey took the black volume from her.

"Now you know why we're here. I hope to find someone who can translate it."

Kelly gave an up and down gander at the unimpressive hallway. "Good luck."

Whoosh, smack. A man's giggle.

Mickey jerked his head behind him. "Did you hear something?"

"No," Kelly said.

"What?" Dennis asked. Mickey didn't answer. He stared at Dennis hoping for an ally, a colleague, someone who could experience whatever it was Mickey was experiencing.

"Did you hear it?" Mickey asked.

"I heard a ball," Dennis said.

"Going through the air and hitting something."

"Yes."

"And then a man laughed."

Mickey moved to a door, held the knob, but didn't open it.

Whoosh, smack.

He opened the door and found a stairway leading to a basement. Doddering chatter rose to greet him. Mickey began to descend. Dennis motioned for Kelly to go next. Their footsteps were anything but soft.

"Hello? Who's there?" a man called from below.

"We come in peace," Kelly joked and Mickey smiled.

A man appeared at the bottom of the stairs. Because there was little light in the stairwell, but plenty in the basement, the man was more or less in silhouette. He bent to the side, as if that could somehow help him see who was intruding on his space. His hands bounced up and down in a bit of a nervous gesture, although Mickey didn't feel that the man was nervous. Until he got closer, the only other thing Mickey could tell about him was that he wore a lab coat.

"I thought I had that door locked," the man said. Mickey expected a frown, but the man giggled the moment Mickey and friends reached the bottom of the stairs.

"It wasn't and we heard noise," Mickey responded.

"Were we that strident?"

The man had a mischievous sort of smile on his unassuming face. He had thick brown hair that was white at the temples. He looked like he was fifty, but Mickey sensed that he was much older and wiser than he wanted people to think. At least the people present. His eyes were dark, bright, and happy.

"Not so strident," Kelly said. Her tone showed amusement at the man's choice of words. "I didn't hear a thing."

The man looked at her and his smile widened. "Well, my, my. That's excellent then. I'm delighted to have visitors." He turned in a manner that assumed everyone would follow, hands waving in the air, index fingers pointing toward the ceiling. "Unbiased minds. That's what I require."

"He's like the absent-minded professor," Dennis whispered.

I don't think so, Mickey thought, hoping Dennis would hear him. Practice made perfect and intuition was telling him he needed Dennis to be connected as much as possible.

"We're conducting experiments, Thomas and me. I. Me. Which is it? Oh, it doesn't matter." His hands fluttered as they walked past a clear plastic partition into an area set up for whatever experiments he and Thomas were conducting. A long table, the sort with retractable legs for portability, was parallel with the partition. There were only two chairs for sitting. A computer purred softly upon the table, a large monitor to its right. There was a yellow note pad with calculations on it. Beyond the table was a second clear partition, apparently for protection from what happened in the rectangular area beyond it. A lean, good-looking man of forty or forty-five stood in the north portion of the space. On the south end were two machines, dissimilar in design. One was clearly a ball-throwing machine. Two small cameras were mounted on the walls.

"We have visitors, Thomas," the man called.

Thomas waved with a slight Cheshire-cat grin. He was tall and wore tight black jeans and a black shirt. His hair was dark and neatly trimmed. He was clean shaven.

He's glad we're here, thought Mickey. *More than glad. Ecstatic. Why should that be?*

"Hi, Thomas," Kelly said. The smile on her face and the gleam in her eye said she thought he was one good-looking guy despite the age difference. "I'm Kelly. This is my husband, Dennis. This is our friend, Mickey." She looked at the comical figure in the lab coat. "And you are?"

"Oh, goodness, you want to know my moniker." He put a hand to his forehead as if he'd forgotten it and had to think. "Call me Ray."

Mickey wondered if Ray was putting on some sort of act. If so, to what purpose?

"We're on the brink. The verge. The precipice. Yes, we are." He turned and faced Mickey squarely. "Perhaps you'd like to try."

Mickey's brow creased as he studied the man's eyes. There was strength in them. He saw a knowledgeable person, not a bumbling fool. "I don't even know what you're up to," Mickey said.

"Oh, that's easily rectified." Ray threw up a hand and was back to his blundering, blustering manner. "We're hurling balls at Thomas and he is shielding himself." He sat at the computer and pecked on the keyboard. A tennis ball whizzed from the machine and hit Thomas on the head.

"Hey, Ray!" Thomas called, rubbing his skull. "You're to warn me *every* time."

Mickey heard a muffled snicker come from Ray before he said, "Oh, yes. Yes. Yes. Yes. I'm always getting ahead of myself. So excited you see. He's gotten so very good at it. I expect him to throw up a shield without giving it a second thought."

"Do you allow Thomas to throw balls at *you*?" Kelly asked.

"Without warning or with warning, you mean?"

"Either way."

"On occasion. On occasion. But I prefer it here." He patted the table. "Much safer."

Mickey noticed Dennis raise his eyes skyward.

"Maybe you could explain from the beginning," Mickey said.

"Yes, certainly I could." But then he didn't explain. He said, "Thomas, let's show them. Ready?"

Thomas stiffened his body and closed his eyes. "Yes."

"On the count of three. One. Two. Two and a half." Ray chuckled. "Three." He hit control-shift-t on the keyboard and a tennis ball flew. An inch in front of Thomas' nose it bounced away as if something had intervened.

Ray laughed.

"How did he do that?" Kelly asked.

"We're engaging with thought forms," Ray said. "Thomas visualizes a shield around him and it forms in reality to protect him. Would you care to endeavor yourself?"

Mickey expected Kelly to say no thanks. But she didn't. Her expression said she was intrigued.

"I'll give it a try," Dennis said. He sounded hostile.

That old push-pull of belief-disbelief has you in its grip. Let it go. Let it go, thought Mickey.

"He gets to practice first, right?" Kelly said. "I don't want you knocking him silly. He's been silly enough lately."

"Oh, we don't commence with balls."

"What do you begin with then?" Kelly asked.

"Laser beams. Light." Ray hit control-shift-# on the keyboard and the second machine came to life with a hum. "You don't feel a thing except a slight chill. We've programmed the machine to include cold air so you have a reaction to being hit when you fail."

Ray motioned for Thomas. Then he looked at Dennis. "Go forth and protect thyself."

Dennis and Thomas exchanged places.

"Now what?" Dennis said.

"Close your eyes. When you feel a laser touching you, tell me where."

Dennis closed his eyes and waited. And waited. And waited.

"Are your receptors engaged?" Ray asked.

"What?"

"Are your receptors . . . do you feel anything yet?"

"Not yet," Dennis said. More time passed. Dennis opened his eyes. "Maybe I'm not laser tag material."

"No. You did very well. I didn't hit you yet. A test to see how susceptible you are to suggestion."

"What suggestion?"

"I asked you if you felt anything."

"Let's do it for real." Dennis' impatience was evident.

"By all means. For real this time," Ray said.

Dennis closed his eyes and Ray pecked the keyboard immediately. A red laser hit Dennis in the shoulder.

"My left shoulder," Dennis said.

"Good." Ray chuckled. "Now see in your mind's eye a curtain dropping down to block it."

Everybody watched, but the red beam continued to glow on Dennis' shoulder.

Mickey knew that Dennis was going to have to change his attitude if he was to get anywhere with the experiment.

Relax, Dennis. Relax. Release that cynical side of yourself. Go with the flow and see what can happen.

If you think it's so easy, old man, you come try.

Mickey smiled as Dennis' eyes flipped open. Getting a telepathic response from him was as good as seeing him create a thought form. Better.

"This is ridiculous," Dennis said, coming back to the group. "I don't believe in any of this so-called thought form crap."

"I'm afraid, sir, that your attitude is not conducive to successful experimentation." Ray turned to Mickey. "What about you, sir? Would you like to give it an endeavor?"

"Why can't I go next?" Kelly said.

"Why, you can. You should." Ray motioned with his hand and Kelly walked to where her husband had stood. She shook her arms and legs like a swimmer about to race and cracked her neck one way and then the other. Mickey glanced at Dennis and saw him scowling.

Kelly closed her eyes. "Okay. Let her rip."

Ray waited.

Kelly said, "Nothing. Nothing."

"Don't talk," Dennis said.

"I'm nervous."

Kelly shook her limbs again and finally stilled herself. Ray allowed the laser to beam. It hit her on the hand.

"I feel it," Kelly said. "My hand."

"Of course, she does," Dennis muttered. "It's all that cold air."

"He turned the cold air off," Thomas said and Dennis' brow dipped.

"Now," Ray spoke, "sustaining that relaxed state, image small atoms of energy. See them vibrate, pulse, and grow bigger until they are all around you." He paused, giving Kelly time. "Now those vibrating atoms move. They connect with each other. Ten, twenty, a hundred, a thousand, one-hundred thousand atoms of energy moving together to form a curtain of steel floating in the air."

Everyone waited and after a few seconds the thin red line of light stopped a foot from Kelly's hand. It was startling, but no one said a word. Everyone stared.

Mickey felt Dennis tense with a flare of envy. Kelly had accomplished something he could not. Then Mickey saw that Thomas' eyes were closed and he was concentrating. Dennis saw it too.

"He's helping her," Dennis complained. Thomas opened his eyes. The beam extended and touched Kelly's hand.

"I feel the beam now." She looked at everyone.

"Thomas was doing it," Dennis said.

"Damn!" Kelly exclaimed. "I thought I finally had some of these stupid powers everybody else seems to have."

"You do have them," Ray said. "They're just undeveloped."

"I was giving you confidence," Thomas said. "You have some now, no?"

"'Fraid not," Kelly said. "But let's go again."

For twenty minutes Ray worked with Kelly and finally, somehow, it appeared that the laser beam was blocked of her own doing. She squealed at what she'd accomplished.

"Shall we take it a step further?" Ray asked.

"You mean, tennis balls?" Kelly asked, looking nervous.

"I'll keep the velocity low."

"So that they won't hurt when they hit." Kelly knocked herself in the forehead with her palm.

"It may take a time or two."

"Okay. I'm in." Kelly grinned.

It took an hour, but eventually balls were bouncing away from her as if she were surrounded by a clear curtain of plastic.

Mickey was fine with all the fun, but time was passing. He still hadn't gotten what he'd come for, and it didn't look like Kelly wanted to stop showing off her new-found ability. "One more time!" she called each time she managed to cause the ball to bounce in a direction other than her nose.

It was time to begin what he'd come for. He removed the black book from under his arm and placed it on the table where Ray would see. The daffy scientist paused at the sight of it and turned off the ball-throwing machine.

"Hey!" Kelly said.

"Ever seen anything like this before?" Mickey tapped the book.

Ray picked it up. "*Accordo.*" He opened to the first page and studied it. After a moment he looked at several pages more. "Perhaps. A long time ago. Something similar. I can't say."

Mickey's heart wilted. He couldn't say. Did this man know what an *Accordo* was or not? Was he supposed to help him or not? Could he interpret the pages that were gibberish instead of Italian?

"I'm looking for someone who can translate it."

"May I?" Thomas held out his hand and Ray allowed him to take the book. "Perhaps I can be of assistance."

Mickey felt his nerves tingle with hope. It had never occurred to him that it might be Thomas he was supposed to meet.

Thomas carefully turned page after page. "This is very old script. It would take time, work, to find a proper source to pull forth the meaning."

Mickey's hopes were dashed. This man would research it for him and, as he'd said, that would take time. There was no time. Mickey extended his hand. "May I have the book back?"

"I am offering you my help."

"I know. But . . . thank you." Mickey took the book.

"I can help you, I assure you."

"But not fast enough."

"Oh." Thomas waved a hand as if erasing what he'd said before. "I will do it quickly for you."

"No," Ray said. "I will." His demeanor changed. He gazed at his protégée with a resolve that took Mickey and Thomas—if the shocked look on Thomas' face was any indication—by surprise. Ray's clownish, Ed Wynnian persona had vanished.

Mickey gave the book to Ray. He sounded so assured.

Thomas covered his astonishment with a smile. "My mentor will help you then. He is, after all, the master of *this* domain."

Ray and Thomas stared at each other in a manner that Mickey found fascinating and strange. They appeared to be engaged in a battle of wills, as if they had both drawn a line in the sand. He didn't understand why.

"The matter is settled," Ray said. "I don't believe I need your services any longer."

Thomas' smile widened. He offered an abbreviated bow, said nothing, and lithely made his way upstairs.

"What was that about?" Kelly asked.

Dennis took her hand in a protective gesture.

"This is a significant *Accordo*," Ray said. "I need time with it alone."

"How much time?" Mickey asked, concerned. But something in him told him to trust Ray.

"I will have your interpretation for you tonight. However, I won't tell you not to worry. It may be too late to change the outcome of what has already been set in motion."

Mickey nodded. He'd been afraid of that.

Chapter 27

For the first time in her life Marjorie's daughter, Luce, was afraid of her mother. Growing up, she'd been headstrong and their relationship had always been a tumultuous one. But through it all Marjorie had been vigilantly reasonable, loving and mature. Because of that, Luce was happy to say they'd made it through her teen years as well as the next decade, and could call themselves friends. She loved her mother and could express the affection she felt with an ease she'd never had as a child.

But this woman who had entered her house five minutes ago, and was exploring every nook and cranny like a crazed cat, was not the mother she knew.

"You've been here before," Luce said. "Nothing's changed."

She followed Marjorie into her bedroom and watched as she picked through her jewelry and perfume. "You know, I expected you hours ago. I thought we could go to lunch. But . . ."

Marjorie clasped a necklace about her neck and plunked on a bracelet. She moved to the full-length mirror and admired herself. Luce was stunned. She'd never seen her mother act this way.

"What's wrong with you?"

Marjorie spun around and appraised Luce as if she were a stranger. Her eyes were feral, her mouth an upside down slit. A guttural drone came from her throat. She took a step forward and Luce moved back. Staring at her daughter, her mouth distorted into a gypsy-like pout.

"Mother," Luce whispered.

Marjorie turned back to the mirror and began to pick at her hair, occasionally glancing at Luce in the glass.

Luce felt a tightness in her chest she could honestly say she'd never felt before. Her mother had lost her mind. It was if she was possessed and the idea that this wasn't even remotely her imagination frightened Luce more than her worst nightmare.

That's not my mother.

She raced from the bedroom seeking the cell phone she'd left in the living room. If she'd owned a gun, she would have retrieved it too. But if she had a gun, could she really shoot her own mom? Fear ravaged her nerves the way a toddler hammered a piano. It was ludicrous to think her mother could be a threat. Crazy! But she'd seen how she was acting. She'd looked into those eyes, filled with some sort of insane fanaticism. This woman was not Marjorie. Luce had to be on guard.

Mickey's cell phone went to voice mail and she left a message, her words a whisper spoken hastily. She called the hotel and left a message there, too. Was he aware of Marjorie's bizarre behavior? If so, why hadn't he taken her to a hospital for observation? What was going on? Call her. Call her! She hung up. What now? Decisive action always helped. She'd called Mickey, but now what?

She was still scared. A big part of her wanted to run outside, jump in the car, and drive away. But she knew that wasn't an option. The situation was so foreign to her experience. Should she call the police? And tell them what? Maybe she needed to talk to Marjorie. Talk and talk until her mother broke through. Surely Marjorie was inside her body somewhere.

Luce almost went back to the bedroom, but she went into the kitchen first. She needed to arm herself. As ludicrous as that sounded, she was too afraid not to do it.

She opened a drawer and removed a carving knife. Oh, God. She felt tears in her eyes and bent over clutching her stomach. Now she was insane!

But she maintained possession of the knife, holding it at her side, and walked back to the bedroom.

The light was on but Marjorie was gone. Luce's heartbeat skyrocketed as if jolted by electricity. She stood frozen and almost couldn't breathe. Jewelry lay scattered atop the dresser. Papers for school were haphazardly spilled upon the floor. A lipstick kiss marred the mirror.

She heard soft footsteps come up behind her. Her hand, the one holding the knife, felt clammy as her grip tightened. For several seconds she didn't move. If she turned around, what would she see? If she turned around, what would she be forced to do?

Pound, pound, pound went her heart.

"Luce." It was Marjorie's voice, quiet but not calm. It resonated with alarm.

Luce turned around. A beam of daylight caused the knife in her hand to gleam. Marjorie saw it, but didn't react. Her face was passive.

"What's wrong with you?" Luce gently asked.

"I don't know."

"No?" Luce dropped the knife and threw her arms around her mother. "Should I take you to a doctor?"

Marjorie hugged her back. "I think I should go back to Hollywood."

Luce's eyes were wet. Normally her quick-witted tongue was lavish with words, but in this moment she was speechless, her mind a pile of mush. Fear subsided and she filled with dread. She knew Marjorie and Mickey had come to Los Angeles on another one of Mickey's special missions. This one must have gone wrong. If that was the case, Mickey was the only person who could help and Marjorie did need to get back.

Marjorie pulled away. Her eyes said *I love you* as she backed toward the door. Soon Luce heard the Mercedes engine start. She moved to the window and watched her mother drive out of sight. Then she took her cell phone and called Mickey again. She had to leave another message.

Chapter 28

Mickey looked at the clock in his hotel room and then he looked at his watch as he paced the floor. Luce had left her message over two hours ago. Marjorie should have been back. How could he have let her drive to Brookdale when he'd seen the personality changes she'd been having? What if she'd gotten physically ill and had an accident? What if she'd done exactly what he'd asked her not to do—driven to the mountains and plummeted straight down a cliff?

He was panicking now, thinking up wild scenarios. Sometimes people just wanted to be by themselves. It was possible that was all Marjorie was doing.

Possible, but not likely.

He walked to the window and stared at the street below. Waiting was the worst. He'd called Marjorie's cell phone a zillion times, left messages, and she hadn't called back. It was four o'clock in the afternoon. Where could she be?

As he continued to stare, he felt like he was waiting for the end of the world. He was waiting for word from Ray. He was waiting for Marjorie. He was waiting for signs that told him what he needed to do about Lavinia. He was waiting and nothing was coming through.

His energy deserted him and he sat hunched on the side of the bed.

When had the people on the Titanic realized they were waiting for the end? When all the lifeboats were gone? That was how he felt now. He'd run out of chances. He'd guided his mission into an iceberg. He'd sunk the operation. There was no time left for rescue.

He was the last man standing and he would go down with the ship.

****

Mars stood in gallery seventeen, arms crossed, staring at the portrait of Lavinia. Was there really a phantom attached to this painting that could come from some other dimension when she had the urge to kill?

Really? God's truth? No lie?

Her eyebrows knit. It was preposterous. Laughable. Nuts.

I'm a little acorn nut, sitting on a coconut. Everybody steps on me. That is why I'm cracked you see. I'm a nut . . .

Girl Scout song from when she was a child. She'd thought it funny and enjoyed singing it until one day her older sister had made so much fun of her for doing so, she'd been reduced to tears. Her sister used to make fun of her a lot, now that she thought about it. Was that why she'd become such a hard-ass? Such a stickler for the straight and narrow? *Don't come to me with nebulous theories, Detective. Just give me the facts. Nothing but the facts. Don't tell me something out of the scope of one plus one equals two. I won't believe it. I won't believe anything anyone can poke fun at.*

Then why was she the one who still remembered the murder in the Brahms receiving area? Why was she the one who kept that murder on the back burner instead of the deep freeze?

I'm a little acorn nut . . .

She pulled an earring from an ear. It was ridiculous that she was even standing here asking whether or not a spirit could kill. Totally out of character. And yet, here she was—asking.

Mickey McCoy had sold her a bill of goods and she had gone forward with a down payment. She'd opened an investigation into Avery Weldon's finances. There had been no one to make an objection and it was amazing how quickly certain facts came to light. The investigation into Avery had led her to Miranda Evans, and Mars was at the museum to talk to her, to play a little game—not to stare at a portrait.

The forensic audit had uncovered a payoff. It was as clear as if someone had drawn a map. Just before the loss of the Agostino portrait, six hundred thousand dollars had shown up in Avery's bank account—source unknown. Two hundred thousand of it had then been withdrawn in the form of a cashier's check and deposited in a bank account of Miranda's. If the owner of the painting, John Carroll, had gone to the police, the theft would have been discovered in a nanosecond. Thus far, it didn't appear that John had benefitted from the theft and yet, for some reason, he didn't notify the authorities, and he was killed before he had a change of heart, *if* he was going to have a change of heart.

Miranda had felt so confident about getting away with thievery that she filed a claim on the museum's behalf with its insurance company. Now surely a competent investigation on their part would have uncovered the shenanigans, but a twenty-thousand cash withdrawal by Miranda must have paid someone else off. The museum received two million dollars.

The forensic team had yet to identify who had paid the original six hundred thou. If Mickey was correct, it was Jay Serling. But Mars hadn't been able to get a warrant to examine his bank accounts because no link had been found. He had covered his tracks and the police weren't allowed to fish.

So Mars was there to bluff. She was there to trick Miranda into showing her hand. She was there to lie.

She made her way to Miranda's office, and at the sight of her police badge, Miranda's secretary hit the intercom. "A lieutenant Mars is here to see you."

Mars was welcomed in. She sat in a chair across from Miranda.

"Well," Miranda said. "Made any progress on that poor man's murder?"

"You mean Norman Blick. Yes, as a matter of fact. That's why I'm here. I'm not in a position to tell you all I know, but I've come to give you a chance."

"That sounds ominous."

Mars allowed a pregnant pause. The term was hardly used any more, but it was fitting. A pause gave Miranda's mind time to fill with possibilities she would find threatening.

"You can't mean you think I had something to do with Norman's murder."

Mars shrugged with exaggeration. "We're looking into all possibilities. All connections."

"Oh, please."

"Oh, please yourself, Ms. Evans. You're a thief. Sometimes it isn't a big leap from thief to murderer."

"Now wait a minute."

"No, you wait a minute. I came here as a courtesy."

"It's courteous to tell me you think I'm a thief and I murdered someone?"

"I didn't say I thought you had. I said it was possible and we were looking into it because I know about the money."

"What money?"

"The six hundred thousand you and Avery Weldon accepted for the Agostino portrait."

"Six hundred—" Miranda shut her mouth.

"You thought she'd given you half? There's no honor among thieves."

"I don't know what you're talking about." Miranda steadied her expression.

"And then there is the matter of the two million the insurance company paid the museum for the loss. They are going to want that back."

Mars' knew how to issue a penetrating gaze. She could see Miranda was trying to return one just as tough. She managed it for twenty seconds before she averted her eyes. "It's not true. None of it. And I don't have to talk to you. I want you to leave."

"Not a problem. As I said, I only came as a courtesy." Mars rose to her feet. "But without your cooperation, things will only be worse for you. You won't be able to avoid prison time and it's a given you'll lose your job."

Miranda lost her cool. She closed her eyes briefly and shook her head . "What do you want?"

Mars slapped both hands on the desk and leaned in. "I want you to talk with the person who bought the painting. Get it back and most of your headaches will go away. At least any connection you would have to the murder."

"Why would I kill Norman what's-his-name?"

"Because he worked for the insurance company. He was going to turn you in."

It was a bald-faced lie, but Miranda would never check it out. And if she did, it would help to incriminate her.

Miranda lifted her chin in a last-ditch show of strength. "I'm busy. None of this story is true. Get out."

Mars had given it her all. She walked to the door and paused. "I'll be back with an arrest warrant in the morning."

Miranda appeared to have filled with resolve. "You do what you have to. I have nothing to fear."

Mars left and closed the door behind her. As she strode down the hall she used her cell phone. "It's done. If she calls Serling, we can get our warrant. If she leaves, follow her."

Chapter 29

It was close to six in the evening when Marjorie entered the hotel suite. A wave of relief washed over Mickey at the sight of her. She fell into his arms and cried like a child. Relief was short-lived, however, when he heard what she had to say.

"I'm so exhausted. I don't know how much longer I can fight this." Her chest heaved. She couldn't seem to catch her breath. He held her and let her cry. She wrapped her arms more tightly around him.

"Most of the time I didn't know where I was. But some of the time..." More crying. "I just kept thinking of you whenever I could. I kept telling myself I have to get back. I have to. I have to. Whatever sickness is trying to invade my body, fight it. There were times when I must have blacked out because I don't remember most of the drive and I can't account for all of the time. Mickey. Oh, Mickey. Do you understand what's happening to me? I'm scared. I've never been this scared. I've been trying to be strong, but I'm so scared." She buried her head in his shoulder.

"It's going to be okay. It's going to be fine. We're going home. I'll arrange for a flight tonight. We'll forget about Lavinia and Agostino and compacts and paintings and John Carroll. We'll leave all this mess."

He felt no guilt about running away. He'd unwittingly put Marjorie in danger and that was all that mattered to him now. He had to save her. Take her away from all this. But he knew deep in his soul that distance meant nothing. The damage had already been done. Certain events had apparently already been set in motion and he didn't know if things could be rectified.

She kicked off her shoes and climbed into bed fully dressed. "I need to sleep," she said. "That's all I want to do. Don't wake me. Don't wake me for a long time."

****

At five after six Miranda walked out of her office and watched the museum close down for the night.

"Good night, Miranda," her secretary told her, locking her desk drawer, hoisting her purse strap over her shoulder and stepping away from her work space. "See you in the morning."

Miranda didn't reply. She would not see her secretary in the morning. She had other plans.

Mars was off her rocker if she thought Miranda was going to cooperate. Seek out the buyer? Get the painting returned? Give back her money? No way. She'd spent most of it anyway. Two hundred thousand wasn't such a large amount in today's world. Especially when she'd had to give twenty of it to someone else. She was a lowly museum curator, poorly paid, but expected to dress with class. She didn't feel remorse for what she'd done. Considering there was a recession going on, she hadn't received a raise in more than a year, the cost of gas and groceries had skyrocketed, and big government was trying to increase taxes any way it could, people like her had to take matters into their own hands. Who had gotten hurt, anyway? Only the big insurance company and they had plenty.

The lights dimmed and she listened to the sound of people departing the premises. After another ten minutes all was silent. The only other person in the building besides herself was JoAnn and she knew the guard's routine. A few minutes more and she could make her move. She'd already prepared what she would need.

Carrying her purse and a soft baby blanket, she moved toward the lobby. She avoided camera surveillance as best she could, only because a visual record of her movements could present unforeseen problems for her later on *if* she actually got caught. She made her way to the deserted security console and shut the system down. How fortunate these trying times had forced the museum to cut back on manpower. It would be another twenty-five minutes before JoAnn would discover the breach. By then, Miranda would be well on her way.

With no fear of being recorded, Miranda slipped into gallery seventeen and paused to savor the sight of Lavinia. She had fallen in love. Not just with the painting, but with the woman in the painting, from the moment she'd laid eyes on it.

Beauty, brains, talent and class. Lavinia had it all. A woman who lived centuries ago had her heart. Call her crazy, Miranda didn't care. She thought of the painting as something that belonged to her and she intended to maintain possession.

She stepped across the room, whispering. "You are magnificent and I won't let anyone take you from me." She removed the portrait from the wall and covered it with the blanket. Then she stole away to her car.

After the visit from Mars, Miranda had run home, obtained the blanket, and packed a bag. She had wisely parked in the garage, closed the door, and moved to and from the house out of sight. When she'd returned to work she purchased a plane ticket to Atlanta, Georgia as a red herring. She had an aunt and uncle as well as a number of cousins who lived there. Her hope was to send the police to LAX if they thought she was going to run.

She drove a circuitous route away from the museum, all the while watching the rearview mirror. If she had a tail, she would lose it before arriving at the Biltmore near Union Station. There she planned to spend the night. Tomorrow she would take the Amtrak to Chicago. Once she reached Chicago she would take another train to Buffalo and from there another train to Niagara Falls where she would cross into Canada. She'd chosen travel by railcar out of necessity. Airline restrictions meant Lavinia didn't qualify for carry-on and she wasn't about to allow her out of her sight.

At a little after nine, Miranda settled into her hotel room. She propped Lavinia on the granite countertop in the bathroom and filled the tub with hot water. She undressed and dipped her toe. The temperature was perfect. Immersing her body relaxed every muscle, and as she lathered her skin with soap she'd brought from home, she gazed at the portrait with loving eyes.

"I want you to know that you are worth all of my effort to keep you with me. I feel a connection with you, a kinship that I have never felt before. I know one can't be soul mates with a portrait, but this feeling I have is strong. I can't explain it. Does that sound foolish?"

She soaked the washcloth in the water and wiped it along an arm. Then she soaked it again, lifted the arm and squeezed the cloth so that water dripped upon her neck and chest.

"Mmmm. I wonder. Am I sexy to you?" She stared at Lavinia. After a while she looked at the light above the sink. "The light is harsh, isn't it? I wish I'd thought to bring candles. Oh, but there is plenty of time for that when we get to where we're going." She lowered herself in the water and the strands of hair she'd failed to pin up high got wet. She lay quietly for a minute, eyes closed.

"Do you believe in past lives, Lavinia? I think I do. I think I might have lived during your time. I think we could have been great friends. Best friends.

"And I think I could have been Agostino's friend too. Although, I don't know. I never felt the same about him. If I had I don't think I could have allowed his sale. I would have wanted to keep him with me as much I want to keep you. Heaven knows, I needed the money. Everyone needs money. But if the buyer had wanted you I would have said no. I would've had to convince him to purchase something else. I didn't find it all that difficult to sell Agostino."

She stopped talking and allowed herself to enjoy the warmth of the water. She rested an arm on the lip of the tub.

"Tu?"

"Hmm?" she said, thinking herself so relaxed that in her twilight state of mind she was experiencing an audible dream.

"Tu pensi che ci apparteniamo?"

"Is that you, Lavinia? Are you speaking to me?"

And with eyes closed, she continued to smile, the water soothing her nearly to sleep.

****

With drapes opened just a smidge allowing for the light of the moon, Mickey sat in one of the chairs at the round table on the far side of the bed and watched Marjorie sleep. She looked peaceful now. She looked like herself. He hoped it was true and not wishful thinking. He loved her with every breath he took, with every charge of every neuron in his body. To think that something awful was happening to her because of him, made him sick.

He'd made plane reservations for eleven o'clock the next morning and could hardly wait to get on the plane. He would have liked to pack their bags, wake Marjorie, and run right then, but he thought it best to let her sleep.

He watched her breathe. He'd been watching her for three hours. She barely moved. He'd set the thermostat to seventy-four degrees so that she would be comfortable, and yet he felt a chill. It didn't come from the air. It came from within himself. He was chilled to the bone because he was afraid.

"I love you," he whispered. "I know I don't tell you enough, but I do." He could feel tears collecting in his eyes. Finally one trickled down his cheek and he wiped it away. "There's no reason to cry," he whispered. "She's going to be fine. Once I get her away from here, nothing can touch her."

But he didn't really believe it and that was what scared him. He didn't know what to do. He didn't know if there was anything he could do.

Marjorie opened her eyes and smiled at her husband.

"You're awake," Mickey said, moving to the bed. "How do you

feel?"

"Better. Much better. What time is it?"

"Nine twenty."

"Oh. I think I'll sleep some more, if that's okay."

"Of course, it is. Of course." He stroked her head.

"It's just that I'm so very tired. I don't think I've ever felt so exhausted." She closed her eyes and Mickey's chin began to quiver.

****

A crowd was gathered outside Miranda Evan's room at the Biltmore.

All was quiet now, but seven guests had been drawn from their rooms by what they all described as a woman's blood-curdling scream. More than one person had called to report it, prompting Howard Egan, the head of security, to respond. He'd contacted Brad Hilcourt, the night manager, and Brad was rapping on the door.

"Hello? Ms. Evans." He'd ascertained the name of the guest before taking action. "Is everything all right?"

When he received no answer he nodded at Howard. The head of security stuck a keycard in the door and opened it until the metal safety rod engaged to stop entry. The manager told the concerned guests to go back to their rooms. None of them complied.

The head of security kicked in the door and the rod easily gave way.

"Ms. Evans? Hello," called Brad. He cautiously walked inside the room while Howard stayed back, eying the closed bathroom door. Light shown where it gapped above the rug. He pushed it open and froze. He'd worked security for many years, but he'd never seen anything like what he saw before him now.

"Mr. Hilcourt. You need to come here."

Brad walked behind Howard and peered inside the bathroom. He drew a shocked breath and held it for just a moment before he took out his cell phone and called 911.

****

Police arrived within minutes. They'd been watching the hotel, maintaining surveillance on Ms. Evans. An officer had been stationed in the lobby. Another had been in the parking garage keeping tabs on her car just in case she made it past the cop in the lobby. Too bad they hadn't been stationed outside her door. She might not be dead.

A member of the forensics team took pictures from every angle. Miranda Evans lay in a bathtub filled with red water—literally a bloodbath. Stab wounds were evident in her chest. Her face had been slashed and there were defensive wounds on the arm that hung over the side of the tub. The hand showed defensive cuts as well. For all that, Mars was certain there were additional wounds that couldn't be seen below the opaque, red water.

The photo session ended and Mars came in for a closer look. Miranda's eyes were open and the expression on her face was one of horror. This poor woman had been butchered; it wasn't an easy death.

Mars removed an earring and rolled it back and forth in her hand. She was of the opinion that no one ever got one hundred percent used to murder, even those whose job it was to deal with it day after day. She was good at keeping her emotions in check. Good at pretending she was looking at an object instead of a human being. And the earring helped. It allowed her to release corralled feelings in a small, quiet way. Some homicide detectives found crass humor did the trick, and once in a while she found the jokes funny. But mostly she found it juvenile and annoying. Mars preferred a stoic face and a bauble in her hand.

This murder was going to affect her differently because she felt she had a hand in it. Twinges of guilt were riding her spine, starting at the neck, departing at the tail bone, only to begin again. If she hadn't tricked Miranda into making a move, Miranda wouldn't have come to this hotel room. She wouldn't have stolen Lavinia's self portrait. She wouldn't be dead.

Mars turned her eyes to the painting propped upon the counter, leaning against the mirror. Her blood ran cold. She saw it now—the loathing in Lavinia's eyes. She saw, too, the satisfied smile on her lips.

"What do you think, lieutenant?" one of her team asked.

Mars squeezed the earring in her hand so hard it hurt. At the same time she shook her head. She couldn't express what she thought. What she thought was fantastic. What she thought was wild. What she thought was something that would have never entered her head a few days ago. Now everything had changed and it frightened her. She thought she had seen it all—every strange, wicked thing that happened to the human race. She hadn't. Not by a mile. There was no video this time, but this murder was certainly the work of the person . . .

Person? Had she thought this the work of a person? Lavinia wasn't a person. She was an image in paint. She was a thing and she had killed before.

She felt herself breathing faster and hoped no one else noticed. Acid caused her stomach to grumble. She hadn't eaten in a while and she wouldn't eat for a while more. She might be hungry, but her appetite was gone. The world had turned upside down. It contained things beyond belief and she didn't know how she was going to live with that.

"Lieutenant?"

Mars turned her eyes on the pestering detective and didn't answer.

"The security door chain was latched. The manager had to kick the door in. The windows don't open so no one got out that way. And where's the knife? The victim is the only one here. She couldn't have done this to herself. This one is a real puzzler."

Mars said nothing. She nodded and rolled the earring in her hand.

****

Someone tapped on the door of Mickey's hotel suite. He jumped to his feet, his heart pounding, and stood glued to the floor.

"Mickey McCoy." The voice was familiar, but he couldn't think. He moved closer.

"Who is it?"

"Ray."

Ray? Yes. Ray. The man he'd given the *Accordo* to. The man who was to decipher it. He'd forgotten about him because Mickey's mind was on Marjorie. He looked at her sleeping in the bed. He no longer wanted to have anything to do with that book. He wished he'd never come to Los Angeles.

Ray was patient. He didn't tap again and for a second Mickey thought his hesitation had sent Ray away. He hurried over and opened the door. Ray walked inside. His manner was completely changed. He had a no-nonsense aura and his expression was somber. He stood with both feet planted squarely on the ground and he held the black book with two hands.

"Can we turn a light on?"

Mickey moved to the table that wasn't near the bed and switched on the lamp. He tapped the table indicating Ray should sit and spoke in a low voice, "My wife is asleep."

Ray glanced at her then put the book on the table and slid it to Mickey.

"It's a simple contract. Lavinia wanted the man she loved tied to her for eternity. In exchange, she left her estate to The Practitioner who drew up this compact and promised she would bring more suffering to the world. There are no specifics as to what sort of suffering."

"She chose murder," Mickey said.

"A common choice."

"It doesn't spell out how many men she must kill?"

"No. And it doesn't spell out men. She can kill anyone she

pleases."

"I'd been led to believe that she only killed males."

"Could be that's all she has killed. But if so, that was by choice."

Mickey nodded. "No one is safe around her."

"No one is safe."

It almost didn't matter to Mickey. He looked over at Marjorie again. Ray talked on.

"She may have wanted to be with her love forever, but she also wanted to live with him in this world. She needed a portal between here and the other dimension—the dimension where she could mingle with Agostino and create whatever she needed or wanted for their pleasure with one another. She thought portraits of herself and the man she loved fitting. And this held another appeal. The portal needed a guardian. She chose Agostino's new love interest, Catherine Del Rosa. Catherine would see them together for the rest of her life."

"And if Catherine destroyed the paintings?"

"A pox upon her life."

Mickey thought of Avery. She had separated the paintings and died in a plane crash.

"Now," Ray said, "It would have been wise for Lavinia to have made one painting with both their images. She didn't and, thus, created a problem for herself. If the portraits are separated, she can't reach Agostino either in this world or the other."

Mickey rubbed the back of his neck to relieve tension. "Why not? I don't understand that."

"The Practitioner who drew this up was perverse. If Lavinia could reach her love at all times, she would lack the inclination to kill. He wanted to enrage her. Vex her all he could. He had to do so within the confines of a seemingly balanced contract."

"Agostino soothed her savagery." Mickey nodded, thinking of his wound and Kelly's burn. "Agostino was, is, a powerful healer. Just his presence must have had a positive effect on Lavinia's base nature, her sick soul. It prevented her from killing."

"Lavinia was smart enough to know there was the possibility the two paintings would be separated. She was smart enough to know that the Practitioner was as wicked as she was and probably relished the idea that she wouldn't get what she paid for, while he would still have his half of the bargain. And so she demanded consequences if the paintings became separated. That would be a breach of the contract."

"Consequences for keeping her from Agostino."

"That is correct."

Ray opened the book and pointed to the large number one on the last page.

"This number," Ray said, "tells me that the paintings have been apart for more than a year. In fact, today is the last day of the thirteenth month that they have been apart. If they are not reunited by midnight, then the contract is fully breached."

"Which means?"

"Lavinia is free to do several things. She can maintain her attachment to her image, the painting, and roam this earth in search of the man, or rather, the essence of the man she loves. He, however, is free to hide from her or refuse her should she find him."

"And if she finds him and he refuses her?"

"That could be dire for Agostino. If she gets angry and recants her love, he will return to his body."

"His body? But it's close to four hundred years old."

"We'll get to that. Now, there is another choice for Lavinia."

Mickey felt his heart jump. He had sensed this was coming.

"During this thirteenth month, Lavinia must decide what she wants to do. Remain attached to the painting with no guarantee she'll be reunited with Agostino, or . . ."

"Or she can take possession of another person."

"You already know."

"I feared."

Ray remained still, waiting for Mickey to continue. When he didn't, Ray went on. "The person must be selected by the

Practitioner, or a descendent of his. Lavinia can try the person out and ask the Practitioner to select another if she so chooses as long as this is done within the thirteenth month, by the stroke of midnight."

"A charming Cinderella story," Mickey said softly, sarcastically.

"If she is in the body of the person at that time, the body is hers. The soul of the person is forced out."

"And you have a flesh and blood Lavinia in another's form." Mickey understood. He felt the blood drain from his face.

"Lavinia can *never* go back to the painting then."

"She will grow old as this person and eventually die," Mickey murmured.

"No. That would make her mortal and go against the original agreement. She has the option to change bodies every thirteen months. She can also stay where she is and wait an additional thirteen months if she so chooses. It's up to her. In this way, she can live forever."

Mickey's agitated fingers tapped the table. "She's chosen my wife. There's nothing I can do to stop this?"

"You would have to convince Lavinia your wife is a poor choice so that she goes back to the painting."

"Marjorie has been fighting the takeover of her body and with every fight she gets weaker."

"There *are* drawbacks for Lavinia, choosing to live in human form."

"Such as?"

"If, ah . . ."

"Say it," Mickey said.

"If the human—"

"My wife."

"Yes. If she died while possessed, Lavinia's soul would return to her body. And so would Agostino's."

"Their bodies? Their dead bodies?"

"The bodies are still alive. They are buried somewhere safe, in a state of suspended animation. Once the souls return, the suspension would cease. Effectively, they would be buried alive and die horribly."

"I wouldn't want that for Agostino. But Lavinia? I don't care what happens to her." Mickey's heart had hardened. He couldn't help it.

"If someone intervened and opened the caskets quickly enough they would live. It would be as if they'd awoken in this century and would live out the rest of their days."

"That's too good for Lavinia."

"And not at all what she wants."

Mickey felt his breath grow shallow. Ray's words were fantastic and yet he had no doubt they were true.

"The ideal thing," Ray said, "would be to burn the painting while Lavinia is attached to it. If you can do that before midnight tonight her soul will be forced to return to her body."

Mickey looked at his sleeping wife. "Is there a chance this can be done?"

"Realistically? I don't know. You have less than two hours. If you do succeed . . ." Ray's voice trailed.

Mickey looked at him. There was more. Something dire. Something he hesitated to say. "What?"

"I think it's best we take this one step at a time."

"What aren't you telling me?"

"There isn't time. I will be praying on your behalf remotely. If you're able to destroy the painting as I stated before, we'll talk again."

Ray headed for the door. Mickey nearly chased after him, but thought better of it. Ray was the expert. If he thought it best to keep certain facts for later, that's how it must be. All that mattered was the next two hours. All that mattered was finding a way to destroy the portrait while Lavinia was attached.

Chapter 30

It was only ten fifteen p.m. The team had finished processing the crime scene and Miranda's body had been taken away. Mars had made them rush.

"You sticking around, Lieutenant?" Detective Yanez asked her. There was perplexity in his voice.

Mars knew it looked odd for her to be the last to leave. She was never last. She always took a close look at a crime scene and then allowed her team to do their job. But this time her team had been unaware of the danger they were in and she had rushed them out. She had to be the last to go.

She looked at Lavinia's portrait. *There's your killer, detective. A painting. You believe me, of course.*

"Lieutenant?"

Afraid, she reached out and placed her hand on the frame of the portrait. She paused. Nothing happened.

Thank God.

She breathed a sigh of relief. "I'm taking this with me. It's too valuable to leave here."

"That creepy thing?"

Mars' heart jumped. *Don't insult her. Please don't do that.*

"How much you think it's worth?" Yanez asked.

"I don't know. A million or two."

"For that? I wouldn't give you a nickel for it."

Don't listen to him, Lavinia. He doesn't know what he's talking about.

"And I wouldn't take one. Neither would the owner." She lifted the painting and was glad to find it didn't weigh much.

"She stole it, didn't she?" Yanez said. "The victim. I remember that painting from the museum. The other murder."

"I remember, too."

"You think that painting is the key to this?"

Mars hesitated, then shrugged.

"Of course, if the killer wanted it, why not take it with him? Or her." Yanez made a face that said nothing made sense.

"I don't know," Mars said, stepping toward the door.

"I don't know either. I can't figure this one out. Hey, you want me to take that to Evidence for you?"

As much as she didn't want to be alone with the painting, she didn't want to pawn the task of transporting it off on unsuspecting Yanez. Besides, she wasn't taking it to any evidence room.

"No. I'll handle it."

****

Mars put the painting in the trunk of her car. It made her feel safer, although she couldn't say she actually felt safe. Her confidence was gone. Her belief system had been shaken to its core. A painting that killed. It was insane. She wondered if she should rip the thing up there in the parking garage. And what would that accomplish? Would it stop Lavinia from killing again? Would Lavinia kill her if she tried to . . . Sonofabitch! Could Lavinia read her thoughts?

Now you are being paranoid. But what are you going to do? Where are you taking her? Home? What? So she can kill you in the shower?

She hopped into her car, placed her hands upon the steering wheel and allowed herself to melt. She emitted a huge sigh. What was she going to do? For all her reliance on the left side of her brain, she hadn't a clue.

****

Mickey pulled a chair beside the bed. The only light in the room was the light at the table where he'd been sitting. Marjorie lay on her side under the covers, facing him. She was in shadow, but he could see that her eyes were closed and could hear the soft rise and fall of her breath.

He stared at her. Was she his beloved Marjorie? Or was she Lavinia? He watched her sleep.

Marjorie. Only Marjorie could look so angelic.

He reached out and touched her hair. She opened her eyes. She didn't speak and neither did he. Her eyes were empty, but they were Marjorie's. She looked tired. Despite the sleep, she was drained. She closed her eyes and he stroked her hair. Was this how it would end? Her lying in bed? Him stroking her hair? Until . . .

Marjorie's eyes opened again and this time he saw a glimmer of Lavinia behind the stare. Her distorted, manic smile emerged upon Marjorie's lips. He didn't withdraw his hand. Maybe his presence would give Marjorie strength to ward of Lavinia's diseased soul.

"I love you *Marjorie*," he whispered.

She closed her eyes and sorrow overwhelmed him. He felt the tears that had been confined race to the surface and spill upon his face. He let them fall.

Moments passed. He stared at Marjorie and allowed every emotion he was feeling to be present: Love for Marjorie. Hate for Lavinia. Self-pity for his situation. Fear for what was to come. Anger at feeling helpless . . .

Resolve replaced tears. He couldn't just sit here and do nothing. Time might be short, but that was no excuse for giving up. That was no excuse for going down without a fight. All was not lost yet! He needed a plan.

He stood, walked into the bathroom, and snapped on the light. He stared at himself in the mirror.

"It's up to you. It's *all* up to you. Think of something. Ask the Universe for help."

The sound of people talking filtered in from the hall.

"Think!"

The voices grew louder as the people approached. They stopped outside his suite and carried on with animated conversation and laughter.

Quiet down or move on! I need to think.

The sounds grew raucous and interfered with his thought process. Mickey shut the bathroom door. With the noise now muffled, he leaned on his hands, took a deep breath and lifted his eyes skyward. There were two things he needed to accomplish. Get Lavinia to return to her portrait and then burn it. The painting was in the museum. The first thing he needed to do was move it to where it could be burned. How dangerous would that be for someone to accomplish? *Who* could he call to accomplish it?

Lavinia preferred to kill men. She probably wasn't attached to the portrait now anyway. The person should be safe.

Mars.

He took his cell phone from a pocket and called. She answered immediately, but sounded strange. She said hello instead of her name.

"This is Mickey McCoy. Please hear me out."

He paused expecting resistance; he received none.

"I'm listening," she said.

"My wife's life is in danger. I need you to get the portrait of Lavinia and take it to Heart House. Pull your badge and claim police business. Pull your gun if you have to. Whatever you have to do to convince security to let you have the portrait, do it."

Dead air. Had he shocked her into silence or had she hung up on him?

"Are you there?" Mickey asked.

"Are you saying this because you know I have the portrait in my car?"

"You have it now?" Mickey's adrenaline began to pump. This was good news.

"You sound surprised."

"I am."

"There was another murder."

Mickey was silent.

"Aren't you going to ask who? Or do you already know?"

"If you have the painting it must be Miranda."

"You're ten for ten."

"No. Right now I'm batting zero. And we're wasting time. Take the painting to Heart House. The code for the gate is one seven four nine nine. If I can't get hold of Morris, ring the bell until he answers and explain. He'll let you in. Ask him to show you the study. And there needs to be a fire. Don't worry about Lavinia. I don't believe she's in the painting."

"What?"

Mickey became aware that the noisy people in the hall had dispersed. He heard the sound of doors slamming closed—including his own.

"Mickey? Did you say Lavinia isn't in the portrait?"

Mickey didn't respond. He lowered the phone to his side and hung up. Part of him was afraid to open the door. What if Lavinia stood there waiting for him?

You're a fool, he told himself.

He reached for the knob. He turned it. He opened the door. No one stood before him and he felt relief. He walked out of the bathroom and looked at the bed. The covers were lumpy. He wasn't sure, but it looked empty. Quickly he opened the door and checked the hall. He saw his wife disappear into the alcove where the elevators were located.

"Marjorie!"

Chapter 31

She stepped off the elevator and tried to remember where she had parked the car. Had she driven it to valet? Of course, she had. That is what Marjorie would have done. But is it what Lavinia would have done?

Lavinia wouldn't even know how to drive a car.

Marjorie couldn't remember. So much of the day was a blank. For all she knew, the car had been driven over a curb and left askew on Sunset.

She heard garbled Italian in her brain, an echo inching its way closer. Her head was pounding with pressure in her cranium. It was as if it were too full of something about to burst out. Her soul? Her essence? Her consciousness? Was it about to leave her?

Fight! Lavinia's energy can't win.

She put her fingers to her forehead and realized she had a slip of paper in her hand. The valet ticket. She'd pulled it from her pocket without even knowing.

"Are you all right?"

Who asked her that? She could hardly keep her eyes open enough to see. Someone, a stranger, a guest of the hotel, or a worker. She didn't know. She didn't know! Someone was holding her shoulders, keeping her from falling.

"Are you sick? Do you need a doctor?"

Marjorie didn't have the strength to answer. She stumbled away. Where was she? Inside? No, outside. She had to get to the car. Without knowing how she'd found it, she reached the valet.

The worker took her ticket and told her something she didn't catch.

She needed to sit down. Was there a place to sit?

A second valet approached her. "He'll be here with your car in a moment, but you don't look good. I'm not so sure . . ."

His voice suddenly sounded like someone talking under water. She concentrated on his words. Not what he was saying, not the meaning. She just wanted to hear them. Hear them as Marjorie.

Concentrate. Be conscious. Know who I am. I'm Marjorie. I'm Marjorie. I hear you. I need my car. I need to fight.

"Hey, Jason. I don't think we should . . ."

Under water. His words were drowned.

Faintly, sounds bobbed to the surface. "What did you say?"

"I said, she's too sick to drive."

You can't stop me. I have to go.

She sprang to the car and was inside after two sloppy attempts to open the door.

"Hey, lady. It's your funeral!"

How right you are, thought Marjorie. *My funeral. I have to do this. I can do this.*

"Marjorie!"

Mickey.

She was dizzy. She heard more Italian gibberish in her head.

Go away. Go away. But you won't go away, will you? It's up to me to make you stop. I heard what that man said. I can make you not want me.

She started the car and put it in gear. It jerked forward.

"Marjorie, stop!"

It was like the world had gone dark. She was blind except for two small holes that allowed her to see only straight ahead. She had no peripheral vision. And her head hurt. Oh, how it hurt.

I am woman. I am strong.

"Rrrrrrr!" she roared.

Hear that. Now see me drive. Think. Think about what Lavinia's trying to do. Think of what she wants. Be strong. Don't let her in.

Squeeze her out. Oh, my head. Somebody, please drill a hole in my head. Relieve the pressure. Lavinia? Lavinia can you hear me? You don't want me, because I will never let you be in control. I will never do what you want. You will not win.

"Marjorie. Stop the car. Stop! You're going too fast. You're running red lights."

Is that you Mickey? Are you in the car with me? I better not look. I can't turn my head. I have to look straight ahead. Clutch the wheel. Hold on tight. Get this right. Get this right!

"Marjorie . . ."

****

Wearing her sexiest, powder blue, baby doll pajamas, Kelly looked at herself in the bathroom mirror. The fall weather had changed from hot to cold in the blink of an eye. It was sixty-three degrees inside the house and the chilly air gave her native Californian skin goose bumps. She didn't adjust the thermostat though. She and Dennis believed in living green, as much as they could.

She felt silly dressed as she was, but flannels would not accomplish what she wanted to accomplish tonight. This was going to take feminine wiles.

He's been in a snit long enough. He's been ignoring me long enough. And if these skimpy PJs don't snap him out of it, I will surely turn into a nag.

Even with the air feeling like ice, she walked slowly to her side of the bed, paused, and cleared her throat. The only light in the room came from the lamp on Dennis' nightstand. He held a book in his hands, eyes steadfastly focused on what he was reading. He turned the page.

Kelly cleared her throat louder and he still didn't acknowledge her. They hadn't spoken for hours. Dennis wasn't himself. Hadn't been since he'd been stabbed in the museum. She knew she'd done nothing to make him mad at her and his attitude had something to do with his father and his upbringing and all the stuff he'd never been able to resolve. But, dammit, he was acting like he didn't love her anymore and, quite frankly, she was starting to wonder if he did.

"Dennis," she said.

"What?" he grumbled, eyes on the book. "I'm reading."

If he thought he was going to get away with ignoring her, he had another think coming. She jumped into bed, threw the covers over her, and snuggled against him. She grabbed his arm, disturbing his grip on the book.

"Kelly."

"Dennis." She pulled the book away from him and put it on her nightstand. "Kiss me."

He actually smiled. He leaned over and kissed her on the mouth. When he tried to pull away, she took hold of the back of his neck and guided his lips to hers. This time the kiss was more passionate.

"Good," Kelly murmured. "You don't hate me."

"What?" Dennis jerked away. "Why did you say that?"

"Well. You don't talk to me. You won't tell me what's wrong. You seemed mad that I could block those tennis balls from hitting me when you couldn't."

"That a-hole of an assistant helped you."

"Only at first. And, besides. Who cares?"

"Give me my book back." He reached for it and she pulled him on top of her.

"No. Talk."

His face remained gruff and she started to tickle him. Unable to stifle a laugh he rolled onto his back and wouldn't allow her to climb on top. He was much stronger than she was. All she could do was sigh and relax.

"You won't talk to me," she said.

"What do want to know?"

"Why you're so angry. What you're thinking about when I see that far away look in your eye. Why we haven't made love since that night in the museum."

Dennis didn't speak for a few moments. Finally, "That's true, isn't it?"

"If I did something wrong, I could try to make up for it—"

"You didn't do anything. But that guy you brought into our lives—"

"Mickey McCoy? I didn't bring him into our lives. He found me. And he saved you."

"You keep saying that and I hate it."

"Why?"

"Because! Because . . . I don't know."

They were quiet for a moment. Then Dennis reached for Kelly and held her close. "I guess I felt . . . I . . . I can't seem to . . . I've always had these psychic experiences and I've always been able to explain most of them away. When I started this ghost hunter thing, it was a lark. I thought, we'll investigate some places, expose a few frauds, and if anything strange happens, maybe we'll even make some money. I never ever thought we'd be put in any sort of real danger. Never. And when I had this overwhelming feeling that my life was in danger and when I did hear that Mickey McCoy's voice in my head . . . Well, I didn't want to investigate the museum. I thought, man, what a wimp! And so I decided we'd go through with it, putting everyone's life in danger. And when I chickened out and wore that vest . . ."

"Thank God you wore that vest."

"I know. But I was the only person I was protecting. What if that thing had come after you or Elyse or Jugs or Carl? My judgment was . . . impaired, to say the least. And now I'm . . ."

Kelly flipped to her stomach and crawled on top of him. She stroked his nose and his cheek with her finger. "You didn't put anyone but yourself in gallery seventeen."

"Not because I was being protective."

"I don't believe that."

"I was trying to prove to myself that I wasn't scared. The vest gave me confidence."

"So."

"So, I think I'm still terrified."

"It's not a crime to be terrified."

"It is to me."

"Is it that you're scared you won't get over it?"

He didn't answer. Kelly took that as a yes. "I bet Mickey could help you with that."

"I don't want his help."

"Why not?"

"Because I shouldn't need it."

"Oh. You shouldn't need it. Do you need me?"

"Maybe."

"Do you need this?" She kissed him.

"Maybe."

"Maybe!" She tickled him again.

"Okay. Okay. Yes!"

"You admit that you need my kisses."

"I admit I need you."

"How about if I help you?"

"I think you already have."

"No. Close your eyes. I've been reading. I want to try something."

Dennis scrunched his lips in a teasing expression. "Something you read, huh?"

"Yeah. A little bit of hypnotherapy to make you feel better about yourself."

"Kelly."

"It can't hurt." Using her finger and thumb she made him close his eyes. "Now relax. Take a deep breath and let it out with a great big sigh." His eyes popped open.

"Do it. Close your eyes," Kelly said.

"Okay, boss." He did as she asked.

"Now picture yourself gathering every care you have in the world and dropping them inside a canvas bag."

"Why canvas?"

"Dennis! Are you going to do this or not?"

"All right. I'll do it for you. Canvas bag."

"Every care. You can pick them up later if you want. But for the next few minutes, they are contained and they don't belong to you."

She saw her husband's muscles let go. His breathing grew rhythmic.

"You are floating. Floating through the air and you feel good. You haven't a care in the world and you know that everything is as it should be . . ."

A dark thought reflected in his face. Kelly saw it. But he didn't open his eyes and he didn't protest that he didn't want to do what he was doing. He remained still for a few seconds and then his eyes squeezed in a manner that said he was trying to concentrate and his body wiggled.

Kelly didn't ask what was going on and she didn't continue her homegrown hypnotherapy. Something was happening with Dennis. Maybe it was his own devilish thoughts that he needed to wrestle with. Maybe it was something else. Whatever it was, she watched and didn't interfere.

* * * *

The Mercedes careened around a curve high in the Hollywood Hills, hit a patch of gravel, and fishtailed for a moment before Marjorie regained control. She heard herself laugh. But it wasn't her laugh. It was Lavinia's.

Her mind screamed. *I am in the car. I'm driving. Not her!*

"Marjorie, can you slow down?"

Yes, Mickey, call me by name. Let her know who I am. She can't take over. I feel her trying. She wants my body. But she can't have it. With every ounce of strength I can muster, I will stop her. Until the right time . . .

"I know what I'm doing," Marjorie found her voice. That was

good. It confirmed she was still in control.

"Then stop the car."

Yes. She'd stop the car and make Mickey get out. Then she'd drive on and when she was in a place where she could direct the car over the side of the mountain, she'd allow Lavinia to possess her. But it would be too late. The car would fly into the air, crash, and that would be that. She didn't want to die. But it would be worse to be taken over. Would she know it? Would some part of her be aware that Lavinia was running the show, while she remained a helpless prisoner? She couldn't live like that. Even if she wasn't aware, she didn't want to be the vehicle for someone else to cause the world pain.

"Marjorie, please. Stop so we can talk."

She stopped the car and allowed it to idle.

"Mickey, get out now."

"Let me drive."

"No. I know what I have to do. Please get out of the car."

"Marjorie—"

"You know this is necessary."

"I won't let you kill yourself."

"I know it's madness, but what else can I do?"

"Let me take the wheel. We'll drive to Heart House. I'll destroy that painting."

Marjorie let loose with a torrent of Italian.

****

Dennis lay still as a stone. He didn't even startle when he heard a barrage of Italian in place of Kelly's soothing voice. He listened calmly in a peaceful, suspended state, and when Mickey's voice came forth, he didn't reject his ability to hear someone else's conversation without being present.

Fight her, Marjorie. Think about us. Think about where you are. Tell her to get out . . .

An image rose in his consciousness, like objects rising through a pool of rippling water, and when they became clear he saw Mickey in a car with his wife. It was as if he were watching them from the back seat. She sat in the driver's seat, hands white knuckling the wheel. Her head was turned toward Mickey, his head toward her. Through the windshield the night sky glowed with lights of the city below. Through the side passenger window he saw a beautiful home built into the side of a hill. The car was parked on a mountainous road.

This must be remote viewing, he thought. He'd never experienced it before and it was happening without any effort on his part.

Marjorie began to sob. "I've been fighting her all day and all night. She comes and goes. Sometimes on her own, sometimes because I have enough will to force her to go away."

Mickey unbuckled his seatbelt and reached for his wife. He held her shoulders. "We'll fight her together. Mars is taking the painting to Heart House. If we can get there and I can burn that painting before midnight . . ."

"No. No! There's no time. I have to let Lavinia take over . . ."

"Marjorie, if you kill yourself, it will be for nothing. She'll leave you before you crash and go back to the painting. You'll be dead. She'll be free to roam."

Marjorie jerked away from Mickey's grasp.

The scene vanished, but Dennis remained peaceful. He didn't understand everything, but he knew Mickey needed his help. In his relaxed state, he realized he'd been sullen and babyish long enough. He was wrong. There were things beyond the five senses that couldn't be explained away as nonsense. He could live with the fact that he'd been doing things wrong, but he wouldn't be able to live with himself if he did nothing to help Mickey.

He concentrated and sent Mickey a message, mentally: *I'll go to Heart House. I'll go right now. I'll find a way to burn that painting.*

****

Marjorie clutched the wheel, the car in park, the motor groaning. She stared straight ahead. "Are you going to get out?" she asked. She looked at her husband, but received no answer. His sight was focused downward, eyes moving back and forth. He was doing something. Thinking? Listening? Something.

She needed him to get out of the car. She could feel Lavinia pressing her again. It was a cold feeling mixed with a rage she'd never known. She didn't know how much longer she could fight. Every time Lavinia came back, she seemed to be stronger. Marjorie had to get moving with her plan before it was too late. She couldn't waste any more time. She didn't want to take Mickey with her, but if he left her no choice, she would.

"I'm staying with you," he suddenly said.

Marjorie felt tears in her eyes as she put the gear in drive, took her foot off the brake, and pressed on the gas.

"Then we'll die together," she said.

"Marjorie, I want you to do as I say. I know you feel her inside of you . . ."

"It's horrible."

"Just drive the car. Stay on the road and fight her until I tell you to let go. Do you understand?"

"I'm sorry. I'm running this show. When the moment is right, when I feel her at her strongest and I see a place to let go of the wheel so I know the car will go over the side—"

"That's exactly right. But I'll tell you when."

Marjorie was too exhausted to answer. Lavinia was working to gain control. Her insides felt as if they'd been stored in a meat locker. The ire she felt was all-consuming. In this moment she hated the world. She hated Mickey—

"Lavinia, can you hear me? I don't speak Italian, but maybe you understand. Marjorie is not going to save you. You'll never have what you want. She is willing to die rather that allow you to live in her."

Marjorie opened her mouth and heard a stream of Italian.

Yes. Yes! She heard it. That was the key. She—Marjorie—was still present.

"Step on the gas. Not too much."

Marjorie felt her foot do as he'd instructed.

"Lavinia, we're picking up speed. Feel that? We're going faster. And when it's too late, the car will fly over the side of this mountain and if you have possessed Marjorie, you'll die. You'll never be with Agostino again."

More Italian. Angry, violent in tone.

Marjorie screamed in pain. She was fighting to maintain her own space and it hurt.

"You don't know how to drive a car, Lavinia. You can't stop it. And when the time is right, the first break in the road Marjorie sees, she is going to drive over the side. Do you understand? All of us will go over the cliff. We will all die. *Addio,* Lavinia. *Capisci?* You will be no more."

Marjorie's foot pressed the accelerator. The car reached fifty miles per hour. She heard a *Noooooo!* come out of her mouth. They were headed straight for the edge of the cliff. It grew closer with every spin of the tires, and her heart was hammering at a frenzied rate. She heard Mickey talking, but she couldn't understand. She felt faint and sick at the same time. She felt as if she might vomit.

The next thing she knew the car was spinning. She knew she must have blacked out. The sick feeling had been replaced by sheer terror. They were still on the road. They hadn't flown over the side, but the car was revolving, tires squealing. A three hundred sixty degree spin. She saw Mickey's hands on the wheel and found her voice.

"What's happening?"

Mickey didn't answer. She saw his leg was on her side, gently pumping the brake at intervals. The car's spin slowed. They were on the opposite side of the road. Another ninety degree rotation before the rear panel hit the mountain. The car rocked once and came to rest, bits of dirt and rubble raining onto the roof and trunk. Then all was quiet. Her eyes were closed and she felt Mickey put his arms around her.

"She's gone," Marjorie mumbled. "She's gone." She started to cry and then she laughed with relief.

"You were wonderful," Mickey told her.

"I was petrified. What happened?" she asked between breaths.

"I turned the wheel and shut off the motor. I figured we had a better chance hitting the mountain than flying off a cliff. I took a chance that the impact would make Lavinia abandon you."

Marjorie clung to Mickey. "I was never more scared in all my life."

"Me either," Mickey replied. "Me either."

Chapter 32

As she drove toward the gate to Heart House, Mars was surprised to see Dennis and Kelly. Their car was parked and they were standing beside it. She rolled to a stop and stared at them. It was strange to say, and she wouldn't say it, but she felt a measure of comfort in the fact that they were there.

"What are you doing?" she asked. Her tone did not reveal that she was glad to see them.

"Mickey sent me," Dennis said.

"And I wouldn't stay home," Kelly added.

"We're here to help."

The cop in Mars almost told them to go home, but this was no time for false bravado. She was scared and she'd accept their help. She unlocked the doors to her car and Dennis and Kelly hopped in the back.

"The painting's in the trunk," she said.

Kelly cheerfully guffawed. "Like that helps."

Mars felt her flash into anger. Was this girl a moron? She didn't sound afraid. Sometimes stupidity masked as bravery. She entered the code and the gate began to roll.

"When did you talk to Mickey?" Mars asked as she drove toward the house.

"A little while ago. He can't make it here in time. It's up to us."

Up to us to get the painting into the house, and then what, Mars wondered.

She parked the car in the driveway and popped the trunk. "I get the honor," she said, not wanting to be anywhere near Lavinia's portrait, but aware that the job fell to her.

"I'll carry it," Kelly said, jumping out of the car.

Mars glared at her. "Are you a fool, or what? Stay put."

"I'm protected."

"Stop it," Dennis said.

Mars didn't ask her to explain. She walked to the rear of the car and stared at the painting lying face down. She had placed it that way just because how else should she treat a murderer?

"You two. Get Morris to answer the door."

They hesitated.

"Go!" she said and they left her.

Mars took a deep breath and picked up the painting. She wondered if it was her imagination or if the painting had more weight to it than when she'd carried it to the car. Had Lavinia returned? She'd heard that when a person died, the body weighed a fraction of an ounce less because of the loss of the soul. Not that Lavinia had a soul. She was pure evil. Was that adding weight to the frame and canvas?

"If you want to see Agostino again, you won't kill me," she told the painting, feeling silly and scared at the same time. The absurdity of the situation wasn't beyond her grasp. Oh, if the other detectives could see her now, talking to an inanimate object. Wouldn't that make for a great story at her retirement party years from now? Yeah, if she lived that long.

She joined Dennis and Kelly at the door.

"We've rung three times," Kelly said. She eyed the painting. "I wonder if there's safety in numbers?"

Mars struck the door with her fist. It swung open on impact.

"I guess he left it ajar for us," Kelly said, leading the others inside. "But which way to the study?"

Kelly and Mars both looked at Dennis. He shrugged. "I don't know."

"Morris!" shouted Mars.

They waited. Mars wondered if the two she was with could hear her heart pounding. She didn't hear theirs. Was she the only one terrified? Of course, they hadn't seen Miranda and Norman's bodies. But then, Dennis had actually experienced an attack. Maybe they were scared and it just didn't show.

"Morris!" she called again.

They heard footsteps approaching. Soon Morris emerged from the hall. He stared at them, almost as if he were in a stupor.

"Morris?" Mars asked.

"I'm Morris. You're supposed to bring the painting to the study."

"We know that . . ."

Morris turned and headed back the way he came. The three quickly followed. Morris walked slowly, like he was heading for an execution—his own—and maybe he was, thought Mars. Maybe they all were.

"Could you move a little faster?" Mars said.

Morris kept his steady slow gate. "She won't hurt you. She only kills men."

"Maybe that used to be her MO, but today she killed a woman."

Morris looked over his shoulder as he walked. His expression never changed.

"I made a fire, like Mickey said."

At the entrance to the study the four of them stopped and looked in. A fire blazed in the fireplace.

Mars felt a rumbling in her hand and she dropped the painting. It had vibrated. That hadn't been her imagination. Lavinia was definitely in the painting. Was it a signal she was about to kill? Mars wasn't brave enough to pick it up. "Agostino is coming," she said in a halting voice. "I know where he is and I'm working to get him back to you."

Before anyone was aware enough to stop her, Kelly grabbed the painting, rushed inside the study, and slammed the door. Mars heard a click and knew she'd locked the door.

"Kelly!" Dennis shouted, both hands trying to twist the knob. "What are you doing? Get out of there!" He rattled the door.

"Where's the key?" Mars asked Morris.

"There isn't one." He shrugged with no more reaction than that. It was as if he were lobotomized.

****

Mickey drove out of the hills and reached Sunset Boulevard. He glanced at Marjorie who was sleeping. It was seven minutes to midnight and it would take longer than that to get to Heart House. He was out of time. It was up to Dennis to burn the painting and it wouldn't be easy.

The twisty mountain road had spotty cell phone service. Fortunately, Mickey had spoken briefly to Morris before the signal cut out. He hadn't been able to reach Dennis by phone. Telepathically he'd told him to meet Mars at Heart House and burn the portrait with her and Morris' help. As far as Mickey knew, Lavinia didn't kill when there was more than one person present, but then she hadn't been known to kill women and she had murdered Miranda.

All sorts of scenarios played in Mickey's head. What if Mars had changed her mind? What if she decided to play by the rules and had logged the painting into an evidence locker?

Or, what if she had taken the painting to Heart House, but Dennis wasn't able to convince her or Morris to help him burn it? Morris owned the painting, and it was worth a fortune. If he didn't cooperate, Mars might balk at destroying a million dollar piece of art she didn't own. After that, Dennis might be too afraid to deal with Lavinia on his own. If the painting wasn't destroyed by midnight, the portal would close and while Lavinia would not be able to take possession of a person's body, her spirit would be free to roam forever. She would wreak havoc any way she could. No one would ever be able to convince her to cross over.

Just as Mickey pulled into a parking lot and grabbed his cell phone, it rang.

"Where are you?" Mars was practically shouting. Mickey heard banging in the background.

"On Sunset. What's going on?"

"Kelly grabbed the painting. She's alone in the study with the door locked."

"What?"

"There's no key."

"And there's no time," Mickey said. "Put Dennis on the phone."

He heard Mars call to Dennis and then another bang before he came on the line. His voice was filled with desperation.

"You son of a bitch! Kelly's gonna die and this is your fault—"

"Calm down. Rants won't help. You know that."

Dennis let loose with a few other choice words before he was quiet.

"Listen. Does Kelly know to burn the painting?"

"I don't know what she knows. Kelly!" he screamed, his mouth away from the phone.

"Dennis!" Mickey shouted.

"Son of a bitch. Son of a bitch! I didn't even want her to come with me. I told her to stay home. This was a man's job."

Mickey didn't have time to groan at the sexist remark. No wonder Kelly came along. "If she doesn't know, then you have to tell her. And then you have to stay calm. Remember what we saw this afternoon?"

"That was bullshit!"

"Tell her Dennis. Tell her she needs to burn the painting. This is too important."

He heard banging again and Mars came on the line.

"What did you say to him?"

"It doesn't matter. Make sure Kelly knows she has to burn the painting. It must be destroyed that way and before midnight. I have to go."

Mickey hung up. Marjorie was looking at him now. "Is it too late?" she asked.

He checked his watch. "No. There are still a few minutes. I have to be quiet now. I have to—"

"You don't have to say anything." She smiled weakly.

Mickey closed his eyes. It was tough to relax under a deadline, but he needed to try. He told himself to be calm. He took several deep breaths. When he felt serene, he visualized Kelly. He visualized energy. He made it grow strong . . .

Chapter 33

Now that Kelly was standing in the study alone, staring at Lavinia's self portrait lying askew against the couch, she wasn't feeling so brave. The bizarre vibration of the painting had startled her and she'd thrown it across the room. It had landed so that it faced her and the eyes had taken on a disturbing hateful quality. Maybe hateful wasn't the correct word. Smugness mixed with malice, like it welcomed a showdown because it knew she—Kelly—couldn't win.

"Calm down. Calm down. Calm down," she told herself. She shook her arms and her legs.

She heard Mars shout, "Kelly! Mickey says to burn the painting. It has to happen before midnight."

"No! Just come out of there," Dennis cut in. Fists pounded, the door rattled.

"Stop that banging!" Kelly yelled.

She needed to get control of herself. She heard a scuffling outside the door and the banging stopped. She checked her watch. Two minutes to midnight. She took a step toward the painting and stopped immediately. A woman's evil laugh filled the room.

"So you're here," Kelly murmured.

She heard something in Italian.

"Oh, God." She gulped. She had planned to run in the room and rip the picture to shreds before Lavinia knew what had hit her. She'd stashed Dennis' Swiss army knife in her pants pocket. A fat lot of good that would do her now.

Just go for it, she told herself. But she couldn't get herself to move. If only she could see Lavinia, she'd know which way to move. Maybe.

Now. You have to do it now!

She rushed toward the painting and immediately felt a horrible sensation. Stopping in her tracks, she looked at her arm and saw a deep slash four inches long. Blood poured profusely. Tears of pain filled her eyes, but there was no time to cry. She had to ignore how she felt.

Get mad. Get even. Keep moving, keep moving. It's harder to hit a moving target.

Swoosh.

The sound of the knife slicing the air was right before her. Lavinia laughed. Kelly's heart thumped wildly as she backed away. *White light of protection.* If only she'd practiced in the car on the way here what she'd learned this afternoon, she'd be safe.

Swoosh.

She heard another laugh. Lavinia was playing with her. Toying. Taking her time. She only had to keep Kelly away from the painting until midnight.

What happens at midnight if I don't succeed? Kelly wondered.

You have to succeed.

She moved her feet more quickly. A plan formed in her head. Keeping her arm on the back of the couch to guide her, she closed her eyes and visualized a shield of energy before her. It had worked this afternoon with tennis balls. Of course, an invisible knife was another animal all together. But, hey, an invisible knife and an invisible shield. Maybe it would work.

Swoosh.

Just keep backing away, around the couch and you'll come to the painting. Believe the energy shield will keep you safe and you'll be able to reach for it.

She came to the end of the couch. She rounded it, keeping her leg against the piece of furniture to know where she was going.

Swoosh.

The sound came from behind her this time. Lavinia meant to block the way. She started walking forward.

Her arm throbbed and her eyes watered. She wasn't feeling peaceful at all. The fire was crackling as if to say, "Here, you're supposed to throw the painting here. What's taking so long?" She heard the knife cutting the air, and with her eyes still closed, she saw Lavinia's smug face in her head. She saw her dark, vile eyes. Italian ripped the atmosphere.

"I win, you lose. Is that what you're saying?" A flood of anger hit Kelly. She couldn't allow her brash rush to save the day be a mistake. She couldn't! The painting was there, only three feet away.

As quickly as the anger had come, it melted away and a sense of utter serenity overtook her. It was as if she was filled with nothing but peace. Something had happened to change everything. She was protected. She knew it and just as she was thinking it she felt the air cool before her face as the knife swooshed toward her. This time she knew Lavinia meant to kill. But Kelly felt nothing. The knife had been stopped.

Angry Italian filled Kelly's ears. Lavinia was mad. She screamed.

The clock in the room began to chime.

Dong.

Kelly grabbed the painting.

Dong.

Rrrip. Lavinia was going for Kelly's heart but the blade caught the canvas.

Dong.

Kelly charged the fireplace and fell.

Dong.

"*Impacciato come un bue.*" Lavinia laughed.

Dong.

Kelly got to her feet and flung the painting into the fire. Flames caught the varnish and the crackling blaze grew loud. Lavinia's laugh turned to a high pitched scream.

Dong.

"Kelly!" Dennis called through the door. "Are you safe?"

Dong.

"I'm fine," Kelly said, quietly at first, eyes transfixed on the fire consuming the portrait.

Dong.

"Kelly!"

Dong.

"I'm fine!" Kelly called.

Dong.

Lavinia's shriek grew faint as the canvas curled into blackened ash.

Dong.

Kelly smiled.

Dong.

As did Mickey on Sunset Boulevard, still in his car.

Chapter 34

If everything Ray had explained to Mickey was true, the *Accordo* was dead, Lavinia's soul was back in her own body somewhere—buried alive, and Marjorie was free. Exhausted, but free.

However, Ray's words haunted him: *I think it's best we take this one step at a time . . . If you're able to destroy the painting . . . we'll talk again.*

Where was Ray? He'd called the Points of Light and hadn't been able to reach him. He'd left messages and Ray hadn't called back. Did that mean something? If so, what?

Marjorie slept most of the time. Mickey didn't want her to travel until she was better and so they remained at the Roosevelt for the time being. She'd been through hell. She needed time to stabilize. In a couple of days they'd head for home.

Luce drove from Brookside to see her mother. "She's still not right," she told Mickey when they were alone. "I'm not scared of her. She's not psychotic. But she has no energy. She's lethargic and she hardly says a word. She pats my hand and smiles and goes back to sleep."

"It may take some time," Mickey told her. "I was scared; I can't imagine how much worse it was for her." He didn't mention Ray and his cryptic words about taking things one step at a time. He didn't tell her he wasn't certain Marjorie's escape from possession was complete. He didn't tell her he feared a part of Marjorie's beautiful spirit had died.

Luce stayed with Marjorie while Mickey went to the Brahms.

Mars had called. She wanted to meet. Agostino's portrait had been recovered. A link to Jay Serling had been found and he'd turned it over without much fuss once detectives pointed out it was considered stolen property and said it would be a shame to tear up his beautiful home looking for it. Charges against Jay were being reviewed by the District Attorney. Jay claimed he thought Avery was the rightful owner of the painting and he'd bought it in good faith. It was conceivable that was true. Avery would have said anything to have things her way.

Mars had yet to see the portrait. She was going to the museum to have a look. She had phoned Kelly and Dennis as well.

Mickey arrived first. He entered gallery seventeen and recognized Pete, the guard he'd spoken with the first time he'd visited the gallery. Pete stood where he was supposed to stand—closer to where the Agostino portrait hung. It appeared he was no longer afraid. Mickey smiled.

"Hello," Mickey said. "Remember me? We spoke a couple of weeks ago."

The guard eyed Mickey. "I see so many people every day that I can't say I recollect."

"Fair enough." Mickey motioned toward Agostino. "Lavinia's portrait used to hang where he is, and you used to stand over there." Mickey pointed.

The guard grinned. "Ah, yes. I remember you now."

"How is it with this painting here instead?"

"Much better. And I'm not the only one to think so."

"Good vibes now?"

"No vibes. She's just gone." Pete chuckled.

Mickey walked closer to Agostino and stared. He felt nothing out of the ordinary. It was as Ray had said. Agostino must have been released. He hated to think about where he might be. Agostino had been the innocent in all this and had paid dearly. Was he lying in a coffin somewhere waiting for the end to come?

Mickey felt a tap on his shoulder and turned around to find Kelly grinning at him. She gave him a hearty hug. Then Dennis shook his hand.

Kelly's eyes traveled the gallery. "You didn't bring your wife. I wanted to meet her." She looked disappointed.

"Her daughter's with her. Marjorie's still recovering."

"I'll bet," Kelly said. "Me too." She lifted her arm. A bandage covered the deep knife wound Lavinia had inflicted.

"Still hurt?" Mickey asked.

"Some." She looked at the Agostino portrait. "So that's him. Handsome." She stepped closer to the painting and stood a moment, admiring. Then she glanced around to see if anyone other than Mickey and her husband were watching. The three of them, plus the guard, were the only people in the room. She whispered to Agostino, "Thank you for healing my hand the last time." She lifted her arm. "Think you could help with this?"

Mickey glanced at the guard. He was watching Kelly with a perplexed expression.

Kelly rejoined Mickey and Dennis. "It's not going to work this time, is it?"

"He's not attached anymore," Mickey said. "You freed him."

"Too bad. I mean, not too bad he's free. Too bad it didn't happen after he healed my— Oh, forget it. He was trapped long enough."

Kelly noticed the guard looking at her. "Hello," she said. "How are you?"

The guard nodded. He refocused his attention when other patrons entered the gallery.

"Where is Agostino?" Dennis asked.

"He could be anywhere on the planet," Mickey answered, skirting the horrible truth.

"On the planet? He's a spirit, right? Couldn't he have crossed over?" Kelly said.

"I'm not certain. He isn't dead, so maybe not."

"What do you mean, he's not dead?" Kelly looked awestruck.

Mickey sighed. He hadn't explained everything to them and

wasn't sure how much he should say. "He's not dead."

"But Lavinia is, right?"

He looked at Kelly with her wide-eyed, childlike stare. How would she cope with the news that her actions had sent Lavinia, and Agostino, back to their coffins?

"She's . . ." Mickey searched for the right words. "Her body . . ."

"What?" Dennis said.

Kelly lifted her chin and her face lost its quizzical stare. "Think Edgar Allen Poe, Dennis. *The Cask of Amontillado. Fall of the House of Usher.*"

"She's buried alive?" Dennis whistled.

"Unless someone freed her," Mickey said.

"Well, we don't want that," Kelly quickly said. "And yet, um, ah . . ." She crossed her arms. "I don't care."

Mickey could see that she didn't wish such a cruel fate on anyone, even Lavinia.

Dennis put an arm around his wife. "She made her own bed, she can lie in it. You have nothing to feel bad about."

"Uh-huh." Kelly stared at the floor.

"Hello everyone," Mars said, joining them. Mickey was surprised to see her dressed in black jeans and a turtleneck sweater. It was a work day and not her normal cop attire. She shook everyone's hand.

"What happened?" Mickey asked, motioning at her, hand moving up and down.

"Yeah," Kelly said. "You look human. Where's regulation-uptight?" She laughed.

Mars pursed her lips in good humor. "I've been suspended."

"What?" Dennis, Kelly and Mickey all said.

"Yep. For a week."

"Why?" Kelly asked.

Mars eyed Agostino's portrait, took off an earring, and began rolling it in her hand. "Because of that little stunt we pulled. So this is the other half of the dynamic duo."

"The good half," Kelly quipped.

"You told your superiors we burned the painting?" Dennis sounded flabbergasted.

Mars continued to eyeball Agostino. Finally, she returned the earring to her ear and looked at Dennis. "I had to. And don't worry. None of you are in trouble."

"Then why are you?" Kelly asked.

"The interim curator, here at the Brahms, asked about it. She wanted to know when she could get the painting back."

"The painting belongs to Morris," Mickey said.

"That's true. However . . . when my boss discovered the painting wasn't in the evidence room where it was supposed to be, he didn't care who owned it because it had been at the crime scene and he's convinced it's the motive for Miranda's murder. I got called on the carpet. He phoned Morris to ask for the painting back, and Morris, being the innocent he is, told them everything."

"How did that get you suspended?" Mickey said.

"Well . . . my boss, in his infinite wisdom, thought I should explore the possibility that Morris killed Miranda. I wasn't about to waste my time with that nonsense. I told him everything Morris had told him was true. To which he replied I was to take a week off without pay."

"Can he do that?" Kelly asked.

Mars nodded. "I didn't put the painting into evidence and I was being insubordinate. He did change his mind about the money. Said I would get paid. He wants me to get a psych evaluation."

Kelly giggled and Mickey smiled.

"It's funny," Mars said. "I sort of agree with him."

"Why?" Kelly asked.

"Because even though I saw what I saw, all is back to normal again. And . . ." She looked at Agostino for a long moment then released some tension with a sigh. "I'm starting to think it was all baloney again."

Dennis laughed. "Exactly."

"Let me tell you, my cut is real." Kelly raised her arm. "I consider it a battle scar, and you know what? I've decided to get a tattoo. In Mickey I trust."

Mickey shook his head. "No. No."

"Yes. Yes," Kelly said.

Dennis reached out his hand. "I'm sorry for calling you a son of a bitch. I was . . . terrified."

"I've been called worse."

They shook hands.

"I don't know what I'd do if I lost her." Dennis squeezed Kelly to him and kissed her cheek. "I love you," he told her.

I know the feeling, Mickey thought, watching the two of them display affection he hadn't seen them display before. And he thought of Marjorie back at the hotel. Would she ever be the same?

Chapter 35

The morning sun splayed light through the windows into the great room where Mickey sat on the couch in his sweats. A light snow had fallen during the night and the view outside was postcard perfect. The world looked bleak to Mickey, however. He and Marjorie had been home for five days, and Marjorie remained a shell of her former self. She rarely spoke, lacked an appetite, and had no interest in seeing friends. She forwent her habit of crack-of-dawn walks and slept until Mickey insisted she get up. A visit to her doctor had revealed no physical problems. She was given a prescription for antidepressants which Mickey didn't fill. Chemicals, he felt, would only make things worse.

He moved into the kitchen to check on the progress of the coffee maker.

He was having no psychic visions, no intuitive directives, and was growing more and more restless. A constant scowl deadened his face and self-condemnation ripped him internally. Marjorie would be fine if it weren't for him. He as good as got her killed. How could he have let this happen?

He poured himself a cup of the caffeinated brew and decided to call Ray once again. The man was his only hope. He had said they would talk again. Why hadn't he returned Mickey's calls?

"Points of Light," the woman who always answered said.

"Ray La Tour."

"Ray has taken a leave of absence. Can someone else—"

Mickey didn't hear the rest of the sentence. A leave of absence? How could that be? The thought that Ray might know how to help

Marjorie had been buoying Mickey like a life preserver. Now all hope was gone. He felt like he'd been sucker punched.

Mickey moved back to the great room and eyed the *Accordo* lying on the coffee table. He hadn't looked at it since getting it back from Ray. He didn't have the heart. What he wanted to do was rip it to shreds and burn it, just as Lavinia's portrait had been burned. He hadn't followed through with his feelings in case Ray needed it. Now Ray appeared to have deserted him.

He sat on the couch and slowly opened the book. Turning pages, he felt a knot in his belly. And then the last page shocked him. It had a new number: 4.

Four? Four days until what? He stopped staring at the book and put his fingertips to his face. The *Accordo* had entered a new phase, and this was the part Ray had yet to explain. Mickey knew this—sort of. But to see an actual number printed on the page added urgency to the situation and filled him with anxiety.

"Mickey?"

He looked up. Marjorie was standing in the doorway, dressed in her nightgown without a robe. Her feet were bare. She looked frail and chilled, even with the thermostat set at seventy-four. He'd done this to her. He'd made her sick.

"Mickey, what's wrong with me? I can't seem to feel anything." Her tone held no fear, no anxiety, no anger.

"I don't know. Lavinia damaged you in some way." He felt a tear trickle down his cheek. He turned his head so she wouldn't see.

"Are you mad at me?"

Her question shocked him. He wiped his face. "What! Of course not."

"Then why are you crying?"

He stared at her. *Because I love you so much. Because I need you so much. Because you are such a wonderful person and don't deserve to be hurt the way you've been hurt.* These tender words stuck in his throat and instead he said, "Come sit by me."

She didn't move at first. It appeared she was deciding something.

Finally she turned and left the room.

Mickey began to berate himself. *Damn you for going to Los Angeles. Damn you for not flying home the moment John Carroll kept his secrets to himself. Damn your conceit, thinking you're some kind of hero who is supposed to save the world.* Four days. He had four days to do what?

He heard Marjorie reenter the room. This time she clutched a large envelope. "We can go if you want." Her voice was low.

Mickey got off the couch and went to her. The envelope was addressed to both of them. He took it and found two round-trip airline tickets to Italy along with an itinerary inside. The flight left in the morning.

"Did you make these arrangements . . ." He looked up to find that she had gone back to the bedroom.

Mickey decided she must have bought the tickets and organized the trip before coming to Los Angeles, never telling him. She didn't act like she wanted to travel now, but something told him this was what they should do. And even if it wasn't, even if it was just wishful thinking on his part, they'd be out of the house. They'd be doing something besides sitting around waiting for the other shoe to drop.

He went in search of their passports and found them in the office. When he went into the bedroom he found Marjorie in bed. He let her sleep. He'd do the packing for both of them. She'd be better once they were on the plane, once they were in Italy seeing the sights. At least that's what he told himself.

****

The plane ride was uneventful except for the moment when Marjorie told Mickey: "I didn't make the arrangements. I thought you did."

He hadn't. And if neither of them had bought the tickets and neither of them had reserved a room in an Italian country villa, who had?

Mickey's euphoria that Marjorie might be a little better soured. She'd thought he'd bought the tickets. She'd thought he wanted to go. She was being compliant. That was all. She had no interest in Italy or travel. Her spirit was not making a comeback.

He looked at her. She wasn't curious about the matter. Her eyes had that vacant, dull quality that said she was running on empty and was doing well just to breathe. A mysterious someone bought them airline tickets. A mysterious ...

Ray? Could Ray have arranged this? If so, that was good.

"Where did you get the envelope?" he asked.

"It was under my pillow when we arrived home from Los Angeles."

Mickey leaned his head against the seat. If Ray had bought the tickets, why wouldn't he have just handed them over? Something didn't make sense.

****

"*Benvenuti.*" A woman in her mid-sixties stood behind a mahogany check-in counter ready to be of assistance. She was a petite woman with friendly, light blue eyes, her hair a flaxen brown with wisps of delicate gray. Her stature and warm manner reminded Mickey of Marjorie and he liked her immediately.

"McCoy," Mickey said. "I believe we have reservations." At least the itinerary that had been included with the airline tickets said they did.

"Si. Welcome to my villa, Mr. and Mrs. McCoy. I am Anna Dibiasi. I am proprietor and happy to serve."

So it was fact. Whoever had bought the plane tickets had also made arrangements for them to stay at Anna's bed and breakfast— Villa Di—in the country outskirts of Florence. Before leaving home, Mickey had checked the Internet. It was an appealing, renovated farmhouse with two suites and five rooms for rent. Arriving at night hid its charm beneath a blanket of darkness. But come daylight, he knew the allure of the hotel with its surrounding gardens, cypress trees, olive groves, and glorious mountain views would be evident.

"Mickey," Marjorie murmured.

He looked at her and saw she was extremely pale. "Do you need to sit down?"

She nodded.

He guided her to one of the sturdy, plush-seat chairs in the lobby, and made sure she was comfortable. "This won't take long." He patted her thigh.

She leaned her head against the wall and closed her eyes. Mickey returned to the counter.

"A too long plane ride?" Anna said, concerned eyes on Marjorie.

"Yes," Mickey said. "Too long. Ah, paperwork?" He motioned with open hands.

Anna pressed a sheet of paper toward him. On it were typewritten words. Italian, then a translation in English. Mickey read it then signed.

Anna spoke. "I give you a most beautiful suite with two rooms. Enchanting view. A fireplace. Jacuzzi bath. Anything you need, *per favore* ask me. I and my grandson Paulo live on these premises."

Mickey slipped a credit card from his wallet, but Anna waved it away. "Already taken care."

"By whom?" Perhaps now he would get some answers.

Acting as if she hadn't heard the question, she picked up the receiver of an old-style phone. "It is very modern. Just looks old for looks." She smiled, pressed a button and the phone served as an intercom. She said something in Italian and a moment later a door to the right of the check-in opened and a handsome young man emerged. He appeared to be in his late teens, had short, light brown hair, the same blue eyes and smile as Anna, with dimples in each of his cheeks.

"My grandson, Paulo. Paulo, meet Mr. and Mrs. McCoy."

"*Molto lieto*, Mr. and Mrs. McCoy. Pleased to meet you."

"Call me Mickey. And this is Marjorie."

"Take luggage to their room," Anna said. "I give them number four."

Mickey and Marjorie's luggage sat in a heap on the lobby floor, deposited there by the shuttle driver who had driven them to the hotel. Paulo grabbed the bags and placed them on a cart as Anna handed Mickey the key.

"Grazie," Mickey said, hesitating before he added, "Anna. We didn't make our own reservations. If it's paid for, you must know who paid."

Anna continued to smile, although Mickey thought he detected a flash of anguish in her expression.

"*Si*. A cousin of mine."

"Does this cousin have a name?"

"He say not to tell you if you ask until he speak with you."

"And when will that be?"

"Tomorrow. Paulo will give you a ride."

Mickey's forehead creased with concern. Why keep his name a secret? It made him nervous. This trip had all the trappings of trouble.

Mickey moved to Marjorie and gently took her arm to help her stand. They followed Paulo into the hall. It was a short walk to their room.

"I like this quarters best," Paulo said. "It is not the biggest, but is the nicest."

There were two rooms and a bath. In the sitting area was a couch, a table flanked by two wing-back chairs, and a TV. In the bedroom was a fireplace, a wooden chest of drawers, a table with chairs, and a Neo-Renaissance queen-size bed. Drapes were closed for the night. Marjorie lay down on the bed and closed her eyes.

Paulo lifted the largest bag and placed it on a luggage rack in the bedroom closet.

"You can leave the rest where it is," Mickey said. The remaining bags were small and he wasn't sure where he wanted them yet. He handed Paulo a generous tip.

"*Grazie!*" Paulo said.

"You're to take us to see someone tomorrow?" Mickey said.

"*Si*. I have a nice car. Tomorrow." Paulo motioned at Marjorie. "Is she no well?"

"It's been a hectic day."

"Because my cousin say to bring you both."

Mickey nodded. What choice was there? He wanted to meet their benefactor and learn what this trip was all about. He felt Marjorie should be fine to ride in a car after a good night's sleep. She'd survived a long plane ride. "What time?"

"After breakfast. Ten, okay?"

"At ten."

"Ciao!"

Mickey sat down on the bed and placed a hand on Marjorie's hip.

She stirred, sat up suddenly, and put her arms around him. "I'm afraid."

Mickey held her. He was afraid too, but thought it best they see this cousin of Paulo and Anna's.

****

In the morning Mickey opened the drapes revealing a large window with a panoramic view of rolling hills and distant mountains. In the foreground were dark green lawns and a garden of rosebushes. The weather was misty and even though it was November, roses were in bloom. A door beside the window opened to a stone terrace with patio furniture.

Mickey was pleased that Marjorie had slept peacefully through the night, and that she wanted to get up and get dressed. They enjoyed a breakfast of toast and jam accompanied by cappuccino in the cozy dining nook and at ten Paulo appeared. He led them to his white Fiat 500 two-door compact. Marjorie squeezed into the back and Mickey buckled her in as if she were a child before he settled into the passenger seat.

Paulo turned the key and put the Fiat in first gear. "Hang on to your hat!"

The day was cool, barely in the fifties. A mist blanketed the hills, vineyards, and tree groves, lending a mystical quality to the terrain. The sky was slate blue, in places pearl white. It blended in with the sparse, frail clouds.

"It is beautiful, no?" Paulo made polite conversation. "I grew up with all this. I want to see the world. Travel. *Si*. But I will always be here. This is home."

He never asked about Marjorie's strange, absent behavior and Mickey wondered if Paulo was merely being gracious, or had he and Anna been told to expect a woman in a near zombie-like state?

Mickey glanced over his shoulder as much as he could. Then he slid his eyes toward Paulo. "This is a cousin you're taking us to?"

Paulo's smile vanished. "*Si*. My cousin Tommaso."

Tommaso? Mickey tried to think. "I don't know a Tommaso."

"He say you are in a predicament and you need his help."

A realization hit Mickey. "I met a Thomas recently."

"*Si*. Thomas. My cousin Tommaso."

The road curved and the car shot through the hills, past old, picturesque farmhouses and small villas. The mist formed dew-like rain on the windshield and Paulo pressed the switch for the wipers.

Thomas sent the tickets? Mickey never would have thought. He was a stranger . . .

"Are we going to his house?"

"*Si*. You talk at his home, the Zanetti Quercia Villa. It is more than four centuries old."

"Zanetti? As in Lavinia Rossi Zanetti?"

"*Si*. It was hers. It is a famous estate."

Mickey heard Marjorie stir behind him. He pulled down the visor looking for a mirror and found one. She was staring at him, eyes fearful.

"We are here." Paulo pointed as he turned the wheel, directing the Fiat along a gravel road. The villa poked above fall-turning oak and chestnut trees. Marjorie whimpered.

Mickey shifted in the seat and give his wife a reassuring touch. He had to unbuckle the belt to reach her.

"I don't want to be here," Marjorie whispered. "We need to go back."

The fear in her eyes had changed to terror. He turned to Paulo. "My wife isn't well. We need to take her back to the room."

"Oh," Paulo said. "But we're here, and my cousin say today."

The Fiat continued to roll toward the villa and Paulo looked ill at ease. Was he afraid to go against Thomas' wishes?

Mickey turned back to Marjorie. Her already-pale skin had blanched to the shade of whole milk.

"I feel her," Marjorie said. "She's here."

Mickey stared. She couldn't be feeling Lavinia taking over, could she? "Inside you?" he asked.

Marjorie shook her head slightly, eyes still wide with fear. This wasn't good.

"You don't have to go in. You can stay in the car with Paulo. Right, Paulo? In fact, he'll take you for a ride."

"Okay. I can do that." Paulo nodded.

Marjorie closed her eyes.

Mickey faced forward again as Paulo drove the last few hundred yards. Three buildings of gray and creamy-orange stones came into full view. The largest had to be the living quarters. It rose two stories high, with a section of attic making it three. Shutters of dark wood flanked the large windows. Terra-cotta tiles covered the low-peaked roof, one end angling at a definitive rake. Climbing tendrils of a yellowish vine clung to the facade like a spidery hand.

Thomas stepped out the front door. He wore a thin, gray jacket. A Fedora protected his head from the drizzle. He approached the passenger side as it came to a stop and soon his head appeared at the window. Mickey pressed the switch to roll down the glass.

Thomas spoke quickly, glancing from Mickey to Marjorie and

back again. "There are explanations for everything, I assure you. Please come inside and give me the chance."

Mickey climbed out of the car and leaned toward Paulo before closing the door. "Take her away from here."

Paulo looked at Thomas as if asking for permission. Their eye contact didn't escape Mickey's notice. Thomas nodded.

"Be back within the hour," Mickey instructed and closed the door.

Paulo stepped on the gas. Mickey raised a hand and kept his eyes on the Fiat until it was out of sight.

"Don't worry, Mr. McCoy. Paulo is young, but a good driver. Come inside, now."

He wasn't worried about Paulo's driving. He was worried about Marjorie's health, her state of mind, and Thomas' stealthy trip arrangements. Why all the secrecy?

"She's been ill. But I think you already know this."

"I do. And if she is afraid now, it is because this used to be Lavinia's home. There can be no other explanation."

Why don't I feel her? I'm the psychic.

"Why did you arrange for us to come here? I don't understand any of this."

"I know you have a lot of questions. Let's go inside."

Chapter 36

Mickey and Thomas sat across from each other on brown leather chairs in a cozy sitting room with yellow-ocher walls, built-in bookshelves, and a crackling fire in the fireplace. With daylight dim because of the weather, a brass chandelier provided the light.

"I know I'm being clandestine. Plane tickets and no note of explanation. But believe me, I wouldn't have done it if I didn't feel it necessary."

"Well, let's hear it."

"I had to keep Ray off my trail."

"Ray?" Mickey frowned.

"I know how far-fetched the things I am about to tell you will sound. But you must believe me. Ray is part of a sect dedicated to evil. He is bitter now, because he thought it impossible for you and your Marjorie to beat Lavinia."

"He's the one who told me what to do."

"A mistake he is sorry for, and one he is rectifying by keeping your wife ill."

"*He* is keeping her ill?"

"That's right."

"How do you know this?"

"Because, dear friend, I used to be like him."

"Used to be?"

"That is correct. If you would like all the brutal details, I will give them to you. But the short version is—I was once a member of a sect such as his until I came to my senses and now I am not."

A woman entered the room and said something to Thomas in Italian.

"Are you thirsty?" Thomas asked Mickey.

Mickey shook his head.

"Caffè Macchiato," Thomas said, holding up two fingers. The woman left.

"And now you're not. How does that make you want to help me? How would you even know I needed help, for that matter?"

"You're going to force me to display my dirty linen?"

Mickey studied Thomas. The man exuded sincerity, and yet he didn't trust him. Sects dedicated to evil. Devil worship—that was what Thomas was talking about. It made him uncomfortable. He knew nothing about it, didn't want to, and had always considered the practice something demented minds did for show; something weak people did to make others think they had power.

Mickey felt small. If Ray knew how to destroy Marjorie's psyche and Thomas knew how to foil him, then Mickey was a mere babe in the woods. His skills were puny and amounted to nothing compared to the knowledge and capabilities of these two men.

"Your thoughts?" Thomas said.

"If you can help me, I certainly want it. I love my wife."

"I know."

"But . . ."

"You still want my dirty linen."

"Yes."

"Fair enough." He allowed a moment for thought. "It was an ancestor of mine who drew up Lavinia's *Accordo*." He paused as if he expected a reaction from Mickey. "I have my own copy, here in this house."

Mickey felt numb and helpless. He was at the mercy of things beyond his grasp. He'd never even heard of an *Accordo* a month ago, and now one was ruling his life.

Thomas stood and walked to one of the bookcases. "There are many texts here, filled with mystical knowledge penned by masters.

Five volumes are compacts. Four ran their course centuries ago and are no longer something to be concerned with. But this one." He removed a black book that looked exactly like the one John Carroll had given Mickey. "This one, not so. It was my father's responsibility to care for it. And then it was mine. Only by the time my father was no longer capable . . ."

Thomas put the book back. "No. I won't tell you all the evil I saw my father do. It must suffice to say it turned me against him. When the task fell to me to preserve Lavinia's *Accordo*, I didn't want anything to do with it. Sometimes, though, curiosity got the better of me and I would check it from time to time. When I discovered a number had appeared on the last page, indicating the compact was about to end, I reread the *Accordo* and knew I had to act."

"Why?"

"I've already explained that."

"The evil you saw your father do."

"Yes. Lavinia had options that had to be thwarted. I tapped into those powers I'd long turned my back on, and it came to me that someone would bring the *Accordo* to Ray."

"So you sought Ray out."

"Yes. And you brought him the *Accordo*. And, well, you were there. You saw what happened."

"And now I'm here."

"Yes."

"And you can make Marjorie well?"

"Yes."

"And Ray? Will he try to harm her again once she is well?"

"No. He won't know about it, for one thing. But my help, my cure, will be permanent."

Thomas sat again and they remained silent, the fire crackling low.

A permanent cure? Dare I believe it?

The muscles in Mickey's neck tightened, threatening to give him a headache. What choice did he have, but to believe Thomas? Marjorie seemed to be getting worse and he had no idea how to relieve her suffering.

The woman returned with a silver tray. On it were two demitasse cups of coffee. She placed the tray on a table then one by one handed the cups to Thomas and Mickey. She left the room.

Thomas sipped his, peering at Mickey as he did. Mickey held his in his lap.

"Mmmm. It is very good. You don't like?" Thomas said.

Mickey clicked an agitated finger on the cup. Thomas' story sounded plausible, but something wasn't right, and he'd been away from Marjorie for too long. He placed the coffee on the tray, rubbed his face and pushed out of the chair.

"I'm here to help you," Thomas said, rising to his feet. "If Lavinia had succeeded in possessing your wife's body, I wouldn't have brought you here and we wouldn't be having this conversation. But that didn't happen. So now, you must trust me. Your wife will waste away to nothing if I don't act."

Mickey couldn't handle much more. He didn't know if he should trust Thomas. He couldn't get past the question of why this man should care.

Then he thought: *You've gone out of your way to help others. Spent your own time and money just to do the right thing because you thought you were the only one who could. That was what got you involved in this in the first place. What makes you think you are the only one in the world with good intentions?*

Mickey felt ashamed. "Okay," he said softly.

"I will have Paulo bring you and Marjorie back tonight."

Panic jolted Mickey. He hadn't thought about bringing Marjorie back here. "No. I won't put her through that!"

"It's the only way. I'll provide you with a tranquilizer. Give it to her and she'll sleep. She won't know where she is. I don't know how to stress how important this is. I can help you. I can end this nightmare. But you must return with your wife. What we have to do must be completed during the phase of the waxing gibbous moon."

Chapter 37

Mickey stood outside in the drizzle to wait for Marjorie and Paulo. All the while he felt like he might explode. Thomas stood with him, but didn't talk. Everything had been settled. Mickey needed no more convincing. He would return to *Zanetti Quercia Villa* with Marjorie. He felt he had no choice. A tranquilizer for her peace of mind was in his pocket. He almost wished he had one for himself.

It took twenty minutes for Paulo to show.

"What took so long?" Mickey barked.

Paulo looked apologetic. "We drove through the hills."

Marjorie was strapped into the backseat, eyes closed, body limp as a rag. She couldn't have seen much. Mickey climbed in beside her. It appeared that she'd been crying.

Thomas bent down to Paulo's level and spoke to him through the window. What he said, he said in Italian. It took several minutes.

"What did he say to you?" Mickey asked as Paulo drove them back to the bed and breakfast.

"He say to bring you back tonight."

"That's all?"

"I bring you after midnight."

Paulo's expression was somber and Mickey suspected Thomas had issued more instructions than that.

"What else?"

Paulo shrugged. "He say it's important I no be late and to follow what he say exactly."

Back at the hotel Mickey asked for food to be brought to their room. Ham and cheese and a roll would do fine. He had coaxed Marjorie into eating a little on the plane, and she'd had half of a piece of toast for breakfast, but that was all. She had to eat. She needed strength. Her lack of appetite had taken its toll. Her body was almost skeletal, her face white and gaunt.

"Eat, Marjorie. I understand you don't want to. I'm not hungry either, but please."

She put small bites into her mouth and chewed.

"I want to sleep," she said. "All I want to do is sleep."

"Finish first." He put his hands on both sides of her face and looked at her with so much love he thought he would cry.

She forced down as much food as she could and then crawled into bed. Mickey collapsed in the overstuffed chair. His throat felt scratchy and he feared he was coming down with something. He couldn't think; confusion ruled. Normally he would calm himself and ask for guidance, but he couldn't overcome the panic he felt. Away from Thomas, his resolve ebbed. Should he take Marjorie to the villa? Asleep or not, he didn't want to force her into entering a place that terrified her. What if she woke up?

Thomas was adamant it was the only way to help her. And time was running out. Day four: Marjorie had shown him the airline tickets. Day three: they'd flown to Italy. Day two was today. Day one, the final day, after midnight when they were at Thomas' villa.

It wasn't normal for him to rely on someone else's judgment, but this situation was beyond him. Someone else, someone with abilities far more advanced than his, had to be Marjorie's rescuer. But could he really trust Thomas? He didn't know him.

Someone tapped on the door. Mickey entered the sitting room and found it was Anna who'd knocked.

"I come for the tray. But first. How is she?"

Mickey opened the door wider and she came inside. He motioned toward the bedroom and kept his voice low. "She's sleeping. She doesn't look good."

Anna nodded, looking sad. "I say a prayer for her." She picked up the tray that had been used to bring lunch and walked toward the door.

It occurred to Mickey that Anna knew her cousin and she would know if he could be trusted.

"Anna."

She stopped and looked at him.

"Your cousin, Thomas."

She didn't say anything; her face was blank.

"How is he your cousin?"

"I cannot say exactly. A grandfather of a grandfather is his grandfather too. I am told he was a cousin when I growing up. I not know his parents. He always live in that house. He is much older than me, but he no look it. I always just know he is a cousin. But distant. Because he marry my sister. She has eighteen years younger than me and most beautiful."

"He's your brother-in-law, then."

She shook her head. "No more. My sister die."

"I'm sorry. Very sorry. I . . ."

"It a long time ago." She started to leave.

"He says he can heal Marjorie."

Anna paused, her back to Mickey.

"Can he?" Mickey asked.

She turned and looked at him. Then her eyes cast downward and moved back and forth. "He can do whatever he says he can do. The question is, will he?"

Her tone hinted at a secret and provided no comfort. She walked out the door with the tray.

Mickey moved to the bedroom and sat in the chair. If Thomas wasn't the answer, what was? Take Marjorie and run back to Tahoe? Then what? Watch her waste away? Watch her die?

He didn't like Anna's reply to his question. She hadn't jumped up and down and said, *yes, yes, Thomas can help*. Why not? Because he hadn't been able to save her sister? Was she just bitter? She didn't seem bitter. She seemed . . . resigned.

Fear poked at him. Then hope nudged back. Maybe Thomas was driven to help people like Marjorie because he hadn't been able to save his wife.

He meditated and prayed as best he could. As the sun shifted in the sky, he watched the shadows in the room elongate and he knew time was passing. Marjorie lay so still in the bed that at one point he got up to see if she was still alive.

He returned to the chair and closed his eyes.

****

He was seated as he'd been most of the afternoon. He didn't know if he was dreaming. He felt calm, at peace, rested—even though he couldn't move. He felt bound to the chair, as if he were a death-row inmate strapped to Old Smokey with tape over his mouth. Still, he remained peaceful.

I'm going to be zapped with thousands of volts of electricity.

He thought this with no alarm, no panic. Whatever was to be would be.

John Carroll appeared before him. He wasn't solid like the time he'd brought the compact. He was translucent and glowed like fired platinum. He floated in the air the way a person might tread water and when he communicated, it was through telepathy.

I've been told this will all be over soon.

Good.

You must trust in your own judgment.

That's what I've been trying to do. It isn't working.

Not true. You know what you think. You know what you feel. Stop fighting it.

John began to fade.

Give me more than that. Please help me. Really help me.

I'm telling you, you already know. Oh. But I did forget to mention. Fear and hate keep you a prisoner. I have forgiven Avery and we have both crossed over to the other side. I must go now. But when you start to panic, when you start to hate, calm yourself and remember what I said. Fear and hate keep you a prisoner.

John Carroll disappeared. Mickey opened his eyes. The sun dropped behind a distant mountain and the room dimmed to murky, dark gray.

Fear and hate keep you a prisoner. What kind of help was that? Why couldn't John have said, *Mickey, you are supposed to do this—* blah, blah, blah, whatever the correct answer was—*and all will be fine. You and Marjorie will go home and go on with your lives as if none of this happened. Oh, and by the way, God is taking away those blasted sixth-sense gifts of yours so nothing like this will ever happen again.*

The lamp on Marjorie's side of the bed switched on. Startled, Mickey drew a breath and froze. Ray stood in the room, staring at him. Mickey jumped to his feet.

"You're here!"

"I told you we'd talk again."

"I thought it would happen a little sooner than this."

"I had to be certain of Thomas' plans before I came to you. I have been praying remotely to give you and Marjorie strength."

"Pray harder."

Ray smiled. "You're doing better than you think."

"I don't think so. I'm scared. And I hate this!"

"Fear and hate keep you a prisoner."

Mickey stared.

"You continue to question why you can't help your wife. With all your telepathic powers, your ability to leave your body and move through time, your proclivity for visions that foretell events as well as those that give glimpses into the past. Why? Why don't those things mean anything now? All you've wanted to do with your advanced abilities is to help those in need. Why can't you help Marjorie?"

"Exactly! Why?"

"You aren't a healer."

"I'm not..." He'd never thought in those terms. He'd helped heal people's lives—their situations and problems. But as far as health being the issue, no, he'd never paid attention to that. He sat back in the chair with hands together, fingertips under his chin.

"And there is a second reason."

Mickey looked at Ray. "Tell me."

"The part of the *Accordo* I did not translate for you. The bargainer always receives a second chance."

"Lavinia has a second chance at Marjorie?" Mickey felt his heart drop.

"Thomas, too."

"What do you mean, Thomas too?"

"Everything he told you today was a lie."

"How do you know what he told me?"

"I was present even though you did not see me."

Mickey put his fingers to his temples. He'd done remote viewing before. He could believe it. Still, he was overwhelmed.

"Thomas is the Practitioner who drew up Lavinia's *Accordo*, not an ancestor. Yes, that makes him very old. I, myself, am one-hundred and sixty-two. Please don't think that makes us supernatural beings. Both of us are quite human. But we have studied and gleaned from natural laws of the universe how to accomplish certain things."

He paused, allowing time for Mickey to digest his words.

"I've learned that Thomas was part of a sect that set out to do good works. But like many cults or factions, over time, their motivation changed. The power they felt they had over the average person made them feel superior and entitled. Desire for personal gain and easy living made them use their knowledge to harm. They became wizards of the dark arts, so to speak. Energy manipulation. Many of them grew lazy and careless. They lost skills for lack of discipline, study, and practice. These Practitioners died out. A handful remain."

"And you? You're part of a sect?"

"No. That story Thomas told you about becoming disenchanted with his father is actually what happened to me, not him. It is a story that doesn't need to be told. What I will tell you is that I am here to tell you what to do. Try not to be afraid."

Chapter 38

At nearly one in the morning the moon glowed in a dark sky and the narrow road to Lavinia's villa shimmered like a ribbon of silver. Fog rose from the surrounding countryside, masking trees and distant villas. Across some of the hills, tall cypress stood like silhouetted sentries making certain the Fiat didn't turn back.

Eerie and quiet. Out of some horror movie, Mickey thought. *I'm glad she doesn't have to see it.* He looked at the figure turned away from him in the back seat of Paulo's car. She wore a hooded cloak that covered her from head to toe.

Mickey hoped he had made the correct decision returning to Thomas. He'd listened to Ray and come to his decision. This was a roll for all the marbles.

They reached the villa and this time Paulo parked in front of the second, smaller structure. Thomas did not greet them.

"He told you to drop us off here? At this building?"

"No drop off. I carry Marjorie. Thomas say she will be asleep and no wake."

Mickey nodded and allowed the younger, stronger man to take her from the car. The front door wasn't locked and they walked inside. Moonlight through windows was all that illuminated the room. Amid shadows and muted moonbeams Mickey saw oak barrels, grape harvesting equipment, tools, and machinery.

"This way," Paulo said. Mickey followed him to a staircase and their footsteps thudded the wood planks to the second floor. Paulo hesitated and muttered to himself in his native tongue. They were standing in a dark hallway with two doors to choose from. "This one." Paulo pointed with his head. They progressed to the door farthest away. Mickey opened it and they went in.

"*Santa Madre,*" Paulo whispered. The room was a marvel. Windows had been covered, blocking the moon. Lit candles flickered from every surface except for the far end, which was buried in utter darkness. A chill traveled Mickey's spine. He was certain that something hideous was concealed there. His heart began to pound. Two wooden chairs, barely in the light, faced the blackness.

It seemed to Mickey that fright and fascination had Paulo's shoes nailed to the floor. He lingered, eyes taking it all in. Finally, the load he'd been carrying grew heavy. He adjusted her in his arms, moved forward, and carefully placed her in the closest wooden chair. She slumped to the side and would have fallen out if it weren't for the arms on the seat.

Paulo turned to Mickey. His eyes said, *I am afraid for you; good luck.* Mickey nodded in acknowledgement. Paulo left the room, his footsteps fading as he traveled down the hall.

Mickey took a deep breath. He eyed the hidden end of the room before stepping toward the chairs and froze when Thomas unexpectedly walked out of the darkness. Dressed in a loose-fitting black robe that included a hood, he had the appearance of a monk. His expression was kind.

"It is good that you are here." Thomas motioned with his arm. "Please, come forward. Join your wife. Sit in the adjacent chair."

Mickey wanted to take his time and didn't move. He was nervous and not at all sure he had made the correct decision to come here. Even having heard what Ray had to say, he had his doubts. "All this was necessary to help Marjorie?"

Thomas smiled and looked at the slumped figure in the chair. "Oh, yes, Mr. McCoy. Very necessary. And see, she isn't frightened a bit. That tranquilizer did the trick. Soon all of her mortal suffering will come to an end."

One way or the other, thought Mickey. *Do you think I'm fooled, or do you not care?*

Thomas' smile continued as he stepped back into the shadow. His robe became a part of the darkness and all that was seen of him was his face. "Sit down, Mr. McCoy."

Mickey didn't move.

Thomas' smile vanished. "I must insist."

Cautiously, Mickey did as instructed.

Thomas began to recite, his voice a low monotone. *"Ommm. Tutto il Potere. Si concentri in me . . ."*

Thomas stepped out of the blackness, a fresh candle in his hand. He moved to an already lit candle and placed the virgin wick in the flame. Lifting the burning taper, he smiled once again. Light gleamed in his eyes and he looked crazed.

"Io sono questo Potere. Nulla può ostacolarmi. La mia parola è legge."

Then the words changed. Instead of Italian they became the bastardized version found in the *Accordo*. Raising his arms high, as if invoking power from the heavens, wax from the candle dripped to the floor.

A woman's humming joined in, the pitch perfectly blending with Thomas's words.

Lavinia.

Mickey felt loathing, which was quickly followed by dread. His heart beat faster, fear stuck in his throat.

There is nothing to fear. There is nothing to fear. I believe in the . . .

Lavinia laughed and Mickey's eyes went to Thomas, who now smiled with delirium. He took a large candle from a pocket and lit it with the taper. The bigger flame erased the darkness and now Mickey could see that a false wall had been knocked open and a chamber was exposed. Two white, elaborately scrolled, stone caskets filled the space. They lay upright at a steep slant against a support. They were closed. Lavinia's hum came from the one in line with Marjorie.

Thomas said, "You have reached the point of no return. You will sit there and you will not move."

Lavinia's hum grated on Mickey's nerves. He hated her. He hated Thomas. His eyes grew hot and stung.

Don't hate. Don't hate. Ray is right. Hate makes me frail and gives away my power.

"Oh, you poor weak-minded fool. I tell you tales and you come running for my help. How easy you are to deceive."

Don't hate . . .

Thomas moved to the casket in front of Mickey. Lavinia began to shout. He smiled. "She is anxious, when there is no need."

Mickey closed his eyes. *Don't hate. She is a miserable soul.*

"Look at me."

Mickey opened his eyes.

"You are surprisingly compliant. I expected whimpering at the very least. But I can see that you are tired of fighting and since you and Marjorie will be together for eternity . . ."

Mickey eyed the coffins. Thomas grinned. Lavinia shouted and Mickey's heart started to race.

"Be still, impatient one." Thomas moved to Lavinia's casket and placed a hand upon it. She quieted down. He looked at Mickey. "Now, I may show you." He moved to the other coffin.

It had to be heavy, but as was now abundantly clear, Thomas was not an ordinary person.

No. Don't elevate his status. He is as Ray explained. Someone who availed himself of the natural laws of the universe and mastered the art of energy manipulation.

Thomas was able to remove the stone lid without assistance and without exertion. The casket proved to be empty.

"Ah! Yes. Agostino has been released." Thomas put a finger to his lips, puzzlement on his face. Mickey knew it was false and for show. With the destruction of Lavinia's portrait Agostino's soul would have returned to his body. Thomas might have freed him because of his agreement with Lavinia. Killing him would have constituted a breach. Maybe he was a prisoner somewhere in Thomas' house. Mickey didn't know. One thing *was* for certain; Thomas knew. And he would know the consequences for any errant action.

"I had to make room for you," Thomas said.

Mickey closed his eyes and allowed himself to feel all the horror those words were meant to elicit.

Don't fight it. The feeling will pass. You must be strong.

"I see that you are terrified. As well you should be. It would not be normal if you were not." He began reciting foreign words again, this time in a chant, and Mickey was glad he couldn't understand. He directed his thoughts elsewhere and concentrated on what Ray had said.

Fear and hatred keep you a prisoner.

Mickey repeated the thought at least fifty times and then crammed his mind with words of peace. This relaxed him very little. He was too caught up in the moment and what was going to happen next.

Thomas continued to chant, his tone irritating to Mickey's central nervous system.

Fine. Keep up your mantra. Keep playing with me. Each ghoulish moment that passes works in my favor.

Mickey didn't know how much time passed before Thomas stopped and spoke to him in English. "Second chances. For me and Lavinia, but not for you." He moved to the closest window and removed the covering. Moonlight beamed through. "Of course, there are always deadlines. Horrible thing—deadlines." He moved close to Mickey. "This all had to be done by the light of this month's waxing gibbous moon. I don't mind telling you that gave me some concern. I never thought it would come to this. But now that the two of you are here, it's kind of fun, no?"

His face looked eerily like a mask, muscles frozen in glee.

"Lavinia's soul in Marjorie's body?" Mickey said.

"I am afraid that is the price she must pay."

"And me?"

"You are a liability as long as you are alive. You have been blessed with some abilities. Not all that powerful, but enough that you might stumble upon a way to interfere with my activities should you decide revenge is a suitable response for what must happen here. And I would find it amusing, but also annoying, like an irritating gnat. You must be squashed." He rubbed his finger and thumb together.

He moved to Lavinia's coffin. She was humming again. He hummed along for a moment, then finally spoke. "*Sei pronta?* Are you ready, Lavinia?"

Mickey's heart hammered wildly. He knew what he was about to see and was glad Marjorie did not have to.

Thomas removed the coffin lid and before he had a chance to discard it carefully, Lavinia's energy hit the room with the force of an icy hurricane. Mickey turned his head to weather the onslaught which lasted only seconds. Candle flames were extinguished, black wicks emitting spiraling threads of smoke. A horrible smell filled his nostrils and saturated the air.

Lavinia's spirit swayed before him, her hair a mass of wild curls, her eyes dark orbs. Her mouth curved into a demonic smile. All of her was translucent, and through the transparency Mickey saw her physical self in the coffin, the fetid beginning phases of decomposition all too apparent. Once her soul had to return to the body, the state of suspended animation had ceased. Either Thomas wasn't home to release her from the crypt or his soulless nature didn't care if she suffered prior to bringing her back.

This was the future Thomas planned for Marjorie? Her soul was to enter this already putrefying body?

Don't hate. You have the upper hand. You do.

Mickey looked at the unmasked window. The moon had traversed the sky and could not be seen. He glanced down at his watch. According to Ray, Thomas needed to complete his maniacal ritual within the next ten minutes. It was time for this farce to end.

He stood up.

Lavinia's head jerked in a weird cartoon-like motion. Both of her hands rose in the air, the fingers appropriately curled like a witch.

"You cannot stand!" Thomas shouted.

"It seems that I can."

"Sit down!"

"You got overconfident, Thomas. Look at the moon."

Thomas laughed. "You are stalling for time. So what if you can stand? A few minutes are all I need and I have met my deadline."

"Really? How long do you think it takes to get to the Villa Di and back?"

"What does that matter?"

"It should matter a great deal to you." Mickey turned to the slumped body beside him. "Because this is not Marjorie."

The person sat up straight and removed the cloak that hid her face. Anna rose to her feet.

Lavinia shrieked. Her features warped as if the molecules that formed them couldn't maintain proximity to one another. She snapped her translucent distortion-for-a-face toward Thomas. "Do . . . some . . . thing!" Lavinia's voice was guttural and indistinct.

Thomas moved toward his cousin. "Anna! My own flesh and blood. You betray me!"

Anna spat. "Your flesh is stone. Your blood is ice. You are an abomination. How long I have wanted to speak those words to your face. Don't accuse me of betrayal. What about my sister? She ran away, but you find her. You destroyed her. You play with all our lives and find joy when you make misery. You dictate and punish and are easily bored." She pointed with an extended arm. "How many lie in that boneyard because of you? How many lost their homes, their land?"

Thomas' eyes were full of venom. He stepped toward her, but Mickey pushed him. It was as if he weighed nothing. He stumbled sideways.

"See how weak you are?" Mickey said. "The transformation has already begun."

Thomas held out his arms and looked at himself in confusion.

"You chose the wrong victim. The compact is finished. The *Accordo* is dead. And you know what that means. Not only is Lavinia destroyed, but so are you."

Mickey motioned toward the window.

"The moon has crossed the sky. Marjorie is not here. She was your choice and you cannot change your mind."

Lavinia commenced to howl a strange hollow reverberation as her figure grew fainter and fainter. Candles began to extinguish themselves.

"Time's up," Anna said. "I do this for my sister."

Thomas tried to speak, but his words were cut off. "I . . ." He began to gulp for air, as if his lungs had stopped working. His face turned gray and grew spotted with age. Then it puckered like a dried apple and his hair thinned to mere wisps."

Anna moved closer to him. "Do you know what I think? You feel pain. All the pain you ever inflicted on others is in you."

His jaw dropped and a wail emitted as if confirming her words. His muscles atrophied until his arms and legs were meager sticks. Unable to hold his own weight, he stumbled backward and tumbled into Agostino's casket. The jaw dropped from his face, limbs from his torso. His skin disintegrated, then bone. He became a pile of ash.

Lavinia's howls stopped. Mickey looked to where she'd been. All that remained was her decaying corpse—an unholy sight propped inside her coffin.

Chapter 39

Mickey entered the bedroom of his two-room suite and cracked the drapes to allow a bit of predawn light. Looking around, he saw no sign of Ray. He moved to the bed and peered at Marjorie. She still looked sickly pale and as thin as a malnourished prisoner of war. He stepped back. There had been a cleansing of energy in the room. He could feel it. Lavinia's intended onslaught and Thomas' dark plan had been thwarted. Pending doom had been annihilated. The air felt light.

Still, Marjorie did not look well and for some reason, probably wishful thinking, he'd hoped to find her sickness had been annihilated as well.

He went into the sitting room where Anna and Paulo sat. "She's still asleep," he told them. "And Ray's gone. He must have known she was safe."

"Everything he told us turned out to be true," Anna said. "I am so grateful."

Paulo said something to his grandmother in Italian and she answered back. Paulo looked at Mickey with serious eyes. "This mission was dangerous, no? I no like that you put my grandmother at risk. If I know it was her, I don't think I take."

"I didn't like it either," Mickey said.

"He did not put me at risk. It was my choice to go. Thomas long needed to be stopped. But until this time, there was nothing I or anyone knew how to do. Mr. McCoy is to be thanked."

Paulo looked grim and unconvinced.

Mickey folded his hand into a fist and held it against his mouth.

Substituting Anna for Marjorie had been Ray's idea. He never would have thought of it. And even if he had, he would not have asked for her help. It *was* too dangerous. Only after Ray convinced him there was no running away—the problem had to be dealt with head on—only then did Mickey accept Anna's help. Ray had talked to her and according to him, she had looked at him with keen eyes and said yes without a moment of hesitation.

"You are young," Anna said to Paulo. "And I always fear Thomas one day set his eyes on you."

Paulo frowned. "You never say."

"Of course, I don't. Children, teens—they no listen to their grandmammas. I must be wise in what I say. Guide you away."

"I was scared of him all my life," Paulo said. "I confess."

Anna patted his thigh.

"It was a risk," Mickey said. "If he had decided to look at you when Paulo placed you in the chair, I don't know what would have happened."

Anna shook her head and her eyes took on a steely strength. "I was never afraid."

Mickey smiled. "You are strong and braver than I am." He sighed. "You have my eternal gratitude. *Grazie*."

Anna pawed the air with one hand. Apparently she could withstand danger, but not heartfelt praise.

"Now Marjorie will be well?" Paulo asked.

Mickey glanced at the bedroom door. "Ray said to be patient. All happens in good time. I asked him what that meant and his answer was 'when the time is right.'"

"What you do?" Paulo asked.

"I'm concentrating on the words 'good time.' We're in Italy. I'm going to believe that Marjorie will get well. I'm going to see that she eats and gets stronger. Then we're going to see the sights. Only we'll go into the city this time. Florence first. No more scenic countryside drives to historical villas with mysterious owners and deadly secrets. No more mystery."

Paulo feigned shock. "None at all? No the statue of David? It a mystery. How Michelangelo release him from that marble?"

Mickey chuckled softly. "Your point is made. How about if I hire you as our guide?"

Paulo grinned. "How much this job pay?"

"Oh, big *denaro*," Mickey said. "Big." He suddenly yawned. "But first I need some shut-eye. Let's talk about this tomorrow."

****

Mickey's dream was filled with the joy of being a tourist in the company of the woman he loved. Marjorie was healthy, energetic, and enthralled with life again. She reveled in all that Italy had to offer. Florence, Rome, Verona, Milan—the two of them marveled at famous sights, lingered in charming cafés, and gazed at each other while dining in romantic restaurants. They climbed the Tower of Pisa as if their legs were twenty. They ogled art in museums and roamed Pompeii, awestruck. Marjorie's skin went from pale to gold sunbathing on a beach in Amalfi. While in Venice they delighted in a gondola ride at sunset. Everything happened in a matter of hours, as can only be done in a dream.

And then Mickey woke up. He rubbed his eyes. The dream had been vivid and while asleep, had seemed wondrously real. He smiled as he lay on his back immersed in a feeling of absolute bliss. He pictured Marjorie's hand in his and tried to replay the dream journey. He saw them laughing as they immersed their hands in the Trevi Fountain. He saw them walking across piazzas and looking aloft inside the Sistine Chapel. Magically they transported to Milan's *Teatro La Scala,* front row center, and the emotive, powerful tones of a tenor reached his ears. The mouth of the singer opened wide. He had a beautiful, dramatic voice. Mickey felt captivated. The mouth opened wider and wider until there was no face and now Mickey felt peril. All he saw was the black void of a mouth rushing toward him, swallowing him, and the song became a scream. In this dark space a small round shape appeared, like the opening at the end of a tunnel, but as it drew closer, Mickey saw it was a head. Closer and closer it flew until he could clearly see it was Thomas' face laughing at him.

Mickey's eyes snapped open. The nightmarish showdown with Thomas flooded his mind. He didn't want to think about it, but the memory clung. His head tossed back and forth. Had that really taken place? Were there really the remains of two lost souls sealed in coffins in that second floor hole in the wall, ready to be properly disposed of? When he remembered Lavinia's horrific presence swaying before him like a demon, it all seemed an illusion. But it wasn't.

He rubbed his face. The room was dark because the drapes were drawn. He rose on an elbow and checked the clock. It was one in the afternoon. He switched on the lamp and looked at Marjorie's side of the bed. She wasn't there. He could see the bathroom door was open with the light on.

Flipping the covers aside, he stepped into his slippers and hurried to see if she was there.

He found her crumpled on the floor and dropped as quickly as his creaking knees allowed. He took her in his arms and she emitted a short, low moan.

"Marjorie."

Her eyes opened weakly. She looked at him and closed them again.

"Are you hurt?"

Her head moved back and forth once. "I can't walk." He saw pee on the floor. He wasn't strong enough to lift her and he didn't want to drag her back to the bed. He went into the bedroom to phone for help.

Chapter 40

"Look at you," Mickey said, joining Marjorie on the terrace of their hotel suite. Her hair was neatly combed and she wore a light touch of makeup. She was dressed in black wool slacks and a warm pullover sweater. She looked ready to go out. He kissed her cheek and she smiled at him, but her eyes did not gleam with cheer. "This is the big day." He sat in one of the wrought iron chairs across from her at the round table. Marjorie was seated in a wheelchair.

"Breakfast should be here any second," she said. "And I will do my best to eat every morsel. I asked if I could have eggs."

"Wonderful." Mickey smiled and held back a sigh.

It had been a full week since he'd found her on the bathroom floor. She'd needed to use the toilet and instead of waking him for help, she'd tried to get there on legs too withered to carry her. She'd managed a few steps, crawled the rest of the way, and collapsed. A doctor had been summoned and she was admitted to a hospital for five days. When her strength increased and her bodily functions tested normal, she was discharged. They returned to the Villa Di for continued convalescence at Anna's insistence. She felt it her duty to help Marjorie regain her health.

Today would be their first day of sightseeing. Mickey was disappointed it wouldn't be an excursion like those in his dream. Marjorie would have to be pushed in the wheelchair and she was only doing it for him. She'd said she would go only after a bit of convincing.

Her strength had returned enough to ride to Florence and see as much as she could. She needed to get out of the room. Mickey didn't want to wait until she desired a trip into Florence for herself. That might not ever happen. She was stronger, but far from well. Skittish, she jumped at unexpected noises and cowered at shadows. She stayed close to the room. Fear ruled her expression when she thought he wasn't looking. Twice he tried to broach the subject of Lavinia and Thomas to assure her she was safe. Each time she cut him off and redirected the subject to something benign. The old Marjorie would have asked questions. She would have wanted to know everything that had happened. She would have been proud of herself for defeating Lavinia, not once, but twice. She would have had harsh words for Thomas and lavish praise for Anna. She would have been raring to beat the sickness that had her in its clutches and been leading the charge against it.

Mickey didn't try to explain things a third time. Instead he teased. "I know. You've been here a hundred times and its old hat."

The healthy, happy Marjorie would have corrected him. She would have said *I've been here once.* The sickly Marjorie, the one with the injured spirit, didn't respond.

He would have to be content that she was better. *All in good time,* Ray had said. So Mickey would bide his time. When she started to ask questions—that's when he would know his Marjorie was back and all was right with the world again.

He looked at her and was overcome with emotion. His nose stung and his eyes grew hot.

Oh, Marjorie. I love you so much. You have no idea.

"Ponte Vecchio."

Mickey looked around. He'd been staring at Marjorie and she hadn't opened her mouth. Besides, the words sounded like they'd come from a man. He saw no one on the grounds near or far from the terrace. He checked the window to the sitting room and saw no one inside the suite. He looked at Marjorie. She was eyeing him but didn't ask why he was so fervently examining their surroundings.

The old Marjorie would have immediately wanted to know—

A mass of tower bells rang loudly. This he knew had to come from inside his head. Out of instinct he put his hands to his ears and the ringing softened. He smiled, removed his hands and it grew loud again. He covered his ears . . . removed his hands . . . covered his ears. Marjorie didn't ask what he was doing.

"Do you hear that?" he asked to see what she'd say.

"Hear what?"

The old Marjorie—stop!

He couldn't keep comparing her to how she'd been. She would get well. She would! Because that was the natural order of things. He had to believe that. The spell, the compact, the presence of Lavinia, Thomas—whatever it was that had killed her spirit in the first place was gone. There was nothing to keep her sick.

The bells' deep tones came to an end.

"Duomo," something whispered in his ear.

His eyes swept the grounds. No one. He almost laughed with glee. These were signs, directions from that sixth sense of his that had been seemingly dead for too long.

There came a tap on the suite entrance door.

"Breakfast," Marjorie said.

"Come in," Mickey called.

Paulo entered with a tray. Smiling, he joined them outside and placed it on the patio table. "I bring and I happy, at your service."

"We are happy too," Mickey said after a beat. It was something Marjorie would have said if . . .

"Where you want to go first? After you eat."

"The *Ponte Vecchio* bridge," Mickey said without hesitation.

****

The wheelchair was not large and could be broken down for portability. Just the same, Paulo borrowed Anna's car for its larger size. The wheelchair would go in the trunk and Mickey would have plenty of room in the back with Marjorie.

"*Ponte Vechio* a good place start," Paulo said. "Everybody want go there."

Mickey looked at Marjorie. She had her eyes closed and looked distressed.

"She miss lovely scenery," Paulo said.

"I—" Mickey stopped. There was no point in explaining. The Italian countryside was indelibly associated in her brain with Lavinia. She'd felt her presence at the villa the day Paulo had taken her for a drive. This phobic terror was another sign Marjorie was far from well.

"What you say?" Paulo asked.

"Nothing," Mickey responded. "She's saving her strength."

"Oh." Paulo drove without speaking for a short while. He glanced at Mickey in the mirror. "You never want to see *Zanetti Quercia Villa* again?"

Surprised by the question Mickey answered with a fair amount of animosity. "No. Why ask?"

"It burn."

"What?"

"*Si*. While at hospital. You gone."

Mickey looked at Marjorie. She wasn't squirming. Perhaps this was something she needed to hear.

"What happened?"

"It no the big house. The small one where—"

"I know which one." Mickey took Marjorie's hand and held it tight. If she felt comforted, she didn't show it.

"Okay. It burn to the ground in the middle of night."

"How?"

"Nobody know."

"What about . . ."

Marjorie shifted in the seat. Was she listening or blocking it out? He decided that he hoped she was listening. He wanted her to feel safe again. Perhaps this conversation with Paulo was the vehicle to make her hear and know all was okay now.

"What about Lavinia and Thomas' remains?" Mickey asked, still holding Marjorie's hand. He felt her tense up.

"They find something, but they know not what."

He'd seen Thomas dissolve to powder. Lavinia still had flesh and bone. If she'd been burned enough, reduced to splinters and ash, would they think her remains Thomas'? He was missing now. It would be a logical assumption. Could they prove or disprove it?

"Who start fire must be very clever," Paulo said.

"It's been ruled arson, then?"

"No. But how else it can start?"

Mickey gazed at Paulo's face in the rearview mirror. He saw the resemblance to Thomas now that he was looking for it. Did he realize he was his son? Had Anna finally told him? And had she then wrapped things up by having someone—herself or even Paulo perhaps—create a funeral pyre? He couldn't see her doing that, but then again, she had reason.

"Paulo," Mickey watched him carefully in the mirror. "How well did you really know your . . . cousin? This is just between you and me. Your grandmother doesn't need to know."

"I know him more than she know I know. I spend time."

"A lot of time?"

"I don't know, a lot."

"And you looked up to him."

"*Si*. I think."

"You thought he was a good man?"

"Hmm." Paulo shrugged. "I thought."

"Powerful? Influential?"

"*Si*."

"You want those things for yourself?"

"Everybody want. But my grandmother explain. And I no want to be like him."

The subject was dropped and soon they reached Florence. Paulo needed no map to know where to go. He drove to a parking lot at the *Piazza Piave* and accepted help from a man who directed him to a space. The man then tried to collect a parking fee. Paulo winked at Mickey and then began to yell in Italian as if he were the angriest person in the world. The man yelled back and both made offensive hand gestures. Another car entered the lot and the man abandoned his argument with Paulo and hurried over to help the new driver.

"Scam artist," Paulo said pointing out a pay machine to Mickey. "No want expensive ticket."

"No," Mickey agreed. He left Paulo to reassemble Marjorie's wheelchair and lift her into it while he paid to park. He placed the ticket inside the car and made certain it was highly visible through the windshield.

"The bridge no even kilometer away. Easy walk," Paulo said.

It was a cool day and the stroll was pleasant. Paulo pushed the chair while Mickey walked along side his wife. Her eyes were open, but didn't seem to connect with what could be seen. She was clearly disinterested.

They found the bridge crowded. It was a popular tourist destination and Mickey knew it would be. He would have liked to bring Marjorie at sunset or sunrise, but felt the effort would have required too much. He was happy just to have gotten her to come at all.

Ponte Vecchio was lined with jewelry and goldsmith shops, all of the merchandise high priced. They paused to window shop. The glittering gold and gems elicited no response from Marjorie.

"No buy here," Paulo said. "Pay too much."

"I think if we found something Marjorie really wanted we might splurge." He looked at her and she said nothing.

Paulo launched into a history lesson as they moved on. "It rebuild many time. This bridge build in thirteen-forty-five. These gold shops most owned by descendants of first owners."

He motioned at an enclosed elevated corridor atop the store roofs. "Cosimo I de'Medici build this part over the shops. He go between his *Uffizi* and his palace and no be in crowd."

"It was more efficient for him," Mickey said.

"*Si.* And he no like be in all the fuss. After it build, he no like smell." Paulo held his nose. "P. U." He laughed. "He get rid of butchers and tanners and replace with golds. Smell better and he make more money too."

Mickey nodded. He looked at Marjorie. She sat contentedly. He couldn't tell if she was listening or contemplating her own thoughts.

"This bridge only bridge over the *Arno* no blow up by the Nazis."

"I heard that," Mickey said. "They blew up surrounding buildings instead to block the way and slow the Allied forces coming after them."

"*Si.*"

They reached the middle of the bridge and paused to listen to a violinist playing for change. Here the shops took a break and the Arno River could be viewed from open terraces on both sides.

"I show you this and I have surprise." Paulo led them to a terrace overlooking the river. There were old-fashioned horse-hitching rings and railings nearly unrecognizable because of hundreds of brass, key-operated padlocks fastened to them.

"What's this?" Mickey asked.

"It be way to make your love last forever. A tradition."

Almost on cue a young couple snapped a padlock to one of the locks already there. They laughed and threw the key into the river. Mickey watched them kiss and a few moments later stroll away with arms wrapped around each other's waist.

"You like?" Paulo took a padlock from his pocket and handed it to Mickey. Grinning, he looked at Marjorie. "Hmm?"

Marjorie looked at the lock and said nothing.

"It's like carving our names on the trunk of a tree," Mickey said.

"I already scratch you initials in." Paulo pointed his effort out to Mickey. Then he handed Mickey the key. He looked around quickly. "No be caught. They fine you now." Mickey felt it was worth the risk for love. Without waiting for Marjorie to show signs she agreed, he unlocked the lock, shackled it onto another and threw the key into the water. He couldn't explain it, but the ritual made him feel good.

"Too bad city worker come by and remove."

"Ah," Mickey said. "Always a catch." He looked at the other side. It too was covered with a daisy chain of locks.

He looked in the direction from which they'd come and saw the Duomo in the distance.

"What you want to do next?" Paulo asked.

"The Duomo, I think. Or is there something you'd like to see, Marjorie?"

She offered no opinion. They walked to the end of the bridge and then turned back in the direction of the cathedral church.

"You want me tell you about it?" Paulo asked.

"Sure," Mickey said.

"The Basilica di Santa Maria del Fiore take one-hundred-seventy years build. It begun in twelve-ninety-six and finish in fourteen-thirty-six on site of crumbling cathedral from early fifth century. The dome design by Brunelleschi. He buried inside the cathedral. The campanile design by Giotto. It have seven bells, different size . . ."

As if calling the bells to life by talking about them, they began to chime. Fascinated, Mickey stopped walking. These bells—exactly this sound—is what he'd heard this morning on the terrace of his hotel suite.

"You like very much?" Paulo asked.

Mickey nodded as a warm feeling coursed through him. He watched the activity on the bridge and everything began to move in slow motion. He'd experienced this phenomenon before and knew something important was going to happen. Paulo spoke to him again, but this time the words were stretched and low as if they were made of taffy and were being pulled until filled with holes.

People moved bit by bit, and sounds gurgled with low-pitched effort. Mickey looked up toward the *Duomo*. The chimes still echoed although not with their normal tone or tempo.

Through the throng of tourists, a man and woman caught Mickey's eye. He was dressed oddly—in boots and breeches and a cape. He had a dark, well-trimmed beard and his hair was long. He looked to be in his thirties. The woman was younger, in her twenties, and was dressed in stylish black jeans and a lightweight winter jacket. They were sharing gelato despite the cool fall weather. She dipped a spoon and fed him a bite. The man's face twisted into an exaggerated expression of delight and the woman laughed. She took a bite and as they drew closer, activity on the bridge returned to a normal speed. Mickey's heart began to race. He recognized the man coming his way.

"What you find interesting?" Mickey heard Paulo say.

He didn't answer and he didn't move. The couple was paying more attention to each other and their flirting than they were to where they were going. Mickey allowed the man to bump straight into him.

"*Scusa,*" the man said. And he tried to walk on with his girlfriend.

"Agostino," Mickey said.

The man turned back. *"Mi conoscete?"*

"Agostino," Mickey said again.

The man stepped closer.

"My name is Mickey McCoy."

They stared at each other.

"You don't know this, but you healed my arm."

Agostino's forehead scrunched.

"Tell him, Paulo."

Paulo translated. Agostino responded.

"He say you voice familiar."

Mickey snorted. "He was in a closet, but he heard me. You don't need to tell him that. Tell him, I helped to free him from her."

Paulo translated again.

Agostino stared. Slowly, a smile came to his lips. He took Mickey by the shoulders, and kissed him on one cheek and then the other. "*Grazie,*" he whispered. There were tears in his eyes.

"This is my wife, Marjorie." Mickey touched her shoulder.

"She's been ill."

Agostino looked at her in the wheelchair and then he knelt down. He looked up and said something to Mickey. His eyes shifted to Paulo.

"He say, can she no walk?"

"No," Mickey said.

With care, Agostino raised his hands and showed them to Marjorie as if asking for permission. She looked at him, but it didn't appear that she really understood. Still, she didn't protest and Agostino placed his hands on her thighs, just above her knees, and left them there for five seconds. Then he stood.

"Thank you," Mickey said, nodding his head in mighty jerks. His eyes stung.

"Siete il benvenuto. Il piacere è mio. È bello essere vivo."

He bowed, took his girlfriend's hand and walked on.

"What did he say?" Marjorie asked.

Mickey looked at her, wiping his eyes.

Paulo answered. "He say, you're welcome. My pleasure and it good to be alive."

Marjorie looked at Mickey with questioning eyes. "Do we know that man?"

Mickey smiled. Her first question. No! Her second.

"Mickey? Do we? I wasn't paying attention before. Who was he?"

More questions. Mickey started to laugh.

"What is so funny?" Marjorie asked. But his laugh was infectious and she too started to chuckle.

"You have a secret," Paulo said. "No?"

"No," Marjorie answered. "I don't. But Mickey does. Are you going to share it with us?"

"That was Agostino. He's over four-hundred years old. Looks rather good for his age."

Marjorie and Paulo stared at him.

"Come. I'll explain as we walk. We have a lot to see. Unless, you aren't interested, Marjorie. I know you've been here a hundred times."

"I've been here once," she said. "Once. One time. I want to see it all."

And we will. Just like in my dream. Because by three in the morning, you'll be on your feet, and that wheelchair will be history.

Made in the USA
Charleston, SC
20 October 2012